My BEST FRIEND'S GIRL

Blythe H. Warren

Bella
BOOKS
2015

Bella Books, Inc.
P.O. Box 10543
Tallahassee, FL 32302

First Bella Books Edition 2015

Editor: Julia Watts
Cover Designer: Linda Callaghan

ISBN: 978-1-59493-462-9

About the Author

Blythe H. Warren teaches English to college freshmen, and she has a terrible reputation for infecting English-weary composition haters with her love of writing. They enter her class dreading the written word and leave thinking that writing can actually be fun. When she's not busy writing or shamelessly converting young minds, she enjoys (yes, actually enjoys) running marathons. She and her partner live in Chicago with their three cats and their dog.

Dedication

To Sue, my co-conspirator and the best
partner a girl could ever ask for.

Acknowledgments

This book owes its existence to an amazing collection of people, and my heartfelt gratitude goes out to all of them. First, to my partner, Sue Hawks, thank you for suggesting that I would have fun writing a romance. You were right. To my sisters Jennie Tyderek, who strongly suggested that others might enjoy reading this book, and Heidi Krystofiak, who kept me on track with revisions, thank you. To all of my sisters—Jennie, Heidi, Amy Cook and Kathy Rowe—and my entire family, your never-ending love and support means more than you can ever know. I also want to thank Sherrlia Bailey for inspiring me to make Jessie a drummer. I tried to make her almost as kick-ass as you. Thanks also to Chely Otero for always answering my questions, no matter how ridiculous they've been, and for teaching me the tiny bit of Spanish I've picked up in sixteen years of friendship. Thank you to my editor, Julia Watts, for asking great questions and trying to subdue my considerable love of adverbs. I truly appreciate your input. Finally, I want to thank everyone at Bella Books for helping me realize a dream and for making this such an easy, fun experience. I can't wait to do it again.

PROLOGUE

Her school day finally over, Jessie Durango trudged home, reluctant to go inside and start her schoolwork. Normally, she had to do her homework as soon as she got home, and once she finished her assignments and left them on the kitchen table for her mother to review, Jessie was supposed to start her chores. Every Monday through Friday homework then chores filled the time between school and dinner, and Jessie always followed the ritual. But today, the first nice day in a long string of lousy ones, the sun beckoned her to stay outside and play with her friends, though she knew that she wouldn't. Facing her mother's disappointment and anger was far worse than missing out on rare pleasant weather, so she dallied as much as possible, extending her enjoyment of the outdoors.

A block from home, though, she spotted her Papa Nestor's truck parked in front of her house. As usual, her *abuelo* had filled the bed of his truck, but since he had put a tarp over the lumpy contents, she couldn't tell what treasures he had found. Forgetting about the sun and the warm, gentle breeze playing with her hair, Jessie ran the rest of the way home.

She burst through the front door of her house, dropped her backpack on the floor and ran to the kitchen. Her grandfather sat at the table reading the newspaper. He had, as was his habit, turned on the radio, and the spacious and pristine kitchen was warmed by the sounds of jazz mingled with her Papa Nestor's soft, harmonic humming. Nestor Durango inhabited a world filled with music, and even the most mundane aspects of his life took on a fantastic appeal thanks to the addition of his own soundtrack. Like him, Jessie eagerly explored the harmonic world around her. Recognizing a kindred spirit, Papa Nestor had impressed upon Jessie the importance of Latin musical influences, but they had also explored classical music, the blues, gospel, country and, with the help of her *tia*, some rock and roll. Though he preferred Coltrane and Count Basie to The Clash or The Cure, Papa Nestor indulged his youngest grandchild and musical ally to develop her burgeoning interest in his great passion.

"Papa!" Jessie squealed as she leapt into his lap and threw her arms around his neck, inhaling the faint aromas of pipe tobacco, leather and Old Spice, the smells of her *abuelo*. "What are you doing here?"

"I came to see you," he said and groaned a little as he set her back on the floor. "I brought you something."

"A present? Can I have it now?"

"Jessie!" her mother, home from her job as a high school Spanish teacher, called from the front door that Jessie had left wide open. "I've told you about leaving your things all over the floor. Come pick up your bag and start your homework."

Jessie crossed her eyes and offered a comically pained expression, to her Papa's amusement, but before her mother had to call her again, Jessie obeyed. "Sorry, Mom," she offered as she reached for the bag, dreading the math worksheets it contained. "I just got so excited when I saw Papa that I forgot."

"Your Papa is here?" Her mother's bewildered expression sent Jessie's thoughts back to Papa Nestor's surprise visit to deliver a surprise present and save her, at least temporarily, from homework and chores.

"*Buenos tardes*, Silvia," Nestor's velvety voice sounded from the doorway. "I brought Jessie an early birthday present, but I don't want to distract her from her studies."

"Not a difficult task, Nestor, believe me."

"Please Mom?" Jessie grabbed her mother's arm. "I promise I'll do all of my homework and my chores right after. Please can I have it now?" Her tenth birthday was still three weeks away, but as usual her *abuelo* had started the celebration early. Jessie knew she'd never be able to concentrate on her homework until she found out what Papa Nestor had gotten her.

Silvia Durango smiled at her youngest child and nodded. "I expect you to finish your homework before dinner, *mija*."

"I promise," Jessie swore, hand on heart.

Nestor took a long, slender, newspaper-wrapped packet from behind his back and handed it to his granddaughter. "The rest is in my truck," he told her, smiling at the quizzical expression on her face as she held her first pair of drumsticks in her soft, small hands. He laughed gently as he caught Silvia's wide-eyed reaction to his gift.

Together Jessie and her *abuelo* walked to Papa Nestor's pickup truck. He pulled the tarp from the mysterious lump in the bed of the truck, and Jessie squealed again and climbed up to inspect her gift more closely. Before her sat a used but well-loved four-piece drum kit. She ran her hand over the finish—a pearly light blue, now her favorite color—and gently tapped the snare with the sticks her *abuelo* had given her. More than anything she wanted to sit down, start playing and not stop until she had mastered this instrument, but she saw her mother watching from the front door of the house and knew she would have to wait.

"You love music with your soul, like I do, Jessie. We've always shared that, and we always will, even when I'm not with you, *mija*. Remember that."

"*Gracias*, Papa," Jessie said and hugged her grandfather tightly as he lifted her from the truck. They held hands as they headed back inside for Jessie to keep her promise to her mother.

She forgot her Papa's words as she worked on her assignments and tended to her household chores, but a month later, when her parents broke the news of her beloved grandfather's death to her and her brother, she remembered what he said. After that, whenever she practiced, she felt close to him, and she felt that she could keep him alive just by making music.

* * *

The thick air in the hallway closed in on Zoey, its overpowering stench of beef and onions gagging her. Still, that wasn't why she found it so hard to breathe. Looking past her best friend rather than at her, Zoey focused on the sweating window beyond Angela's wildly wavy brown hair. Outside the rain blew almost horizontally in the brutal wind, but there in the hall outside the Tuckers' apartment the still air grew even more stifling. Angela's accusation hung between them, oppressive in its weight.

"You don't think he's good enough for you." She folded her arms across her still flat chest and set her jaw, daring Zoey to deny the truth of this statement. In four years of friendship Zoey had seen that look only a few times, but it was enough to know things never went well for the person on the receiving end.

"No, Ange, that's not it."

She'd been best friends with Angela since the fifth grade when the Tuckers had moved into the apartment below Zoey's family. Zoey'd spent so much time in their home that they'd become a second family to her, with Angie's older brother, Ian, filling that void in her own life. Even now that he was a senior and she was a lowly freshman, he always talked to her at school. He'd even helped her make it onto the cross-country team, running with her and offering friendly advice after his own varsity training finished for the day. A standout athlete, he knew what would help her and didn't hesitate to suggest improvements. He was a sweet, wonderful guy, and she loved him. Just not that way.

She searched for the words to explain, but Angela's stern expression short-circuited Zoey's brain. "Ian's a great guy," she offered apologetically.

"Just not great enough for perfect Zoey Carmichael," Angela sneered.

"That's not why I said no."

Again focusing on the harsh weather, Zoey recalled with anguish Jake Morris, the other cross-country star and the reason she'd started running to begin with. Jake Morris, the boy she loved with all her heart, Jake Morris, the junior that every girl, including seniors, wanted to be with and whom she had been with for two beautiful months. She remembered his brutality, and still she loved him. She saw herself confessing her feelings and heard him agreeing, "Me too," in that soft, low voice before she gave herself to him entirely. He'd been her first, and a week later he'd dumped her for Julie Mott, a faster runner on the junior varsity team.

She'd skipped practice that day—not caring what fresh torment Coach would have for her—and had run all the way home, straight to Angela's bedroom where she poured out her soul and sorrow to the only sympathetic ear she needed. She'd cried for hours, wailing so fervently that Ian, finally home from practice, took one look at Zoey and, rather than giving her a hard time, just smiled sympathetically and walked away.

She thought Angela should remember the hurt, would understand why, even after all these weeks, she just couldn't go out with Ian. Disappointed, hurting, she voiced her concerns. "After the thing with Jake, I don't want to date anybody. I don't want to hurt like that again." She risked a glance at her friend and saw that Angela's expression had softened. She did understand. Zoey grabbed her best friend's hands and, squeezing them, said, "Besides Ian's like a brother to me. It would be weird, I think, and then if things didn't work out, I might lose your friendship. I couldn't bear to lose you, Ange. You mean more to me than having a boyfriend."

Angela's face hardened again, and she pulled her hands from Zoey's hastily. "Ian *is* my brother, and that's way more important than any friendship." Angela turned toward her apartment door, her hand reaching for the knob.

"Wait." Zoey grabbed Angela's arm, keeping her in the hall. "Angela please." She choked on her tears. "Please, Ange, I'm sorry. What can I do?"

Turning slightly to face her pathetic friend, Angela told her, "You can't do anything, Zoey. You really hurt Ian, and he doesn't want to see you around here anymore." Wheeling back to the entryway, Angela said to the door, "Neither do I."

Just like that she walked away from their four-year friendship. Zoey thought she'd heard uncertainty in Angela's last comment, and hoping that wasn't just wishful thinking, she tried repeatedly to make amends. Angela rebuffed her at every turn. By the time Angela's family moved to Park Ridge at the end of the year, any ties they'd had to each other were completely severed. Outside of her family, Zoey felt woefully alone.

CHAPTER ONE

Seventeen years after her grandfather's death, Jessie felt certain he would be proud of her and the passion for all things musical that he had cultivated in her. Over the years, his final gift to her—music—had flourished so that now, Jessie made her love of it an integral part of her existence, earning a respectable following but a small income as the drummer for Nuclear Boots. As would be expected of the determined granddaughter of a never-resting immigrant, she worked tirelessly at her craft, practicing every day whether her bandmates were up for it or not. However, since they all shared an intense dedication to the band, as well as a place in Pilsen, she usually found them as ready to rehearse as she.

The neighborhood's status as a hub of Hispanics and artists on Chicago's not quite fashionable Near West Side meant Jessie and her bandmates could easily afford to rent out a three-story house. The bottom two floors belonged, for the most part, to the guys, but as the first floor held their living room and rehearsal space--which the boys had thoughtfully decorated with taxidermic artifacts and beer paraphernalia and in which the musty scent of stale beer and old sweat socks always lingered— Jessie found herself spending a fair amount of time there. The second floor, where the guys each had a bedroom, was a disaster area Jessie passed through as quickly as possible to get to the third floor, a mother-in-law's apartment that she claimed for herself. For two months, Sean (forgetting or ignoring the fact that Jessie paid more rent) had griped at every opportunity that Jessie was acting like the queen of the band, living in her "palatial suite" while the rest of them shared cramped quarters below her. His complaining stopped when Neal threatened to buy him a pacifier.

Jessie ignored Sean's surliness unless it affected the music. She wanted no part of his drama (even though he tried to hang it on her), and the benefits of their living arrangement far outweighed Sean's attitude. Sharing a house—not a grungy apartment—with her band made almost every aspect of their collaboration easier. On top of that, having her own home within a home provided Jessie with a private living space that her house and bandmates only entered with her permission. She suspected that, at least in Sean's case, this was more out of fear of her overprotective ex-Marine brother (who had made his menacing presence felt the day they all moved in together) than respect for her privacy, but as long as none of them touched her bathroom or kitchen, she didn't care.

Despite, or perhaps due to, her role as the only female in the band, Jessie refused to play the girl card and be thought of as weaker or less valuable than the guys. The band was just as much her baby as theirs, and because of this, whenever they had a show, she always made sure she was involved in every aspect of preparations, from packing up gear and loading it into her truck to setting up at the venue. The harder she worked on their shared dream, the more invaluable she felt, so she was not angered when, almost finished arranging their equipment in the truck, she spotted Neal Murphy, Nuclear Boots's singer and lyricist, strolling up the block with his love interest of the moment. Though he'd been seeing Zoey Carmichael for over four months, this was the first time he'd brought her around the band. He'd confided in Jessie, with an endearing shyness she was surprised to see in anyone as sure of himself as Neal, that though he'd initially seen Zoey, like all the others, as a body, he'd grown to respect and admire her.

"She's smart, Jess, so smart." He'd beamed as if he was somehow responsible for his girlfriend's intelligence. "She's an English professor. She's got a freakin' Ph.D." Quite a turnaround from his usual appreciation for women. Most of his conquests couldn't string three sentences together.

"If she's so special, why haven't I met her?"

"You will. Soon I hope. I don't want to rush things."

"Excuse me? You're like the cheetah of the dating world. You go through women like Paul goes through guitar strings. Since when do you do anything but rush things?"

"Since Zoey," he'd replied so sweetly she didn't know whether to hug him or vomit on his perfectly scuffed shoes. "There's something, I don't know, different this time. I can't figure it out, but—" He stopped midsentence, his eyes getting a dreamy, faraway look. He stirred himself from his reverie and spoke, almost shyly, "You'll meet her soon. I promise." Still it had been nearly a month since their conversation, and this was the first she'd seen of Zoey.

Beyond curious, Jessie stopped what she was doing and assessed the pair that approached her through the waning sunlight of the early spring afternoon. He strode with the same confidence he exuded onstage, completely self-assured and at ease in his lanky, six-foot frame. His comfortably worn, dirty-looking jeans, old green T-shirt, gas station attendant's jacket and biker boots were his compromise between personal style and the rock and roll uniform, and though he kept his shaggy brown hair looking greasy and unclean in the grungy style currently favored by local musicians, Jessie knew it was an act. Neal meticulously groomed himself to look like a slob.

At his side, Zoey—busty and pretty like all the rest—was startlingly tall. No mere doll for Neal's amusement, Zoey had to be five foot ten at least. Jessie eyed her height with the halfhearted disdain she usually reserved for tall girls. (At five foot three, Jessie was the tallest woman in her family but otherwise unenviably short in most groupings.) She wore faded jeans that seemed to fit her slender form perfectly, accentuating strong thighs and a slight curve of hip. Jessie noticed with a mixture of relief at her good sense and further irritation at her height that this girl chose not to mix high heels with jeans, a fashion error that Jessie found unforgivable. Instead, battered Chuck Taylors emerged from beneath the frayed hem of Zoey's pants. Further separating her from all the other cute blondes in their too clingy, immobilizing blouses, this one had donned a soft, pale blue V-neck sweater, highlighting her full breasts and trim waist. Unlike her many predecessors, Zoey walked next to Neal without draping herself all over him. In fact, aside from holding his hand, she showed no outward signs of infatuation. Watching their approach, an uneasiness settled in Jessie's stomach.

"How long do you think this one will last?" Sean Black, tall, wiry and very tattooed, lifted his bass into the truck and gestured toward Neal and Zoey with the barest motion of his shaved head.

"She's hot," Paul Davidson answered as he scrutinized the pair walking toward them. Paul, closer to Jessie's height than Neal and Sean, bore a slight resemblance to Kurt Cobain, a similarity which thankfully ended with their shared love of music, Paul's one true addiction. "Maybe too hot for him. I give it another month before she dumps him."

Jessie cringed and kept her mouth shut about Neal's true feelings for Zoey, understanding that he would be embarrassed if Sean and Paul suspected. None of them had ever known Neal to experience any emotion beyond lust for any woman he'd been with before, and though Jessie was far from experienced, her heart had been trampled before. She remembered the incident bitterly and worried about Neal. She couldn't shake the thought that this, his first adult foray into love, would not end well for him.

Eager to meet Zoey, the better to assess her worthiness, Jessie settled herself on the truck's open gate as the lovebirds covered the remaining distance between them. She drew her knees to her chest and brushed dust from her pants. Jessie wore what she considered her cute punk rock girl outfit: soft gray Dickies, boots, and a girly but not-too-tight dark blouse, with her thick, sable hair curling playfully onto her shoulders from childish pigtails. Though striking with her caramel skin and fine Aztec features, she did not see herself as the type who drove men wild. Not like the woman striding her way.

"Sorry I'm late, guys," Neal said as he eased himself onto the gate next to Jessie. Still holding Zoey's hand, he pulled her closer to himself and the band and introduced her to Sean, Paul and Jessie, pointing at each individual in turn.

Sean nodded and muttered a noncommittal "Hey," while Paul leaned back against the truck and raised the right corner of his mouth. Not quite a smile, but it was about the limit of his investment in Neal's flings. He'd probably already forgotten her name. Jessie, however, smiled and said, "It's nice to meet you," for which Neal sent her a small but grateful grin.

Zoey responded with an easy smile and finally spoke. "I've heard so much about all of you. It's nice to finally put faces to the names." Sean and Paul exchanged raised eyebrows at the thought of Neal spending any time with this woman talking about anything, especially them. Zoey didn't notice but kept speaking. "Really, I'm the one who should be apologizing." Her voice was sultry, warm and inviting, not the high and soft baby voice of Neal's typical woman. "It's my fault that we're late."

"What did you do? Mess up his hair?" Jessie smiled more fully as Neal rolled his eyes and unconsciously fingered a few strands on his forehead.

Zoey laughed along with the band and then spoke. "I wish. Actually, I got trapped at an emergency faculty meeting that dragged on for over an hour, so I was late getting home to change, which means I wasn't ready to go when Neal arrived."

Jessie was about to interrogate Zoey (with Neal's best interests in mind, of course), but Sean and Paul, apparently uninterested in Zoey and ready to leave, strolled over to their motorcycles and brought the once dormant engines to thunderous life.

"We'll catch you over there," Paul shouted before roaring after Sean in a veil of noise.

With Zoey and Neal joining Jessie in the cab of her decades old red and white Ford F-150, Jessie sped off in the direction of the recently opened club where the band would be playing that night. "So," she started simply, "Neal told me you're a teacher. How do you like it?"

Zoey, sitting in the middle of the bench seat, angled her long legs into Neal's portion of the floor to avoid interfering with the gear shift. The tangle their gangly limbs created on the passenger side of the cab, though comical to Jessie, put Zoey at a slightly awkward angle for talking, but she answered readily.

"The hours are crazy, especially when there are papers to grade, the pay isn't immense for the work involved, and several of my colleagues seem prematurely burnt out. But I love it." Zoey craned her neck to look at Jessie when she spoke, and Jessie met her gaze as she paused at a stop sign. Zoey's deep green eyes sparked as she elaborated.

"Much of the time my students seem bored or like they're only in class to kill time until something better comes along."

Jessie cringed inwardly, thinking of her own time in school. All she'd wanted to do was get out and experience anything other than another lecture or a math test.

"But now and then I'll catch the moment of understanding. I'll actually see their faces change as they grasp some concept I've been droning on about, and it's magical. I feel so alive and influential but at the same time insignificant. I can't quite explain it, but it makes all the bad stuff fade into the background." Zoey blushed and then continued, "Speaking of droning on. I'm sorry. Sometimes I forget what a dork I am for loving school."

"It's all right. You were almost making me regret not going to college," Jessie offered. Zoey's love of teaching reminded Jessie of her own mother's commitment to her students. Jessie saw a hint of what would draw Neal so strongly to Zoey, and she put a checkmark in the "pro" column of her mental Zoey checklist.

"Thank you." Zoey smiled genuinely and placed a hand on Jessie's arm in thanks. Jessie felt the warmth radiating from

Zoey's hand. The cab fell silent for a moment as Neal pulled Zoey to him and kissed her.

Uncharacteristically irritated by the impending make out session, Jessie interjected with the first question that popped into her head. "So, what do you do for fun?" She grimaced at the cliché she'd just uttered, but again Zoey seemed eager to respond.

"The usual stuff—books, movies. I run a lot."

"You run? Voluntarily?"

"Yes," she laughed. "I ran track and cross-country in school. It's what paid for most of my college education actually, and now I just feel off if I don't put in at least twenty-five miles a week."

"Ugh. I was late to soccer practice once," Jessie recalled. "Coach Sullivan made me run sprints until I puked. I have never been late for anything else in my life."

"My baby sister thought I was nuts too. She gave me a shirt that said, 'My sport is your sport's punishment.' But then her sophomore year of high school, she joined the cross-country team, so I had to get her a shirt just like mine."

"I used to watch the girls running after school," Neal jumped in. "That was no punishment." Neal's wide grin and flirty wink let them know that he was only partially being a pig. Zoey playfully slugged him in the ribs anyway.

Jessie, enjoying the conversation more than she had anticipated, put another checkmark in the "pro" column of her Zoey list before asking, "How did you and Neal meet? He didn't say."

"It's a funny story actually. I was on a date with another man—"

"Brian," Neal cut in, "the poor bastard." Neal laughed, and Jessie's stomach fell a little.

"Neal just sauntered up and asked me out. I thought that kind of audacity should be rewarded, so I said yes."

"Didn't your date mind?" Zoey's flightiness startled Jessie.

"He was so busy with a 'very important business call' that I'm not sure he noticed when I said goodbye and left with Neal." Neal chuckled and said something about the other guy's loss being his gain. She wondered what Neal could possibly be thinking and was still dumbfounded when she pulled into the alley behind the club where Sean and Paul were waiting to unload the gear.

Zoey grabbed a guitar as atonement for her tardiness and followed Sean and Paul into the club, expressing an interest in witnessing the technical side of the music business. Neal watched them enter the building then pounced on the opportunity to talk to Jessie alone.

"Well?"

He seemed eager to hear Jessie's opinion, an eagerness that Jessie did not share. She understood the complicated laws of dating and friendship and knew that what Neal was really asking for was Jessie's approval. The potential problems that could spring from her total honesty were innumerable, so Jessie simply said, "She's okay."

Neal's face, so full of joy a moment before, fell instantly. "You don't like her."

"I've spent twenty minutes with her. I don't know her well enough to not like her." Jessie stepped carefully.

"But?" Neal asked as he began unloading the truck. He knew Jessie well enough to know that she was keeping quiet about something.

"But I'm worried."

"About what?"

"About you, dummy. What if you get hurt?"

Neal set the amp he held on the ground and looked directly at Jessie. "You're a good friend, but you don't need to worry about me, Durango. I'll be fine."

"I bet What's-His-Name thought the same thing before Zoey changed her mind middate,'" Jessie hadn't meant to say that, but now that she had, she didn't regret it. Neal seemed surprised by her words, which merely strengthened Jessie's resolve to urge Neal to protect himself and his emotions. Someone had to. "I guess she seems nice, but doesn't it bother you that she left her date with another man to go out with you? She just jumps from one warm body to the next. What kind of person does that? She sounds like a—" She stopped herself just before the word *puta* came flying out of her mouth. She had already said more than she should have, and there was no way Neal would forgive her for calling his new girlfriend a whore.

"Like a what?" Neal asked, his voice tight.

"Like a flighty person." Neal's posture relaxed a little, indicating to Jessie that he wasn't mad at her. "Just make sure she's someone you can really trust your heart with."

"That guy she was with was an ass who only cared about himself. I'll be fine," he repeated.

"I hope so," Jessie relented. "You're too much of a wimp to handle heartache."

Neal hugged Jessie, a thanks for her concern and a sign that he wouldn't hold it against her. "Do me a favor," he said. "Get to know her. I think you'll really like her if you give her a chance."

"If it will make you happy," Jessie said, "I will get to know her better." She grabbed the amp he had set on the ground and headed inside the club.

Ears ringing and eyes watering, Zoey prayed the night wouldn't be a complete waste of time. The first band, whose name she'd missed, had seemed some sort of punishment for unknown sins. The singer—and she hesitated to call him that— had shrieked near-incomprehensible lyrics over intense (and apparently intentional) feedback while the drummer had beaten forcefully on anything within his reach. The next group had been no better, and despite the comparatively mellow sound of the band currently on the stage, Zoey's head still pounded from the initial onslaught. Paying minimal attention to this, the third in a line of mediocre to awful bands walking through their sets, Zoey hoped that Neal's band would at least be tolerable so she wouldn't have to break up with him just to avoid another night like this.

Nuclear Boots had performed a number of times since she'd started seeing Neal, but other commitments had always prevented her from attending. And the fact was she shouldn't even be there tonight—the mountain of essays she'd collected earlier in the day taunted her with its overwhelming need for corrections. But Neal had looked so excited and eager when he'd told her about the show that she'd agreed to attend in spite of her workload.

Now, as she stood between Maureen and Carla—the other band girlfriends—she regretted her decision. The volume of the music made conversation next to impossible (though Maureen and Carla didn't seem to notice), and Neal had wandered off because they were up next, so she bought herself another beer and waited for her agony to end.

Easily seeing the stage over the heads of those in front of her, she clapped politely as the third band cleared out, and she sighed, preparing herself for the worst, when she saw Neal and the others walk onstage for the quick transfer of instruments before they began. She'd watched their initial preparations with curiosity, having never before been privy to the backstage world of music and had been fascinated to learn that, for speed's sake, all of the drummers from the several bands playing that night would be sharing the same drum kit. Each drummer provided his or her own sticks, snare and cymbals, which could be switched out much more quickly than breaking down and assembling an entire drum kit for every band. The concept of musicians using each other's instruments seemed odd to Zoey when Jessie had kindly if not patiently explained it. Now, as she watched the band, impressed by the speed and professionalism of their setup, she understood how it simplified the process for everyone. Impossibly soon they went to their respective places and, without preamble, began to play.

Zoey was pleasantly surprised by the sound that reached her ears. From the times she'd heard him sing in her apartment, she knew Neal could carry a tune. But now he infused his songs with passion, demonstrating an impressive vocal range that included a low, sexy growl. She paid minimal attention to the other members of the band, noting with little interest how the near river of sweat running down Sean's face belied the laid-back calm typical of a bass player. Likewise Paul seemed totally at ease and unaffected, but his hands, in unceasing motion, produced a steady stream of notes that ranged from surfer rock to the crunching assault of near heavy metal. It was all so perfectly rock and roll.

It took Zoey until the third song to shift her gaze to the drums. After that her eyes seldom veered from that focal point. Jessie moved fluidly, precisely, filling every inch of the song with percussion, and though her movements seemed unpredictable, every beat fit the music. Far from merely providing background noise or just keeping time, she tackled each song with ferocity, driving the music forward, and when, on one song, she blended her high Spanish vocals with Neal's deep English, her strong, pure voice provided a sharp yet pleasant counterpoint to the rest of the music. Though Zoey had no clue what Jessie sang, the sound of the words, the rhythm they created within her, moved her.

The real beauty of Jessie's musicality, though, lay not in her movements or in the muscularity of the sound she produced, but rather in her face. Her expression indicated an intense focus and revealed the absolute carnal joy she felt making music. Her passion ignited a corresponding joy in Zoey that she felt to her extremities.

Song after song Jessie maintained this intensity as song after song Zoey's focus zoomed in on her, scarcely shifting to the other members of the band. She watched Jessie gulp down water from a plastic bottle as Neal talked to the crowd, but his words barely registered she was so anxious for the next song to begin. Two and a half minutes later Carla's catcalls jarred Zoey from her daze, and she joined the hearty applause of the crowd around her. She watched impatiently as the band cleared the stage for the next group, eager to approach Jessie and congratulate her.

Jessie watched Neal, who stood front and center, looking out at the crowd, good-sized and raucous for a Wednesday. Slightly to his left Paul switched guitars for their final number, and opposite him Sean took a long swallow of beer and wiped sweat from his forehead with the hem of his shirt. At the very front of the crowd Jessie spotted Zoey in a group with Sean's and Paul's girlfriends and their small but loyal fan base. Jessie drank deeply from her water bottle, condensation rapidly coating its outside. As always she would wait until after the show to drink. Setting the bottle down, she returned her focus to Neal. "If it's all right with everyone, we have one more song for you." The crowd made its approval known, and smiling, Neal said, "Here's an old one called 'Lady Truck Driver.'"

With that Jessie let loose a torrent of sound, setting a fast pace for this song Neal had written after he'd learned of her brief stint driving the big rigs. Two and a half minutes later, a decent amount of applause greeted Jessie's ears, and she and the guys began the speedy process of breaking down their gear and clearing the stage for the next band.

Once finished, Jessie, hot, tired and full of excitement, made her way through the congratulatory crowd to the bar for a much-deserved drink. She gulped down a full third of her beer, but it did nothing to dissipate the heat within her. Feeling a tap on her shoulder, she turned, anticipating the usual encounter with some random male fan who thought she was a really great drummer for a girl. The backhanded compliment—typically followed by pointers and friendly advice—she now received with a wry "Thanks." Recognizing the futility of her efforts, she'd long ago given up arguing with anonymous male egos.

So she was surprised when she instead faced Zoey, who had come up behind her. Before the show, Zoey had seemed fascinated, asking questions of all of them about their preparations, and here she was again, ready to talk to Jessie once more. Jessie wondered if Neal had also spoken to Zoey about getting along with his friend. If that was the case, Jessie would do her best to play nice and see the good in Zoey.

"So that's Nuclear Boots?" Zoey took a drink from her beer.

Jessie nodded and took another swallow of her drink. "What did you think?"

"Well, Neal told me you guys were good," Zoey answered. She leaned close so that Jessie could hear over the cacophony of the bar. "But Neal doesn't seem to be the best at self-critiquing, so I didn't know what to expect."

"And?" Jessie grew impatient to know what this woman thought of her music. Zoey's answer would weigh heavily on Jessie's ability to like her.

"And," Zoey leaned even closer as the crowd around them increased in volume. Her lips were inches from Jessie's ear as she said, "You were incredible." Her cool, smooth fingers lightly touched Jessie's forearm as if to emphasize her point. The touch sent chills through Jessie's body even as an unsettling warmth spread across her stomach. "You're kind of like early R.E.M. meets The Pixies with hints of The Ramones and The Jam."

"I'm impressed."

"Don't be. When I found out that he was in a band, I asked Neal about his musical influences."

"He told you all that?" Zoey nodded emphatically. "Typical."

"What?"

"Except for Kim Deal—who I love—he didn't mention any women. What about Patti Smith or Kathleen Hanna or Carrie Brownstein?" Suddenly peevish, Jessie practically shouted, "God, he couldn't even mention Joan Jett or Chrissie Hynde or Debbie Harry! What's with that?"

"He's a guy." Zoey shrugged as if in apology for her boyfriend.

Shaking her head, Jessie grumbled. "I know. It's just so frustrating. I've been working on the boys' musical education for four years now, but I don't know if I'll ever break through their testosterone wall of sound."

"Well, good luck with that." Zoey laughed, and Jessie felt herself warming up to Zoey again.

Silence descended upon them once more. Jessie cast about her mind for something to say, but Zoey spoke first. "So, who came out to support you tonight?"

"The guitar player from my last band said she was going to try to make it, but I haven't seen her yet. Other than that, just some friends, no family. It's not really their thing."

"No boyfriend lurking around here somewhere?"

"No," Jessie answered and crossed her arms over her chest, feeling defensive, irritated and inclined to dislike Zoey again.

"I'm sorry." Zoey seemed to understand her gaffe instantly. She bit her lower lip and scrunched her face in an oddly becoming apologetic expression. "I shouldn't have been so presumptuous." Zoey's face reddened a little, and she looked around uncomfortably. Smiling she spoke again. "You're probably better off anyway."

Still irritated Jessie asked, "How's that?"

"Well, men can be incredible assholes." Just then, Neal came up behind Zoey and grabbed her around the waist, pulling her to him. In spite of herself, Jessie laughed. "This guy, for example," Zoey jerked her thumb over her shoulder at Neal, "I asked him to go to one little poetry reading with me, and he acts like I've signed us up for couples day at the spa." Neal was nuzzling Zoey's ear, clearly not listening to her complaints, and she gently pushed him away with her shoulder. "Yet he regularly torments me with football games, basketball games and threats of baseball."

This didn't surprise Jessie, who had been subjected to Neal's extreme sports fanaticism almost from the start of their friendship. They hadn't even moved in together before he'd dragged her to watch the Cubs. She'd quickly lost what little interest in the game she had to begin with, but it had been such fun watching Neal's childlike enthusiasm as he cheered and engaged with other fans. She found herself eager to attend the next time he invited her, and now they went to at least three games a season together. She hadn't acquired a new appreciation for baseball or Neal's favorite team, but she had so much fun with him that not even the Cubs could ruin her good mood.

"I made plans with my sister a month ago," Zoey continued, "and she just informed me today that she's going to have to work. I don't really want to go alone, but will my boyfriend go with me? No. See how lucky you are to not have to deal with this crap?" Zoey playfully slapped Neal's face as his lips made their way down her neck.

"When is it?"

"A week from tomorrow. Why?"

"Well, if you're desperate for company, I could go with you." Neal, who apparently had been listening, sent Jessie an appreciative smile. Who knew? It might even be fun. Zoey was at least more interesting than Neal's other girlfriends.

"Really?" Zoey's face lit up as she smiled. "That's wonderful. It's at six in Andersonville. I could meet you there around five thirty. We'd have plenty of time to get good seats. Would that work?"

"Why don't I just pick you up?"

"I don't want to impose." Zoey again scrunched her face in an apology. "But since you suggested it, I'd love a ride. I can leave work around five. Is that okay?"

"Sounds great," Jessie answered, and Zoey wrapped her in an appreciative embrace that caught her off guard. Feeling a little uneasy, Jessie escaped the hug and murmured an excuse about finding her friends.

CHAPTER TWO

The next day, after her morning classes ended, Zoey holed herself up in her office and slogged through most of her students' essays. As she expected, they ranged from atrocious abuses of the English language to mediocre attempts at satisfactorily completing the assignment. She'd set aside the papers from her handful of good students for later as a reward for getting through all the garbage. So, kicking herself as she labored over comments that would be largely ignored, she wondered how so many students had advanced to the college level without the most basic knowledge of the English language, without knowing how to construct a complete sentence even. Why were they there if they didn't care enough about their work even to hit the spell check button? She couldn't fathom wasting her time and money like that, but the mistakes were priceless. One student actually wrote about how George Milton "shat his friend Lennie." Just as she was about to write a gently sarcastic comment in the margin, her phone rang.

"Zoey Carmichael," she answered after one ring.

"Hey babe." Neal's deep, warm voice met her ears, and she smiled. "How's it goin'?"

"Great or terrible, depending on your perspective."

"Well, what's your perspective?" he asked with a grin in his voice.

"Both," she sighed. "I've gotten through most of the garbage, I hope, so that's good. But it also means I'll have a lot of slightly less awful revisions to go through in a couple of weeks."

"And that's terrible."

"Right." She twisted the phone cord around her finger and stretched out her long legs, enjoying Neal's attention and this small break. "What's up with you?"

"IT crap. You know. What are we doing tonight?"

Zoey groaned a little. "Nothing, I'm afraid. I promised Grace I'd help her proofread the latest section of her dissertation. Not that I know anything about cellular biology, but I can still be supportive." She said more to herself than Neal, "I should probably buy her dinner too, since she's a starving grad student."

"Oh." His voice grew soft. "I was hoping for a repeat of last night." She could almost hear the wiggle of his eyebrows in his voice. After the show last night their sex had been explosive. She didn't know what had come over her, but even in the cab on the way to her apartment she'd hardly been able to contain herself. Tempting though it was to try again, she couldn't back out on her baby sister.

"Tomorrow night for sure."

"All right." His lighthearted grumbling further warmed her. "Say hey to your sis for me."

Zoey vowed to herself to finish her grading by the next night so they could spend the whole weekend together, and after hanging up she turned her attention back to the unfortunate evisceration of Steinbeck's work with a lighter heart.

* * *

That weekend and into the next week, Zoey became a bit of a fixture at the house in Pilsen. She showed up after band practice on Friday night and stayed for most of the following weekend, puttering around the place with Neal. As Jessie passed in and out on her way to meet friends, she wondered if Zoey was really content to sit in their smelly living room staring at the dead things on their drab walls and talking to Neal and occasionally herself or Sean, but that was no more her concern than what went on behind Neal's closed door at night. And the monotony dissipated a bit on Saturday when Maureen and Carla showed up. Jessie watched in amused silence as all three women commiserated about their cheap boyfriends. After half an hour of pointedly cataloguing the virtues of frugality, they got their way and spent the rest of the night on the town.

But even after a sickeningly lingering goodbye on Sunday night, Zoey returned briefly on both Monday and Tuesday, just to have dinner with Neal before heading to her sister's to help with her wedding. Or maybe it was a paper. Jessie hadn't really paid attention. So when the doorbell rang shortly after band practice on Wednesday, Jessie wasn't surprised to see Zoey on the other side of the door.

"Hey stranger," she said with thinly veiled sarcasm.

"Hi. Neal and I are supposed to go out. He told me to meet him here at seven. I'm a little early." She did that apologetic lip bite thing again as Jessie stepped aside to let her in the house.

"He ran to the store right after practice." Probably to buy condoms, thought Jessie, but she added, "You're welcome to come in and wait for him."

As Zoey settled into the big couch in the living room, facing the practice space, Jessie considered that she should probably entertain her until Neal returned. Paul, normally quiet, had retreated to his room after practice to focus on some work problem, and Sean was socially inept. Plus, Jessie's mother would drop dead from shame if she knew that Jessie had failed to be hospitable, so instead of heading upstairs to finish reading her book like she'd intended, she found herself sitting across from Zoey and making small talk. Their banter, superficial though it was, moved constantly and lightly from one topic to the next. With no awkward pauses as one or the other groped for something to say, Jessie found it easy to talk with Zoey. It seemed almost as if they had known each other for years.

"What's it like living with all these men?" Zoey asked out of nowhere. "I grew up with three sisters and no brothers," she explained, "so this is completely foreign to me."

"It's messy," Jessie answered only half-jokingly. "Well, I have my own space upstairs. I take care of that, and they take care of this, as you can see." She gestured to the beer cans and dishes strewn about the room. "I don't really have to deal with them so much as roommates, except when the rent is due. But it was hard at first, before I let all of this go."

"Do you think they treat you differently than they do other women?"

Jessie wondered if there was any hidden meaning behind Zoey's questioning but answered honestly. "They look at me more like a sister than anything else. An annoying kid sister. It's funny though," Jessie continued, reflecting on her early days living in the same house as her band. "The biggest issue wasn't our genders so much as our ethnicities."

"Really?" Zoey seemed shocked.

"Yeah. It was like they tried really hard to show me that it was no big deal that I'm Mexican, which, of course, made it a bigger deal than it should have been. We had all these bizarre exchanges at first."

"Like what?"

"Well, these guys love Mexican food. I sometimes wonder if they're aware that other types of food exist, but I swear they didn't buy anything Mexican for two months after we got this place, not even tortilla chips. I don't know if you've noticed, but it's kind of hard to avoid Mexican food in this neighborhood. It's like they were afraid I'd scrutinize what they ate or that they'd offend me by enjoying the food of my people or something. I don't even know. But when Paul went out of his way to let me know how great Los Lobos and Santana were, I decided that things had gone too far. So I explained to them that I know they're not racists and that I won't be offended if they eat burritos, but if they ever decided to cover 'La Bamba' I would leave the band."

Zoey laughed, an appreciative cackle whose volume and pitch startled Jessie. "Things got better, I take it."

"Yeah. It's pretty much a nonissue now." Jessie reflected on the awkwardness of their first half year of living together. Though it had seemed unbearable at the time, that discomfort had led Neal to write "Beaner," one of her favorite songs. "Sometimes Neal and Paul joke about my dad's *elotes* stand or my brother being a landscaper. At least once a day Sean speaks really bad Spanish just to piss me off. He's such a juvenile. Sometimes I question if he's matured beyond age twelve. But when I bring up the long line of alcoholics in Sean's and Neal's family trees, we're even."

At that moment, as if on cue, Neal walked through the door with a case of PBR under each arm and a nondescript black plastic bag in one hand. Bidding him and Zoey good night, Jessie headed upstairs to her book. On her way she reflected on how enjoyable her conversation with Zoey had been. Thinking that she may have judged Zoey too quickly, Jessie sincerely hoped that it would work out between Zoey and Neal, and not just for her friend's sake. She wouldn't mind having Zoey around.

The next morning when Jessie cut through the kitchen to the back door, which was closer to her truck, she ran into a disheveled Zoey, who was desperately trying to make the ancient, moody coffeemaker work.

"Morning," she said, startling the other woman. She laughed as Zoey leapt in the air a little, and then, gently pushing her to the side, Jessie stepped in and started brewing the coffee.

"I didn't expect anyone to be up so early." Zoey wrapped her arms around herself in an embarrassed embrace. Though Neal's T-shirt and boxers covered her completely, the obvious reason for her presence seemed to make Zoey feel naked, and she tightened her arms around herself.

"I start work at seven," Jessie offered, amused by Zoey's self-consciousness. "I'll be out of the way in a minute." Zoey still clung to herself, clearly not certain what to do, and finding

Zoey's awkwardness strangely endearing, Jessie decided to linger a while longer. "So we're still on for tonight, right?"

"Tonight?" Zoey allowed one arm to leave her chest as she tucked her hair behind her ears.

"The poetry thing." Jessie couldn't help but smile at Zoey's mortification. Any of Neal's other conquests would be strutting about in the nude without a concern, assuming they ever got out of bed. This woman, though, not only seemed to care about her role in the world outside of Neal's bedroom but also exhibited a refreshing modesty.

"Oh, right. Yes. We're still on."

"Great. I'll see you at five." She started to head outside, but turned back when she was halfway through the door. "Uh Zoey?"

"Yes?"

"I've never been to a poetry reading before, so I'm not really sure about the dress code. Is it formal, or should I wear something more like what you've got on?" Zoey's face turned bright red. She threw a dish towel, but Jessie ducked it and, as she closed the door, called, "See you at five, *guera*."

CHAPTER THREE

"Hey Marco," Jessie called to her brother and boss at Durango's Car Clinic in Lakeview. "I picked up some tamales from Rosita's stand this morning on my way in. You can have them if you want." She smiled and held out the grease-spotted brown paper bag. Though Marco and Jessie would never verbalize such heresy, Rosita's tamales put even their dear mother's to shame (which was why she usually sold out by seven in the morning), and Jessie hoped that a little bribery plus brotherly love would compel Marco to say yes to her request to leave early. She really wanted to shower before she went to hang out with book nerds.

"Hand 'em over." He snatched the bag from her hand and headed to his office.

Jessie leaned against the office doorframe and watched him. The room was small and lacked any sort of interior decoration. The once white walls were now grayish in most places, and the light switch was nearly black from the touch of Marco's greasy hands. Two tall, dark gray filing cabinets stood against the wall to Jessie's right, but Marco's desk, at which he sat along the far wall, still held several large stacks of paper. The only other furniture, a plain but comfortable chair, faced the desk. In deference to Jessie, Marco had removed his slutty girl calendar, which Jessie had happily replaced with something more modest from the Sierra Club.

As Marco devoured the tamales, Jessie spoke over the whir of air wrenches and ratchets from the garage. "I finished the Buick and the Camry, but I'm waiting for parts on the Cherokee, which Al says he can't deliver until tomorrow morning. I already called Mrs. Johnston and explained," Jessie assured her brother. "She's not ecstatic, but she understands. She can't drive it either way, right?" Marco raised his eyebrows and smiled around a large mouthful of food.

"True," he managed to say between bites.

"So, do you think I could maybe cut out now? It's only a half hour early. I kind of have somewhere I need to be, and I'd like to clean up before I go." She gave him her most imploring kid sister smile, praying he'd say yes. Mindful of the impression it would make on his other mechanics, Marco didn't like to bestow too many perks on Jessie.

He licked his fingers, belched, and then asked, "Hot date?"

Though she recognized his innocent teasing, Jessie couldn't keep the defensive edge from her voice. "No. It's not a date. I'm just meeting a friend." She looked down at her work boots to hide her sudden embarrassment. Just like when they were kids and she'd had a two-week crush on Father Martinez, Marco knew how to make her feel supremely stupid about nothing.

"If it's just a friend, what's the rush?" His face looked as serious as the day he'd left home for boot camp. "Can't you meet your friend later?"

"Come on Marco!" She stepped into the office. "Don't be a jerk. You know Junior and Eddie can handle it without me." She looked at him, saw a twinkle in his deep brown eyes and knew he'd been playing with her. "How long were you going to mess with me, gordo?"

"'Till I finished eating," he said as he polished off the last tamale. "Go have fun on your nondate, mija. Just be ready to fix that Jeep in the morning."

"No problem, boss." She gave him a quick hug. "*Gracias.*"

She made it home in record time, allowing her the opportunity to clean most of the grease from under her fingernails and dry her thick hair. Wrapped in a fluffy towel, she began searching through her wardrobe. Her kidding of Zoey that morning aside, what *should* she wear to a poetry reading? Rejecting two dresses and an old pair of slacks as perhaps too dressy, and all of her T-shirts as definitely not dressy enough, she finally settled on a pair of moderately tight jeans and a light sweater in consideration of the likely chill of spring nights in Chicago. Then as she brushed her teeth and applied makeup, she chided herself. "It's not a date, *pendeja.*" Still she had butterflies in her stomach as she headed downtown to pick up Zoey.

Plotting a tough but necessary quiz to revitalize her students, Zoey almost ignored her phone. She wanted to finish typing her questions so she could photocopy them before it was time to meet Jessie, but since she and her department chair had been trading voice mails all day, she relented on the third ring.

"Bad time?" Juliana's voice cut in almost before Zoey finished her salutation.

"It's never a bad time to talk to my favorite older sister."

"I'm your only older sister."

"Yes, and even though you're neglecting your commitment to me tonight, you're still my favorite."

Juliana ignored the dig and got down to business. "That's actually why I'm calling. Have you found a suitable replacement for me yet?"

"I think so. Neal's drummer-slash-housemate, Jessie, graciously volunteered to take your place."

"Neal's letting you go with another guy?"

"Juliana, Neal is my boyfriend, not my lord and master. He doesn't get to *let* me do anything."

"Mea culpa. I'll hand in my feminist ID card immediately."

"Besides, you big sexist, Jessie's a girl."

"Oh. Is she ugly?"

"What kind of question is that?"

"She lives with your boyfriend, and they must spend time together since they're in a band. Either she's a dog, or you're the most confident, least possessive woman on the planet. Or she's gay."

"God, Juliana! If I hadn't grown up with you I'd think you were raised by wolves."

"Sue me for being direct."

"There's a slight difference between directness and crassness."

"I notice you're avoiding the question. She is ugly, isn't she?"

Zoey growled her frustration at her sister's irritating, single-minded focus. "She's amazing actually. She's smart and funny and strong and attractive, and I'm excited to get to know her better. God knows I could use female friends with whom I don't share DNA."

"Then—" began Juliana.

But Zoey cut her off. "Before you ask again, I don't know her orientation."

"Relax Z. I'm just concerned for you." Zoey rolled her eyes as Juliana's muffled voice muttered something to someone near her. "I have to go. They're helpless here without me. Have fun tonight. I hope the drummer lives up to your expectations."

Shaking her head at the frenzy that was her older sister, Zoey hung up the phone. A tiny light next to the voice mail button indicated that she'd missed another, probably more important call while talking to Juliana. Listening to the message she groaned as she heard the department chair's too-calm voice saying they'd talk tomorrow. She glanced at her watch and groaned again. It was four thirty, and she still hadn't finished her quiz. Hopefully the day would improve once Jessie picked her up.

Inching through rush hour traffic, Jessie grew increasingly aggravated. When a tall, skinny Mexican teen thumped the hood of her truck as he and his friends stopped traffic to cross between her and the car in front of her, she gritted her teeth in irritated recognition of the cocky posturing of many of the boys she'd grown up with. Most of them had emanated a confidence that belied the fear lurking beneath the surface. And the ones who didn't act so tough? They were the worst, she recalled sourly, unwelcome thoughts of Andy springing to her mind.

A tall, shy boy a year older than Jessie and a close friend of one of her cousins, he had attended her *quinceañera* and had danced with her. She remembered his clammy hands and the perspiration lightly covering his hairless upper lip. He'd been unable to look her in the eye throughout the dance, moving uncertainly in his father's too-large suit, and she'd been so moved by his complete lack of machismo that she'd kissed his smooth cheek at the end of their dance. Other than a few cautionary words about boys from her father, she'd given little thought to the incident until Andy started showing up at her soccer games. Midway through the season, after a particularly grueling win, he'd approached her.

"You're good," he'd said to the ground, his fists stuffed so far into his pockets she'd worried he'd pull his pants right off. She could see the muscles in his smooth forearms flexing and relaxing as he clenched his fists in his nervousness.

"Thanks," she had replied, still slightly out of breath from her exertion during the game.

"A bunch of us are going to a movie later," he still spoke to the ground. "Do you want to come with?"

"Sure." He finally looked up, meeting her eyes for the first time with gentle brown eyes that reminded her of her *abuelo*. "I'll have to check with my dad, but I think he'll say yes." She gave him her address in Humboldt Park, told him she'd see him in two hours and went home to get ready.

He'd paid for her ticket, bought her popcorn and a soda and sat next to her during the movie, some forgettable horror film with half-naked teens and buckets of blood. Afterward he escorted her home. He walked her up to her front door and made sure she got in safely. Unlike his friends who had been constantly groping the other girls in the group, he hadn't tried to touch her at all. As he turned to walk down the front steps, she ran back out the door and kissed him lightly on the lips, startling both of them.

Through months of similar group dates they grew comfortable in their relationship, easily holding hands and kissing. They never went further unless Jessie initiated things, which she sometimes did, but these experiences always stopped short of sex. She told Andy it had to be perfect if it was going to happen, not in his car or on a friend's basement couch, and he respected her wishes. She suspected how difficult it was for him to stop, and his respect for her virginity and beliefs further endeared him to her.

They'd been together in this relative chastity for about two years when Jessie's senior prom came around. Of course they went together, though Andy was already out of school. Andy did everything right that night. He'd borrowed his brother's convertible (but kept the top up to preserve Jessie's hair), brought her a dozen roses and a beautiful corsage, endured the endless pictures her parents insisted on taking, and even danced through several songs, although he always felt awkward on a dance floor. He'd sat for hours, obviously bored but patient, as she gabbed and danced with her friends. It had just seemed right to go to the hotel with him.

As she'd lain on the stiff, scratchy hotel sheets in just her panties and strapless bra, her black gown a shapeless heap on the dull carpet, uneasiness swirled through her body to her stomach, unsettling her with its weight and persistence. Andy undressed himself quickly and joined her on the bed. They'd never seen each other naked before, and she was surprised by his sinewy body with its random tufts of hair and his total readiness for the occasion. Alarms sounded in her head, and her stomach became a knot as he removed her bra. She tried to relax as his kisses grew more fiercely passionate, moving down to her small breasts. The streetlights, filtered through the gauzy curtain, lent an eerie glow to the ugly paintings of sailboats that adorned the walls. Andy pulled her panties down, throwing them unceremoniously on the floor. Simultaneously the acrid odor of cigarettes smoked long ago, perhaps after similar encounters, assaulted her nostrils. She could smell old sweat and cheap perfume all around her, and her stomach lurched. Her mind reeled. She had to get out of the room. She glanced at Andy, and he seemed a thousand miles away, but at the same time he was suffocating her.

"No."

Everything stopped. She didn't know if the squeaky sound she heard was in her head or if she'd actually spoken until Andy said, "What?"

Her heart raced, and her tongue was suddenly thick and dry. Still she managed to say in a more forceful voice, "No. I'm sorry Andy. I guess I'm just not ready."

He threw himself facedown onto the bed. An animal sound of rage and frustration, only partially muffled by the flat hotel pillow, broke from him. Soon he disappeared into the bathroom where he stayed for what seemed like hours. She had silently dressed herself, putting her ruined stockings and crushed corsage in her purse, and sat on the edge of the bed, waiting for him to emerge. The ride home was silent.

The next day, an hour after he was supposed to pick her up for a picnic with some friends, she called his house. With a chilling detachment he told her they were through. She merely said, "Okay," and hung up. Overcome with guilt, shame and sadness, she went to bed and wept. Four months later, when Andy married a very pregnant Elena Ortiz, she cried tears of rage, and, certain her prom night decision had been the best one of her life, she swore she would remain a virgin until the perfect person found her.

Shaking her head as if to shake away her thoughts, Jessie slowed with the increasing traffic around her. She saw the school where Zoey worked looming ahead and miraculously found a free spot directly across from the school's entrance. She barely had time to put on her hazards and the parking brake before Zoey emerged from the building. In light gray slacks and a white, short-sleeved blouse, Zoey seemed like a different woman. Her professional attire, though it magnified her beauty, made her seem somehow inaccessible, a change Jessie wasn't sure she liked. When she saw the big red truck, Zoey smiled broadly, warming her appearance, and she dashed across the street to climb in.

"*Hola profesora*," Jessie exclaimed when Zoey opened the passenger door.

"*Hola* yourself," Zoey replied.

Jessie waited for her companion to stash her briefcase on the floor of the cab and buckle her seat belt before she entered into the flow of traffic headed toward northbound Lake Shore Drive.

Though they arrived at their destination in half an hour, they still had to search for two seats together, and once they settled themselves in behind a veritable wall of women, they chatted amicably until the poet took the podium.

CHAPTER FOUR

"What an amazing evening. I'm so glad I didn't miss it. Thank you for coming with me." Zoey, sitting across the table from Jessie at a restaurant near the reading, dug into the enormous salad in front of her. "And thank you for agreeing to dinner. I'm starving."

"Me too." Jessie took a hearty bite of her pasta, ecstatic that since Zoey also was a vegetarian she needn't worry about downplaying her nutritional preferences to accommodate people like Neal and Sean, who thought that the five food groups were beef, pork, chicken, beer and pizza. She added, "I should be thanking you. I honestly didn't think that I'd have fun at a poetry reading. Not that I don't read," Jessie said. "I just don't usually think of it as a social event. She riffled the pages of the slender volume of verse next to her plate. Intrigued by the poet's passion and her powerful reading, she'd felt compelled to buy the book and have it signed.

They engaged intermittently in easy, familiar conversation as the waitstaff, casually dressed in everything from jeans and

T-shirts to modern-day hippie dresses, rushed about to attend to the sudden influx of diners pouring in from the reading. Their waitress, a healthy, dreadlocked girl in a rose-colored dress over bell-bottom jeans, brought them fresh drinks before heading off to a noisy table of women and children. As the waitress soothed their fellow patrons, a sudden and welcome quiet provided the illusion of privacy at their little table, and Jessie spoke. "Who's your favorite author?"

"That's such a hard question to answer. So many authors exemplify different aspects of writing that I really respect." Zoey sat for a moment silently considering. "I love Flannery O'Connor's twisted sense of justice and irony. Mark Twain has a razor-sharp wit and social conscience. Faulkner was so experimental with point of view and voice. Sandra Cisneros draws you into her words and really connects you with the characters, makes you care about them. There's the strange beauty of Gabriel Garcia Marquez and Isabelle Allende. I wish I could read them in Spanish to really appreciate them. It must be marvelous."

"My mom made me read *Paula* in Spanish. It was beautiful, but I never read it in English, so I can't tell you if you're missing out."

"Really? I'm jealous." Zoey's left hand hovered in midair, threatening her food with her fork poised at the ready, but silent and still for several moments, she seemed lost in thought. After a moment she resumed her discussion. "I guess if there's one author whose work I can continuously return to and be surprised by and never be disappointed, it's Margaret Atwood. I always find something new in her work no matter how many times I've read it. She's brilliant." Her face radiated warmth and happiness.

Struck by the palpable joy on Zoey's face, Jessie blurted out, "You really like books!"

"I love them."

"It shows."

"It's nerdy, I know—"

"No. I've never met anyone who's passionate about books before. "

Zoey blushed a little and turned her attention to her salad. "It's…beautiful. More people should feel strongly about things and not be afraid to show it." The splotches of red appearing on Zoey's cheeks surprised Jessie, so to preserve this new friendship, she decided to change topics a little. "Do you write?"

"Not unless I have to." Zoey's skin tone was already returning to normal. "I prefer analyzing literature, picking it apart and putting it back together in a new way for myself mostly, but also for my students. I've written two pieces since I finished school, but it's such a laborious, time-consuming process that I haven't even considered future projects."

"Well, what would you be doing if you didn't have to worry about paying the bills?"

"Are you always this inquisitive?"

"Pretty much. My mother encouraged us to ask questions, except where her authority was concerned, so here I am. But we were talking about you."

Zoey exhaled slowly, a slight frown on her face. "I'd like to think the answer is teaching, but I honestly don't know that if I won the lottery I wouldn't just take off on a permanent vacation." There was a silence between them broken after a time by Zoey's return question. "What about you? What would you be doing?"

"Playing drums," Jessie replied without hesitation. "I try to live like music is my career and being a mechanic is just a hobby that pays enough to keep me interested."

"What a great way to approach life. If I ever find my passion, I'm going to use you as my model."

A comfortable silence befell them, and they ate their meals happily and heartily before Zoey interrupted the relative quiet by saying, "I'm glad that we're doing this, Jessie, getting to know one another better."

"Me too." Jessie smiled sincerely. The more time she spent with Zoey, the more she understood what drew Neal to her. She was incredible.

"I have to confess that I found the idea of you intimidating," Zoey said. "I was terrified to meet you. I know how important you are to Neal, and if you didn't like me, well—"

"I think you overestimate my influence on him," Jessie cut in, feeling guilty over her initial reaction to Zoey and her comments to Neal. "Besides, what's not to like?" Jessie winked. "You are good for my ego. I need to spend more time with you."

Their dinner continued, interrupted intermittently by bursts of harmonious conversation. When the check arrived, Jessie, saying it was only fair since Zoey provided the evening's entertainment, paid for dinner, leaving a generous tip for their still overburdened waitress.

As they stepped out of the warm restaurant, the sudden chill of the evening surprised them both. Zoey shivered and rubbed her bare arms to warm them, but she turned down Jessie's offer to let her wait in the restaurant until she pulled the truck around. When they reached the pickup, however, Jessie stood firm in her demand that Zoey warm herself with the oversized work jacket she'd left in the cab. Zoey gratefully snuggled into the sturdy, dark blue workman's coat (a white patch with a cursive "Jessie" embroidered in red over the left breast), thrust her hands deep into the pockets and pulled the coat tightly around her.

"Thanks," Zoey chattered as Jessie started the engine and remarked that the truck would warm up in a minute. "I can't stop shivering. I guess I was too optimistic about the weather."

Moved to a bit of maternal fussing by her companion's trembling body and chattering teeth, Jessie zipped the coat and lifted Zoey's soft full hair out of the collar for her. Their eyes met, piercing green locked with deep brown, and for a moment, though the world seemed to stop, Jessie could still feel it turning in her stomach. The no longer so unwelcome warmth that she was beginning to associate with Zoey spread from the core of her body to her extremities. The absolute perfection of the moment impressed itself upon her, and every cell within her surging with electricity, she knew as they leaned slightly toward one another that kissing Zoey would be the most sublime mistake of her life. Her ears rang, and her alert and seemingly exposed nerve endings compelled her to act. She licked her lips, cleared her throat and from nowhere said, "Neal missed a good time tonight."

The phantom of her bandmate and best friend, called forth by her guilty conscience, rose palpably between them and forced her fully back into the driver's seat, eyes on the car parked in front of her. Perplexed and a little out of focus, Jessie labored over the minutiae of driving. Nevertheless, she jerked forward, killing the engine, as Zoey softly responded, "Yes he did." Her eyes, heavy-lidded and impenetrable, briefly met Jessie's before she glanced away. Jessie swore at herself and successfully maneuvered into traffic, driving north for fifteen aimless minutes before confessing that she didn't know where she was going. Once Jessie turned around and headed toward the Ravenswood address Zoey gave her, the cab fell silent, and neither woman spoke until Jessie pulled up at Zoey's front door.

"Thanks again for coming with me tonight. And for the jacket." Zoey reached for the zipper, and Jessie placed her hand on Zoey's to prevent her from removing the coat. Zoey's hand, warm and soft, stilled beneath Jessie's.

"You still need to get inside, right? So keep it. For tonight at least." Jessie reluctantly pulled her hand away from Zoey's. "Get it to me later. You know where I live." She smiled at the woman next to her, wanting somehow to soothe her, to erase the vulnerability now clouding her expression. Instead she looked away.

"Thanks Jessie. I'll see you soon." With that Zoey grabbed her briefcase, opened the door and was gone, leaving only the barest trace of her heady perfume behind. After ensuring that Zoey made it safely into her building, Jessie, again cursing her deplorable self, headed home feeling alone.

CHAPTER FIVE

Safely inside her apartment Zoey collapsed against the door. "What have I done?" She sighed as she trudged fully into her apartment to drop her keys on the coffee table and her briefcase on the floor next to it. Still in Jessie's coat she sank heavily onto the couch and sighed again.

"How do I keep doing this? What is it about me that messes everything up?" Not for the first time the ghost of Angela Tucker haunted her, sneering at her and their lost affection. "That was not my fault," she told herself without conviction.

Besides, Angela wasn't the only one. Zoey's past was littered with the corpses of her failed relationships with women. She had plenty of male friends and both male and female acquaintances, but it seemed that any time she got close to another woman, something interfered and sent the other woman reeling away from Zoey. And though she always had her sisters (whether she wanted them or not), she saw their wealth of friendships and genuinely wished for similar connections.

How could Laurel, who really was a bitch at heart, have more friends than Zoey? The men and women who populated Laurel's life loved her. They showered her with attention and affection, often offering little gifts and friendly notes in recognition of their closeness, and some of them had been around since early childhood.

Her other sisters, too, had hordes of friends, and that defied explanation as well. Grace was sweet but sometimes detrimentally focused on her work, while Juliana could be overbearing and downright cruel. Yet Zoey, who considered herself a nice, outgoing person, couldn't maintain a lasting, satisfying friendship with a woman. It made no sense.

Shifting her position on the couch, she caught the unexpected scent of Jessie—soap and fruity shampoo with a slight undertone of motor oil—all around her. Like a punch in the stomach, the warm, comfortable smell thrust her back into that moment in the truck when she leaned in to kiss her boyfriend's friend.

Maybe Juliana was right. Maybe Jessie was gay. She had gotten awfully defensive when Zoey had asked her about a boyfriend. Mentally reviewing her recent history with Jessie, Zoey saw how, in her attempts to forge a friendship with her boyfriend's best friend, she'd given Jessie the wrong impression. She'd touched her too easily and too often, an impulse she'd have to curb in the future. She'd obviously sent the wrong signals to Jessie, leading them to that highly charged moment when their lips almost met.

"But what's your excuse?" she asked herself harshly. If Jessie hadn't mentioned Neal, reminding Zoey that she had a boyfriend, who knew what would have happened? What would she be doing right now? Kicking herself even harder, she thought as her stomach jumped not entirely unpleasantly at the idea of actually kissing Jessie.

"Well," she said, pushing herself off the couch, "that's not going to happen again. I'm looking for a friend, nothing more."

Hanging Jessie's coat in the closet, Zoey shivered a little as that smell hit her again. She grabbed her favorite Northwestern sweatshirt and, vowing to be the best friend to Jessie that she could be, she padded back to her couch to settle in with a good, cheesy romance.

* * *

Watching the moon-cast shadows creep their way across her ceiling, Jessie passed hours of sleeplessness unable to focus her thoughts in any one direction. Scenes played before her eyes, images of Neal, Zoey and herself dancing in front of her, confusing her senses with their vivid reality. She envisioned her first meeting with Neal when, just after she finished a show with Used Monchhichi, her band at the time, he'd asked her out. Though they hadn't been compatible romantically, Neal had refused to let Jessie out of his life. Convinced that her skills as a drummer far surpassed her potential as a girlfriend, he'd hounded her for months, calling her at work and appearing regularly at performances, begging her to leave Used Monchhichi and join his fledgling band, Nuclear Boots. Along with an alarming tenacity, Neal demonstrated a sensitivity and intelligence that he typically hid from women. But as he no longer saw Jessie as a potential piece of ass, he felt no need to camouflage himself with blunt humor and overt sexuality. By the time she finally broke down, offering to sit in with the band once to see if they fit together, she had started looking forward to the gentle harassment of his visits. The afternoon she agreed to take a chance on Neal's musical vision, he'd picked her up and swung her around joyfully, and as the room spun around her she knew she had found much more than a band. She'd stumbled into friendship.

That feeling intensified later that night when the guys took Jessie out for celebratory drinks. Paul and Sean didn't stay long, both disappearing with their girlfriends in under an hour. Paul at least had told Jessie how happy he was to have her in the band, but Sean hadn't engaged in conversation with Jessie unless he had to, and then he'd spoken in monosyllabic grunts. He'd seemed irritated as he downed his beer, and he had made zero effort to make Jessie feel welcome. When she had offered to buy the next round, Sean had declined then bolted, leaving Jessie and Neal alone at the bar. When an attractive young woman on the prowl had approached Neal, Jessie had expected him to bail on her too, but he had ignored the other woman's advances in favor of spending time with Jessie.

They'd stayed for hours, drinking and talking about their first concerts (his: Wilco; hers: Yeah Yeah Yeahs), their families (his: disappointing in almost every way; hers: like a fairy tale, even without his for comparison) and everything in between. By last call they'd shared so many confidences that Jessie felt almost as strong a connection to Neal as she did to her own brother.

Crashing in upon that memory, Zoey's unreadable expression hovered before Jessie, teasing her with its mystery and leaving her with the same unfulfilled desire to touch and comfort her. And mingling with that apparition was a scene of Neal and Zoey together around the house over the past week. His face, flushed with joyful contentment as he touched her (even the innocent linking of fingers as they talked), took on an expression she had seen too few times before to disregard. Other visions, less clear but equally disturbing, swam before her burning eyes, confounding and exhausting her.

Finally, after hours of restlessness, Jessie rose, physically and emotionally depleted. The bracing water of a cold shower followed by two cups of black coffee provided a sense of alertness, if not the real thing, and she left her quiet house in the waning darkness of the early morning, the chill of the previous evening having settled for longer than she anticipated. Upon opening the door of her truck, she reached automatically for her jacket, sighing when she remembered just where it was. She quickly climbed in and closed the door to bar the nip of a sudden gust of wind, and after a moment's pause, she started the truck and pulled out into the trafficless city street, shivering as she waited for the truck to warm up.

Despite her cautious, meandering commute, she still arrived at work well before seven, parking on the street halfway up the block though a large section of vacant curb sat right in front of the Car Clinic. The sidewalks, clear and peaceful, would remain largely free of people until, in an hour and a half or so, the bulk of the city's workforce burst onto the streets, everything about them a frenzied rush of tardiness. At this hour, however, she could hear birds singing and squirrels chittering their conflicting requests for food and privacy. Even with the nip in the air, she desperately wanted to rest on some stranger's front porch a while and watch the natural world unfold around her, its beauty and brutality encroaching upon the more unnerving images of the long, dark night. And for a while she did stop to lean on a low fence as two squirrels ran and jumped from tree to tree, finally coming to a rest on a branch several feet above her. Upset at her intrusion upon their morning antics, they joined their small, angry voices in chastising rejection of her. Wondering if this was perhaps a sign of the future of her social life, she summoned her flagging energy and continued on her way. After all, Mrs. Johnston's starter wasn't going to fix itself.

As she approached the shop, she saw a splash of artificial light falling across the cracked and bald cement before her. Without looking inside, she knew Marco would be moving about preparing for the day. He'd probably arrived not long ago and started checking overnight drop-offs. The more troubling vehicles would be brought in first to be puzzled and sworn over before his mind lost some of its freshness in handling the assorted snafus that would present themselves throughout the day. Though she typically enjoyed facing these mechanical challenges with him—dirtying her hands in her approach to a sort of mental cleanliness—today, certain her overtired mind would not allow her to focus for very long on any task, she felt she would ask for the smaller jobs. Perhaps her restless mind and body could somehow be settled by an onslaught of routine activity. If nothing else, she could at least rest assured in her capabilities and solid work ethic.

So, when her brother greeted her with a playful "You look like shit. Must've been some nondate," she only slightly less playfully flipped him off and headed into the momentarily quiet garage. Instantly a cool stillness enveloped her, and the welcome smell of oil and metal, rubber and cement greeted her nostrils. She inhaled deeply as she pulled her thick mane of hair into a tidy ponytail. She loved the garage at this time of day. Her solitary presence among the inert machinery never failed to mollify her, and working alongside Marco for the few hours before Junior and Eddie appeared often brought her back to their childhood when her brother watched over her, strong, steadfast and godlike with his four extra years of life experience. Feeling dangerously close to tears, she welcomed the security of his presence. Once she started dismantling and reassembling faulty autos, she would, she felt certain, work herself free from her emotional confusion. And as she reexamined the Cherokee, her spirits lightened a bit. Soon Al would pop in with his gravelly-voiced yet cheery hellos and her parts, and she would begin her day in earnest, but for the time being she busied herself with the largely unnecessary tidying of her tool box and near immaculate work space.

The first few jobs after her completion of Mrs. Johnston's Jeep were relatively straightforward—mostly flat tires and oil changes. She undertook them with rote simplicity, enjoying the heft of tools and machinery and the musicality of the pneumatic tools' machine-gun purr. By her third oil change, however, the repetition of activities, rather than turning her thoughts away from the persistent idea of Zoey (and the nagging afterthoughts of Neal), gave her mind ample opportunity to wander. She considered again the almost kiss of the previous night. With a heavy heart she realized that what she felt more than anything, more even than the guilt that gnawed at her heart and gut, was regret. Her stomach fluttered nervously at the thought of touching Zoey's pink lips with her own, and more than once she played the scenario out in her mind. She envisioned how their lips would brush together, her own more full lips gentle at first but growing just a touch firmer before they parted barely enough to let the tip of her tongue pass through, faintly contacting Zoey's lips. Perhaps Zoey would respond similarly, and their tongues would brush each other shyly, teasingly, before retreating then emerging more fully to explore one another with wonder and excitement, allowing Jessie to taste the fullness of Zoey's mouth.

But, she reminded herself, she could never discover the exquisite softness of Zoey's kiss because of Neal. Her oversexed friend, who could, and usually did, have any girl he wanted, decided to want this woman, who slipped in and, in just over a week, turned her—mind, body and soul—into a traitor.

Plodding her way through the next four hours—wrenching and ratcheting, completing estimates and calling customers— she battled the specter of Zoey with a disheartening futility, and as four o'clock inched ever closer, she eagerly anticipated the welcome idleness of her home. There, if thoughts of Zoey pressed themselves upon her (and it seemed likely that they would), she could blur the images with alcohol and, hopefully, sleep. So, as she eased the Cavalier on which she'd just replaced the muffler into a tight but legal spot and walked back to the shop in the now warmer spring afternoon, the heat of the sun dancing across her bare forearms, she smiled, knowing she'd soon be home with absolutely nothing to do.

After what seemed like the longest drive of her life, Jessie finally arrived home and crawled up the stairs to her apartment. Stripping as she walked through her living room, leaving her dirty clothes on the floor, Jessie crossed to her kitchen and, ignoring the rumble of her stomach, opened the fridge and grabbed a bottle of beer from the bottom shelf. With just one swallow she was more at ease, and she shuffled over to her bed where, after setting her drink on the night table, she flopped onto its welcoming softness. With a sigh of pleasure she grabbed her new book and snuggled deeper. Soon Sheila E., her fluffy, fat tabby, curled up beside her, soothing her with his warmth and noisy purr. She easily sank into a heavy-lidded repose, but forty-five minutes into her relaxation, a sharp knock jarred her, and as Neal called her name, she remembered. Band practice.

"Fuck," she muttered and then called louder, "I'll be down in a minute."

Hearing Neal's retreating footsteps, she testily left her cozy nest. She pulled worn and comfortable jeans over her slender legs but didn't bother slipping a bra on under the old T-shirt in which usually she slept. Being small-breasted and surrounded by guys who looked at her like a sister had a few advantages.

Entering the living room, she saw the guys gathered together absently handling their instruments amidst an impressive accumulation of beer bottles and cans, which may or may not have been gathering for days. Guessing at their irritation, she scurried over to her drums, grabbed her sticks and looked up to see not only Sean's and Paul's girlfriends staring at her, but also, on a separate couch, Zoey smiling at her.

Shit. This wasn't happening. She hated having an audience for practice anyway, which she repeatedly told the guys, but how was she supposed to focus on playing when the source of her exhaustion and total lack of concentration was sitting fifteen feet away grinning bewitchingly in her direction? Steeling herself, she returned the silent greeting then fumbled her drumsticks, sending one clattering to the floor. Softly, so that only Jessie could hear him, Sean asked, "How do you say 'mistake' in Spanish?" As she moved to grab her errant stick, their eyes—his full of barely concealed contempt, hers embarrassed and glassy—met. And then things turned ugly.

They made it through two songs, quickly working through the few problems that arose. Sean picked up the tempo a bit during "But Not Today," looking back at Jessie in an obvious challenge, which she ignored. But before they began "Bad Goodbye," Sean scowled hard at Jessie and muttered under his breath, "Think you can keep up this time?"

Not wanting to exacerbate the hostility of the situation, she simply nodded, her jaw tightening as she counted off the start of the song. Cursing him mentally while she played, she more than kept up. In fact, she began playing so fast that they had to stop in the middle. She apologized then counted off again, this time remaining focused until the end, but as her exhaustion built, she found it increasingly difficult to concentrate. And the fact that Sean was being such a *culero* was about as helpful as the persistent gaze from Zoey to Neal that seemed also to include her. Every time she glanced in Zoey's direction, their eyes met, sending tiny electric shocks from Jessie's chest to her stomach and back. She fixed her ponytail, as if smoothing her hair would somehow settle her nerves.

Whether or not it worked she couldn't know because, as she picked up her drumsticks for the next tune, a catchy and surprisingly unsentimental love song Neal was writing for Zoey, Sean intensified Jessie's internal fury with another snide comment that only she heard: "Funny. Our old drummer never wasted rehearsal time playing with his hair. Must be a chick thing."

Grinding her teeth she started the song. She again inadvertently picked up the tempo, and though she caught herself almost immediately, still Sean sneered in overbearing recognition of her mistake. But when she dropped her drumstick again just before the second chorus, Neal turned on her.

"What the fuck Durango!"

"Don't Neal." She spoke through clenched teeth, the muscles along her tightened jaw flexing visibly. Her knuckles appeared as islands of white in the furious red sea of her fists. Sean drank his beer and said nothing.

Seeing her anger Neal backed down slightly. "Well, you're screwing up too much to ignore."

"Isn't that why we practice? So we can work through the mistakes?" She threw her arms toward the ceiling in her exasperation, and everyone in the suddenly tiny room seemed focused on her. "I dropped my sticks. I'm sorry. But are we going to stop every time Paul loses a pick or Sean takes a drink?"

Sean stopped midswallow, and Paul snarled at her. "Screw you, Jessie. Don't bring me into this." His words were covered by Neal's response.

"If they forget how to play their instruments, then yeah, we'll stop."

"So now I don't know how to play?"

"Not tonight." Sean finally spoke loud enough for everyone to hear him.

Her head snapped in his direction, and with fiery eyes and flared nostrils, she looked from Sean to Neal a few times, a thousand curses filling her mind and ready to erupt from her. Not trusting her voice to carry her rage, she threw the drumstick she finally realized she still held and stormed wordlessly from the room.

"I guess we're done," she heard Sean say seconds after she left. As she pounded up the stairs embarrassed and enraged, she heard deep voices and muffled laughter, and knowing that they laughed at her, she seethed. Wondering if Zoey joined them in their ridicule and saddened by the possibility that she did, Jessie slammed her door three times in her fury before grabbing a beer. As she stepped out onto her rooftop balcony, she heard another door slam in the distance.

CHAPTER SIX

For several moments Zoey sat with her mouth open, taking in the scene before her. This was supposed to have been a fun, carefree night, just a chance for her to relax after a long week while also spending time with her boyfriend. And her friend. Instead she'd watched the most uncomfortable display of angst play out before her. She'd witnessed Sean's surliness as they all waited for Jessie to show up, and she'd sensed the tension when Jessie arrived. Still, their reaction to her departure seemed callous at best and overtly cruel at worst. Snippets of insults penetrated her disbelief as Sean, Paul and even Neal blamed Jessie's "fiery Latin temper" for the disintegration of rehearsal. She questioned her sanity as, glancing at Maureen and Carla, she saw them giggle at the verbal attack on Jessie. Surely she couldn't be the only one having a problem with this, yet as she looked around her the evidence suggested that she was. Uncertain what to do she held her tongue until she heard Sean, the ass, say, "You know how she gets when she's on the rag."

"Assholes!" Zoey spoke before she had a chance to think, and even as the whole room turned to stare at her, she didn't regret it. "I can't listen to any more of this." She stood, grabbed her coat and headed for the door. Neal ran after her and grabbed her by the arm, but she turned from him. "I can't be around you right now, Neal. We can talk tomorrow."

Outside, twilight had begun in earnest, the sun taking with it the last of its glowing warmth in its slow descent, and Zoey shivered lightly before buttoning her coat against the impending chill of the evening. As she stood trying to decide whether to take a cab home or risk waiting for public transportation, she heard a harsh, tight voice from above her asking where something was.

Utterly confused, Zoey spun around, looking for the source of the exclamation. Spotting Jessie, she called back, her voice thin and tired, "Where what?"

Jessie laughed a little, her voice and posture loosening a bit as she spoke again. "Not 'where,' *gringa*." She adopted a nasal intonation, obviously poking fun at Zoey's misunderstanding and anglicized pronunciation. "*Guera*," she stressed her accent on the Spanish word. "It means white girl."

"Oh," Zoey muttered. She shifted her weight from one foot to the other and folded her arms across her chest, never once looking away from Jessie, who stood, still in her worn T-shirt and jeans, sipping a beer. She rested her arms on the railing and leaned forward.

"What're you doing out here?"

"Leaving, I guess. I'm not really sure where I'm going, though."

"Why don't you come up here?" Jessie suggested it casually, and Zoey weighed the possibilities. Certainly spending time with Jessie would be more fun than riding a bus home to stew in her anger, but the idea of reentering the house and walking past Neal and everyone else on her way to Jessie's room seemed about as appealing as dusting her ass in pollen and sitting on a beehive. Before she could decide, Jessie broke in on her thoughts. "I've got food and beer." That sealed it.

"I'd like to, but I don't really want to go back in there." She shrugged her head toward the front door and grimaced with exaggeration.

"So climb the tree." Jessie said it offhandedly, as if she was suggesting Zoey take a breath or chew gum, and gestured toward the enormous oak towering over the house, its gnarled branches twisting and reaching through the sky.

"The last time I climbed a tree I was twelve, and I broke my arm. I consider myself emphatically earthbound."

"Relax *guera*. I've done it a few times when I forgot my keys. There are strong branches all the way up, and I'll help you onto the roof if you're scared."

Zoey remained still for a few moments, considering this plan. Finally deciding that the risk of falling to her death was minimal, she called out, "Don't make me regret this," and began her cautious ascent. As Zoey climbed, Jessie offered encouragement and guidance, ensuring a safe journey. Surprised at the ease with which she scrambled up the sturdy old oak, Zoey looked almost giddy as she shinnied along the thick, knotted branch that hung over Jessie's porch. Still, she was grateful for Jessie's arms—fiercely strong despite Jessie's small size—supporting her as she lowered herself to the relative safety of the roof. Jessie's unrestrained breasts pressed against Zoey through the thin fabric of her shirt, and they held their half embrace for a moment, the space between them charged with energy and seeming to grow smaller, before Zoey stepped away and spoke.

"That was kind of fun, but I'd really like a drink now."

"The kitchen's through the bedroom, down the hall and to the right. Help yourself to whatever you want." As soon as Zoey disappeared through the door, Jessie called after her, "Sorry about the mess."

Inside the apartment, which was, aside from some dirty clothes on the floor, as clean as her own home, Zoey paused to take in her surroundings. Though small, Jessie's quarters had warmth and charm. She'd painted the walls, something Zoey had wanted to do in her own apartment but had never dared, and the bold primary colors seemed to make the space come alive. Two bookshelves, nearly as crowded as her own, stood against the walls, and a worn but cared-for acoustic guitar rested against one set of shelving. The minimal furniture—a love seat and coffee table—looked old and comfy. The most prominent feature of the space, though, was a monstrous stereo system with every means imaginable for playing music. Zoey thought she even spied an eight-track. Surrounding it, Jessie had amassed more music than Zoey had seen collected in any one place outside of a record store. Curiosity stirred within her, but she was more thirsty than nosy. She redirected her attention and headed down the hall to the kitchen.

After opening two beers (better quality than Neal's swill of choice), she returned to the roof where she found a fat, fluffy tabby working itself in a figure eight through Jessie's legs and curling its tail around her calves in an affectionate cat hug. Jessie sat down to pet the cat, and as Zoey handed off one of the beers, the cat flopped on its side at Jessie's feet, pulling her hand to its ample chest for a reciprocation of affection, which Jessie gave.

Zoey sipped her own beer then sat on the roof beside Jessie. She enjoyed two full swallows before Jessie asked, "So you just popped in for a free concert, or did they do something to you down there?"

Zoey hesitated before answering cautiously, "They were trying to decide if your ethnicity or your hormones prompted your outburst."

"Oh," Jessie responded noncommittally.

For a time neither of them spoke. Instead they drank their beers and watched the cat chase bugs that the human eye could not detect. But eventually curiosity got the better of Zoey, who asked softly, "Are they always like that?"

"Nah." Jessie showed no signs of elaborating as she continued drinking and watching her cat.

"Then what happened?" Zoey gazed out at the city beyond them.

"It's a lot of stuff. I haven't been myself the last couple of days." Catching a flicker of movement in her peripheral vision, Zoey turned her head back to see Jessie wrapping her arms around her shins and resting her chin on her knees. "Sean's friend Russ used to be the band's drummer. He's a great guy but a second-rate musician, and he'd be the first to admit that.

So when Neal found me and had me play with the band, they all agreed that I should take Russ's place. I refused to come in unless everyone agreed because I didn't want to deal with anger and jealousy. Even Russ was okay with it. He had a brand-new baby at home and no time to practice. I think he was relieved."

"But?"

"But sometimes Sean still gets pissed at me for replacing his friend. If I screw up he's the first one to let me know. Sean's a good friend, and I love him, but if I'm not perfect, we can't stand each other. And tonight I sucked. I couldn't concentrate."

"Why not?" Zoey probed.

Jessie remained silent for some time, apparently considering her answer. After a time she said without conviction, "Who knows?"

"Aren't you angry?"

"Of course. I'm pissed at him for being such a prick, and I'm upset with myself for being off and for letting him get to me. But we'll both forget about it by tomorrow night, and our next practice will be great. It's just how we work."

"Well, what about Neal? Is he usually so uptight?"

"Not at all," Jessie chuckled and shook her head as she answered. "He'd kick my ass for telling you, but that last song I screwed up is a love song he's been working on for you." She glanced at Zoey and laughed harder when she saw her wide-eyed expression. "I'm sure that's not how he envisioned you hearing it for the first time, so he let me have it." Zoey's mouth hung open in a blend of shock and horror for a full minute. Unable to speak, she made no response, and Jessie patted her shoulder in mock comfort. "It'll be okay."

"Shut up you jerk." Zoey playfully pushed Jessie's pleasantly warm hand away. "I've never had a song written for me. I've barely even had love notes written to me. The closest I ever came was in my sophomore year of high school when my boyfriend copied the lyrics of an Iron Maiden song and gave them to me. This is a little weird." She smiled as she spoke.

"The life of a future rock star's girlfriend. Think you can handle it?"

Zoey's eyes lingered over Jessie's face as she answered quietly, "I guess we'll find out."

The silence between them grew again, electric but not uncomfortable, and for a time they merely sat together drinking their beers. The cat strutted back and forth between them, mewing its requests for attention, and though they both stroked its soft fur as it passed by, its cries grew louder, almost shrill in their intensity. Abruptly the cat sat directly in front of Jessie and screamed at her. In response, she sang softly in that same sweet voice from before, "Shut up, little Sheila, shut up. Shut up, little Sheila, shut up." And as she sang the cries quieted, and the cat curled itself between them, expecting love from both women.

"That's so mean but kind of sweet." Zoey rubbed the soft, thick fur on its chest, her fingers almost lost in the long, striped tufts.

"It's not mean. It's my special Sheila song, and he loves it. Don't you Sheila?" A purr roared from the cat's throat as a trickle of drool ran down his chin. "See?"

"He? Isn't his name Sheila?"

"Yeah. I found him under a car when he was just a teeny kitten, and with all his long, pretty hair I thought he was a girl, so I named him Sheila E. But when I took her in to be spayed, I found out that she was a he."

"And you didn't change his name? Doesn't he mind being called Sheila?"

"Nah. He knows Sheila E. is the shit."

Zoey grinned and continued to pet the cat, shivering a bit as she did so.

"Are you cold?" Jessie asked.

"Aren't you?"

"No. I'm still too angry to be cold." She swallowed the dregs of her beer. "But since we both need more to drink, I guess we should go inside. Unless you want to climb back down."

Zoey blinked several times. "Not particularly."

Inside Zoey talked and gestured with her fork intermittently as she ate from a carton of leftover Chinese takeout. After helping Jessie grab food and more drinks, she'd kicked off her shoes and settled on Jessie's old blue love seat. She positioned herself sideways and tucked her sock-covered feet beneath her, completely at ease, and Jessie, disarmed by her guest's ability to be absolutely at home in a new environment, sighed in pained contentment as she took the seat next to Zoey. She would have liked to keep a greater distance between them, but in truth there was nowhere else to sit except the bed. So she gave herself over to circumstance and enjoyed the closeness.

Jessie listened intently as Zoey spoke of growing up the second oldest of four girls on the far north side of the city. Her working-class parents had endured decades of physical labor and austere living conditions in the apartment on West Lunt so that their girls could achieve whatever successes they desired. For each daughter the Carmichaels had scrimped to set aside a modest but respectable sum of money to provide either a very small, unpretentious wedding or a good part of a college education at a state school with the promise of all the emotional support necessary to guide them through the challenges of earning, in every sense of the word, their degrees. Each girl— Juliana, Zoey, Laurel and Grace—had opted for the rewarding adversity of college plus full-time job. Zoey and Grace had both surprised everyone by continuing on to graduate school, pushing themselves almost beyond their limits to satisfy their ambitions. Jessie began to suspect that, for Zoey, ambition wasn't easily satisfied.

"Why didn't you go to college?"

Jessie drank some of her beer, considering how to explain her decision to this woman who so obviously valued education. Where Zoey's parents had borne hardships to provide for their children the gift of experiencing what they themselves had never known, Jessie's mother and father, with their degrees and white-collar employment, took for granted both of their children's unsought academic desires. Shifting sideways in her seat to face her companion, Jessie answered carefully, "I guess I just felt that it wasn't right for me. I got good grades in school, and I enjoy learning new things, but I hated being trapped in a classroom listening to what someone else thought I should know in order to accomplish things in my life. I wanted to actually be out there accomplishing whatever it was I needed to accomplish."

"So what have you accomplished?" Zoey maintained an affectionate eye contact with Jessie, who warmed uncomfortably under her direct gaze.

"A lot and not very much." She cleared her throat and took a drink, trying to steady her suddenly shaky voice. "I was in a couple of bands that fell apart because everybody else was more interested in having sex and getting wasted than they were in making music. So I gave up on music for a while and tried to find something else that would satisfy me."

"Since you're back in music, I'm guessing you didn't find anything."

"No, I didn't, but I looked just about everywhere." Zoey's raised eyebrows indicated a desire to learn more, but Jessie found it increasingly difficult to form thoughts or words when confronted with the intimacy of Zoey's deep green eyes. Again she cleared her throat. "I was a truck driver for a while."

"Really? You don't seem like a trucker."

"That's pretty much the reaction everyone had. When I got my license no one believed that a little girl like me could handle much more than a ten-speed bicycle, so I was determined to prove them wrong." She remembered with dulled fury how door after door had closed in her face. Of course, no one had directly come out and offered her size and apparent lack of strength as the reason she couldn't be hired, but after one month of joblessness, she had begun to realize her handicap in the eyes of trucking outfits. She kept up the search for work for another two months, determined that only she would decide which careers she was or was not cut out for. "I finally found a small company way out in Elk Grove Village that was willing to give me a chance, though not a lot of money. Even though I was miserable, I stuck with them for about a year just out of spite."

"That's wonderful."

"I'm so happy my suffering pleases you."

Zoey shook her head emphatically. "Not the misery. That sucks. But you refused to give up. You broke through barriers and proved yourself. That's admirable." Zoey reached her hand across the love seat to give Jessie's knee an apologetic squeeze. Too soon she pulled away. "What did you do after that?"

"Well, I was a waitress for eight months, a bike messenger for three weeks. I think you have to be really crazy or really lucky to stay in that job for long, and I'm not either. After that I drove an ice cream truck for a summer. All those germy little kids with their sticky hands and sweaty money. It was gross. So then I was a welder for a while."

"Very *Flashdance* of you."

"Yeah, but my dancing career never took off." Jessie grinned at Zoey's questioning look to indicate that she was, in fact, kidding about the dancing. She continued, "When I got tired of being hot and stinky from welding, I moved to Alaska for six months to be cold and stinky from gutting fish."

"Yuck."

"Yeah. That's pretty much when I stopped eating meat. Plus, I was so far from my family, and by then I really missed making music. I came home as soon as I could, and I started working at my brother's garage, driving the tow truck and learning how to fix cars."

"All that just to avoid a few lectures." They both laughed.

During their talk she stole glances at Zoey, noting in snippets how her gold and brown hair curled at the ends, forming little inverted question marks that corresponded to her own curiosity. A smattering of tiny freckles dotted the pale, nearly hairless forearms that emerged below sleeves shoved up past Zoey's elbows, and the delicate bones of her wrists popped up and receded with her many gestures. Without warning Jessie imagined herself kissing the soft white skin and tracing the bones and their hollows with her tongue. Her face became flushed, and she excused herself, walking quickly to the kitchen under the guise of getting more drinks, and splashed cool water on her hot face.

Somewhat calmed, Jessie braved the closeness of the love seat again, and as she sat Zoey asked her, "How did you get into music?"

"My *abuelo*." She smiled at the memory of him. "He could sit for hours listening to record after record and picking apart the instruments and rhythms and musicians. He could listen to ten seconds of a song and tell you when and where it was recorded, who wrote it, who played which instruments and anything else you wanted to know. He was amazing. I loved him so much." Jessie grew silent remembering Papa Nestor and how she would sit on his lap and listen to him and the music. The warm smell of him would surround her like an embrace. She wiped a tear from her cheek and went on. "I guess I just grew up with music. Every memory of mine has a soundtrack to it. After my Papa died, a little bit of me did too. I was ten years old, and the only time I didn't miss him was when I played music, so I played all the time. I'm sure the neighbors wanted to kill me, but my parents never made me stop. At that point they were willing to try anything to cheer me up. I probably could have gotten a pony if I'd wanted one."

"Why drums?"

"Percussionists and drummers were his favorite. He said they were the most underappreciated, like immigrants in this country."

While Jessie was talking, Zoey had leaned forward, placing a warm hand on her knee, which she now stroked comfortingly. Her hand stopped moving but rested on Jessie's calf. "He sounds like an interesting man."

"He was." She nodded and smiled sullenly. "I'm sorry. I'm not usually so emotional. Come back any other night, and you'll see a much more even-tempered Jessie Durango."

"No, I'm sorry. I didn't realize I was asking such a loaded question. Now the whole evening's grown maudlin when we were having such a good time." Her face flushed, Zoey quickly pulled her hand from Jessie's leg and stood up. Jessie worried that she'd driven her away with her tears, but then Zoey said, "I have to go to the bathroom, but we'll talk about happier things when I get back. I've got some very funny school stories that might lighten the mood." Jessie watched as Zoey headed down the little hall to the bathroom, trying to ignore the dull thudding of her heart within her chest.

When Zoey returned she brought more beer, some cookies she'd found in a cabinet and tales of students that made Jessie laugh and wonder how anyone could have the patience to put up with them for long. Around midnight, when they both stifled yawns, Zoey mentioned catching a bus home.

"Absolutely not. 'S not safe," Jessie slurred as Zoey raised her eyebrows in questioning disbelief.

"Well, then I'll call a cab."

"That won't work either."

"Why not?"

"Because first of all, you'll never get one to come out to Pilsen at this time on a Friday."

"And second?" Zoey watched in amusement as Jessie screwed up her face in thought that was far too much for her beer-soaked brain.

"Second, I'll drive you home."

"You can't drive anyone anywhere. You're wasted."

"I know that, *guera*. Stay here tonight, and I'll drive you home in the morning on my way to work. Then I'll know that you got home safely."

Zoey hesitated slightly before asking softly, "Do you have something I can sleep in?"

Jessie got up and shuffled tired and drunkenly to a dresser near her bed. From the bottom drawer she pulled out an old T-shirt, much like the one she wore, and tossed it to Zoey. "It might be a little small, but try this."

Zoey headed into the bathroom and emerged a few minutes later in pink bikini briefs and Jessie's shirt, which clung more tightly to her full breasts than it did to Jessie's smaller ones. Jessie stared for a moment at the long, strong legs now bared before her and the chest which remained partly visible through the thin fabric of the T-shirt, then headed into the bathroom herself. While brushing her teeth she worried over the situation, sure she'd made a mistake, that she'd never be able to sleep with Zoey inches from her looking like one of her brother's calendar girls. And when she returned to her bedroom and saw Zoey and Sheila E. waiting for her in the bed, homey and comfortable as anything, her heart raced and her body grew cottony.

"I didn't know which side of the bed was yours, if you had a side…"

"You're fine." Jessie swallowed hard and turned out the lights. Getting into bed she resisted the almost overwhelming urge to lean over and kiss Zoey goodnight, a light peck to complete the picture for this distorted family album. Instead she said, "Goodnight," and turned her back to the woman in her bed. Zoey responded with a soft, "Goodnight," of her own, and for a time Jessie stayed awake, listening as Zoey's breath grew deep and steady with sleep. But slowly the alcohol in her system and her own exhaustion washed away her anxiety, dulled her desire and allowed her, finally, to sleep.

CHAPTER SEVEN

Jessie woke twice in the night. The first time, startled awake by Sheila jumping on her chest, she was alarmed by the other body in her bed. The alarm quickly subsided into a warm contentment as she recalled how she and Zoey, who slept rather soundly, drank too much and formed an impromptu sleepover. Jessie turned to the body next to her, its warmth reaching out to hers. She resisted the urge to snuggle closer to Zoey, instead contenting herself with watching the regular rise and fall of Zoey's chest in the deep relaxation of slumber. Soon sleep consumed her, and her own breaths fell into cadence with Zoey's.

When she woke a second time to go pee, she wished, on her return to the bed, that Zoey would roll over and throw her arm across her in an accidental embrace. She moved as close to Zoey as she felt she could without violating her trust and privacy and fell back into fitful sleep, cursing herself for the weakness that she was enjoying every moment of.

In the morning as she got ready for work, she moved stealthily about her apartment, not wanting to wake Zoey and end her domestic fantasy. At six fifteen Jessie sat on the edge of the bed next to Zoey and shyly reached out to touch her shoulder. It was small and firm, and Jessie let her hand rest on its inviting warmth as she whispered, "Zoey." A slight stirring and a groan of resistance prompted Jessie to shake her companion a little and repeat her name more loudly. At that Zoey's hands came to her eyes and rubbed them as she muttered something incomprehensible that Jessie chose to interpret as "You smell good."

"Morning." Jessie smiled. "It's early, but if you want a ride you have to get up now. Sorry."

Zoey sat up, the covers falling away from her, and Jessie looked reluctantly away. Jessie found her beautiful as disheveled as she was, and rose to put distance between herself and what she couldn't have.

"There's coffee," Jessie still spoke quietly, shyly even. "I don't know if you would even want any right now. Maybe you'd like to go back to bed when you get home. I don't know." Her words trailed off as she felt an awkwardness rising in her that seemed to be manifesting itself in her inability to communicate. She turned away embarrassed, but Zoey didn't seem to notice.

"Is there time?"

"A few minutes."

Zoey shuffled sleepily into the kitchen and stood for a minute sipping from the Frida Kahlo mug Jessie offered her. Still in her sleepwear she stretched expansively, raising the bottom of her shirt to an even more alluring height, and spoke through a yawn. "I slept so well."

"Really?"

"Oh, I'm always like this in the morning. How about you? How did you sleep?"

"Fine." Trying to look at anything but Zoey's body, Jessie checked her watch, and Zoey, reading that as a sign that she should hurry, shuffled into the bathroom.

"Give me three minutes," she said before the door closed the image of her off from Jessie.

But the image was burned in her mind, and she dwelled on it all morning at work, overcome with raw physical desire each time she was assaulted with a vision of long, leanly muscular bare legs or of breasts asserting themselves against thin cotton fabric, suggesting a supple fullness that would more than fill Jessie's hands. Or her mouth. And though it tortured her to do so, the pleasure involved in succumbing to these visions and the fantasies that accompanied them proved too much for her to resist for most of the morning. Finally realizing, however, that this was little more than mental flagellation, she began chastising herself, trying to find some way to purge the want. The best way, of course, would be not to see Zoey again, at least not until Jessie got her hormones in check. But since she was her best friend's girlfriend—and one that he genuinely appeared to care for—the likelihood of that scenario seemed minimal at best. She spent much of the rest of her workday, when she wasn't concentrating on the cars she repaired, trying to devise a plan to release her from her desires. Nothing occurred to her that wasn't ridiculous or impossible until she was almost ready to leave.

Standing in the front of the shop and filling out paperwork, she assisted one or two customers who arrived to pick up their cars. She explained all the costs and the work that had been done, ran through any warranty information the customer needed to know and, after charging them, sent them, dazed or relieved, in the direction of their like-new vehicles.

Swearing under her breath after dealing with a particularly surly gentleman who'd insisted that Jessie not work on his car, Jessie's stifled rant was interrupted by the sound of the front door thudding closed. Looking up, she groaned inwardly but plastered a grin on her face.

"Hi Chad. Weren't you just here a week ago?"

"Hey Jessie." He flashed his perfect white teeth at her, pleased that she'd remembered. "Yeah, you replaced the motor on my windshield wipers."

"So what's wrong now? Nothing big I hope. We close in half an hour."

"No, just a flat. I think I drove over a nail."

Probably did it on purpose, she thought. Chad, who brought his Jetta in at least every other month, had automotive Munchausen by Proxy and used his frequent visits as an opportunity to hit on Jessie. Marco, if he noticed, had never intervened, as he either found Chad as nonthreatening as Jessie found him irritating, or he just didn't want to upset a customer with his thinly veiled threats.

"Give me the keys, and I'll go take care of it for you."

"No need. I saw Marco outside. He's already working on it." Chad smiled again.

Damn Marco. Now she'd have to stay and talk to Chad. Her brain was already fried from trying to figure out how to handle the Zoey situation. The last thing she needed to deal with was Chad's unflagging interest in her. As usual he was grinning at her. She knew what would come next.

"I ask you out every time I come in here Jessie, and honestly, I'm running out of not-too-expensive automotive problems to bring to your attention. Are you ever going to say yes?"

Stunned by his directness, Jessie couldn't help but smile back. At least he'd skipped the small talk. "You never know. Maybe you'll wear down my resistance if you keep asking." Why, why, why was she encouraging him?

"So if I asked if you were busy tonight, what would you say?"

His gentle brown eyes locked on hers, and for the first time in all the months he'd been harassing her, she honestly looked at him. He was tall, not quite Neal's height, but hulkier than her friend. She detected large, well-formed muscles pressing against his crisp white shirt. His hair, short and brown, he wore in a style that was a little too professional for her taste, but he had one of those firm jaws that superheroes and movie stars always seemed to have, and the kindness in those eyes could make a puppy look mean. He was good looking.

"I might say, what did you have in mind?"

For half a second Chad's astonished facial expression registered his obvious surprise. Recovering he answered in a deep voice that Jessie realized was inviting rather than grating,

"Well, assuming the weather holds, a friend of mine is doing this rooftop performance piece. If you're interested, we could start there and see what happens next."

Jessie considered for a moment before answering. He really was cute. If she gave him half a chance, maybe she would stop finding him so irritating. Marco wouldn't like it, but then Marco never liked it when she dated. "It sounds fun, Chad. I'd love to." Had she really just said she'd love to go out with Chad? His enormous grin confirmed it. Feeling a little weird, she wrote her address and phone number on the back of one of Marco's business cards and, passing it across the counter, asked Chad, "What time should I expect you?"

"Seven o'clock?"

"Great. I'll see you then." Hopeful that a romantic interest of her own would get her mind off Zoey, she wandered into the garage to help Marco.

As soon as Jessie dropped her off, Zoey threw on her running clothes and shoes, grabbed a bottle of water and headed out the door. She'd have to go at least eight miles to recover from last night's excess, but she looked forward to the physical release.

At first her sluggish legs refused to pick up the pace. It seemed like there was glue on the pavement or her shoes. Or both. That was probably good, though, since she felt every step reverberating through her aching head. After about a mile and several swallows of water, she began to feel more human. Her strength and rhythm returned, and she sped up, eager to push herself and really enjoy what remained of her run. Comforted by the familiar burn in her muscles, she pushed herself harder, picking up speed nearly to a sprint. The cool morning air tore at her throat and lungs, and with each burning intake of breath and every dull slap of her shoes on cement, she felt more like herself. As she neared the halfway point, she allowed her mind to wander. Unbidden, her thoughts turned to Jessie.

It had been an interesting night. Jessie had been so open about so many things—her accomplishments and ambitions and the loss of her grandfather. Yet Zoey felt there'd still been some distance between them, something that Jessie held back. Of course, they'd only known each other a week, so how much did she really expect Jessie to offer? Especially when she'd revealed so little of herself. There had to be something left to expose over the course of their friendship, and Zoey looked forward to discovering new things about Jessie.

Still, she was bothered by Jessie's reaction to the disintegration of practice. She sensed that Jessie was more hurt by her bandmates' abuse than she'd let on. Instead of showing her pain or even very much anger, Jessie had put on a tough-girl façade, acting as if the events of the previous night were nothing. Zoey didn't really believe that, but she wasn't yet close enough to Jessie to earn the trust necessary to push her into revealing her pain. But she was close enough to Neal to lay into him about how he'd treated Jessie, which she planned on doing later that day.

Checking her watch and her location, Zoey calculated that she'd slowed her pace considerably with all her musings, possibly a minute per mile or more. Shifting her focus back to the present, Zoey picked up the pace again, racing to finish in a respectable time.

Back home, sweaty and out of breath but feeling pure, strong and healthy, Zoey grabbed an apple and more water and headed for the phone. She didn't care if eight o'clock was too early to call Neal. She was ready for a fight. But as soon as she picked up the phone she discovered that she had new voice mail. Allowing Neal a small reprieve, she punched in her code, and seconds later she heard the first of Neal's three apologies and requests for a return call. Though her anger was slightly dulled, she realized that Neal had only apologized for offending her. He hadn't mentioned Jessie at all. Not that he should apologize to her for what he did to Jessie, but she knew that meant he didn't think he'd done anything wrong.

Irritated at his insensitivity she punched in his phone number violently, taking out some of her aggression on her phone. She hoped to wake him and maybe Sean and Paul too and then make him suffer more. That hope dwindled when he picked up after the first ring. He did sound a bit groggy when he murmured an incoherent greeting, so it was possible that, if he'd slept with the phone nearby, she'd disturbed his slumber. But if that was the case, he was likely still in his cozy bed.

"You called?" She hoped her voice sounded appropriately frosty.

"Hey babe." His warm, gravelly morning voice provoked images of him in bed, and she softened a little in spite of herself. "Where'd you go last night? I was worried."

"I stayed with a friend." Why hadn't she mentioned Jessie?

"I'm sorry we pissed you off."

"I'm not the one you should be apologizing to."

"Hunh? Whaddya mean?" His obtuseness refueled her irritation.

"I mean Jessie. You guys were really horrible to her."

"Durango's a tough girl. She can handle it. Besides that's—"

"How you work. I know. That's what she said."

"You talked to her?"

"Yes," Zoey answered feeling suddenly guilty, as if she'd been caught in a lie. "I was worried about her."

"Did she cry or somethin'?"

"No." At least not about that, thought Zoey. "She didn't really even want to talk about it."

"Well, there you go. When Jessie's upset, she lets you know it. Don't worry about Durango. She's tough. She can take care of herself."

Why did it sound so perfectly reasonable when Neal put it like that? No matter how badly Zoey wanted this friendship to work, it really wasn't her job to protect Jessie. "I still don't like it, but I guess you're right. Jessie's an adult and a capable one at that. But could you try to be a little nicer to her anyway?"

"For you babe, anything."

"Thank you." They talked for a few more minutes before Zoey couldn't stand to smell herself anymore. Saying she'd see him later that night, Zoey hung up and headed for the shower.

CHAPTER EIGHT

"We need to talk." Neal opened the door as soon as Jessie put her key to the lock.

Panic rushed through her, and not wanting to ruin her only recently attained good mood with a confrontation, she asked, "Can it wait?" Neal's only response was a shake of his head before striding into the living room. She grudgingly followed, her feet leaden and her heart racing, and saw Sean and Paul lounging on the worn sofa. They looked as unsure as she felt, which actually relaxed her a bit. She sat between them and tried for a light, carefree tone as she asked, "What's up?" The lump in her throat barely allowed her voice to squeak past it.

"I got a call today from a guy named Dino Ryan." Neal, in his own world, seemed not to notice Jessie's nervousness. "His sister caught us at Elbo Room last month, bought a CD and played it for him. He's been trying to get in touch with us ever since." Jessie's emotions split in two. Though she felt it must be good news, she didn't want to give in to excitement just to be let down. What if this Mr. Ryan just wanted to hire them to liven up his kid's birthday party?

"Spill it Neal," Sean demanded. "What did this guy say he wanted?"

"Dino—he told me to call him Dino—owns a record company."

"Shut up!" Jessie practically leapt from her seat, her excitement getting the better of her.

"He said he wants to hear more, so he'll be at Double Door on Thursday to check us out for himself."

At that Jessie did spring up and throw her arms around Neal. She couldn't contain her squeals of joy. An actual record label was pursuing them. Nothing in her life had ever felt as astounding as this moment, standing at the edge of her dream come true.

"Don't get too excited," Neal interrupted Jessie's elation. "There are some drawbacks."

"Like what?" Paul asked with his habitual tranquility. She remembered the day she had joined the band, while Neal had been euphoric and Sean had exhibited an impossible blend of disgruntled surliness and welcoming charm, Paul had merely said, "Cool," with unbelievable calm. At the time she had been concerned about his lack of enthusiasm, but she quickly discovered that Paul, naturally taciturn, rarely spoke unless he had something important to say.

Neal continued, "Like it's a small, independent label, so we won't be getting rich any time soon."

"So what!" Jessie squealed again.

Sean and Paul high-fived each other, and Sean, who was smiling more fully than Jessie had ever seen, spoke then, "We have to practice."

With raw energy borne of their excitement, they ran through their songs three and four times each, striving for perfection. They played until Neal's voice grew hoarse and Jessie, limp, sweaty and exhausted, drooped tiredly over her snare drum. Paul and Sean both swiped at their foreheads and necks, wiping a constant collection of sweat away whenever a moment allowed. Feeling her muscles cry out for a reprieve, Jessie wondered how much longer they should continue, and after almost two hours they felt totally ready, the discord of the previous night purged from them.

Feeling closer to her band than ever before, Jessie said, "We have to go out and celebrate." The guys immediately agreed, and after some debate they decided to meet anyone who wanted to share their joy at nine thirty at Ziggy's, a favorite dive of theirs that offered pool, music and good beer.

"I have a date at seven, but we, or maybe just me, will see you there."

They all stared at her wide-eyed and open-mouthed as if this was a more significant development than the call from Dino Ryan. "You have a date?" Neal teased. "You?"

"Yes, asshole, I have a date. It's not that uncommon."

"You're practically a nun," Paul snorted as he and Sean regressed to third grade, making kissing noises and cooing "Oooh, you're so dreamy. I love you" to one another. She slapped at them to make them quiet, but that simply spurred them on.

Neal, on the other hand, took a different approach. "What's his name? Where'd you meet him? Would Marco approve?"

Rolling her eyes, Jessie sighed, "His name is Chad. I met him at work, and Marco never approves. Any more questions, Mother?"

"Not now, but if I think of any I'll be sure to ask Chad later."

"And this is exactly why I don't date," she commented over her shoulder as she went upstairs to prepare for her evening.

Perhaps because of the guys' teasing or maybe because she needed this date to go well so that she could quit losing her mind over Zoey, or possibly just because she had some time to kill, Jessie groomed herself excessively for her date. She shaved and tweezed and moisturized and applied makeup and perfume. She swept her long, thick hair off her neck and into an attractive knot on her head, a few loose strands framing her face and tickling her neck. She even broke out her little black dress, not caring that she might be overdressed for the occasion. She wanted to look and feel beautiful, and she did. By six forty-five, stunning and ready to go, she ventured downstairs to wait and exposed herself to her friends' ridicule, which continued in the form of catcalls and whistles from Sean.

As Neal commented that Marco would definitely not approve of Jessie leaving the house looking like that, Sean called her *"mucho caliente."*

"You mean *muy caliente*, ass. Why am I surrounded by dumb white boys?" The doorbell rang promptly at seven, and she playfully slugged Sean in the arm before rushing to beat long-legged Neal to the door, no easy feat for a short woman in a dress and heels. Though she tried to rush Chad out before her friends could comment, the boys got in a few moderately embarrassing remarks as she pulled the door closed between them.

"Sorry about them," she said on the walk to the car. "Sometimes they forget that they're not twelve."

"It's all right. Family can be a pain."

"True, but we're not related. They're my band."

"You're in a band? How did I not know that? Are you the singer?"

"Drummer." She was amused by the question. "Neal's the singer and lead pain in my ass."

"That's great, not the pain in the ass part. You'll have to tell me more about it." They had arrived at Chad's blue Jetta, and he paused while opening the car door for Jessie, smiling at her as he spoke. "You look amazing by the way. You're definitely prettier than my last mechanic. I can't believe you finally agreed to go out with me."

"Thank you. I'm actually glad you suggested this. I'm looking forward to it," she said as she settled herself in the passenger seat. Butterflies swarming her stomach, she hoped for the best.

Zoey glanced around her, thoroughly unimpressed by her surroundings. The hole in the wall that Neal had dragged her to looked, smelled and sounded like the VFW that time forgot. The paneled walls sported a stunning collection of beer signs, their various neon hues casting a lurid glow on the pool table. The scarred floors and lingering odor of stale nicotine preserved the memory of the many smokers who'd passed through Ziggy's doors before the smoking ban had forced them outside. And the jukebox—a relic itself—had apparently not been updated since Zoey's birth. Nevertheless, Neal and his friends had dumped a fortune in quarters into the machine to produce a steady outpouring of classic rock.

What the place lacked in atmosphere, though, it overcompensated for with quality beverages. The craft beer options alone overwhelmed Zoey. Obviously the owner had spent the redecorating budget on expanding the beer selection. Halfway through her first pint, Zoey had stopped caring about the lack of ambience.

Neal, happier than she'd ever seen him, looked positively edible as he stretched his lanky body over the pool table to take an awkward shot. He groaned good-naturedly when the cue ball dropped into the pocket after barely grazing the two, his intended target.

"Poor baby," Zoey cooed, pulling him to her for a lengthy, stimulating kiss.

"I guess I don't mind so much now," he answered, his voice low and suggestive.

"I do," Sean grunted as he lined up his shot. "All your lovey-dovey stuff is distracting."

"Oh, I'm sorry Sean," Zoey replied with barely concealed contempt. She was still irritated with his behavior from the previous night. "But once you're beyond emotional third grade you'll discover an array of human experience that doesn't result in cooties or icky feelings."

Maureen giggled, and Zoey honestly wasn't certain that her use of the word cooties hadn't been the cause. When Sean missed his shot, Maureen laughed more fully at him, and though not as jovial as Neal, Sean shrugged it off and retreated to his girlfriend's arms. They had a strange relationship.

Paul and Carla approached the table as Neal lingered over it, scrutinizing the layout of the balls and calculating his shot.

"Hurry up and lose already." Carla handed a beer to Zoey as she spoke. "Zoey and I want to play sometime tonight."

Neal shushed her gently, still lining up his shot. "Don't rush me. I take losing very seriously."

"That's probably why you're a Cubs fan, sweetie. Now take the shot."

Neal sent a friendly growl Zoey's way before obeying her. To everyone's surprise, he made his shot. As the game plodded on, Zoey discovered that, while Sean and Maureen were fairly contemptible, Paul and Carla were actually fun. Despite her idiocy from the night before, Carla's bald humor and general goofiness appealed to Zoey. Of course she'd prefer to talk to Jessie, who was way more interesting than either of these two women, but so far she hadn't shown up. Reflecting on Jessie's absence, Zoey wondered how she was doing. Neal said their practice had been incredible, so she assumed they'd worked through everything. Still, she'd like to find out for herself.

"Is Jessie coming tonight?"

"Yeah," Neal answered to the table. "She's on a date, but she said that she'd be here."

"A date?" Taken aback by the revelation that Jessie was on a date, Zoey couldn't account for her disappointment. Nonplussed by her reaction, she chalked it up to her hopes that the fun she'd had with Jessie the night before would continue tonight, but now it seemed likely that Jessie's date would occupy her attention. "Good for her," Zoey muttered without conviction and settled in to endure the remainder of the bad pool showdown.

* * *

Sitting on the roof of a beautiful old South Loop building newly condemned to its fate of becoming a condo conversion, Jessie took in the wonder of the night around her. A small, skinny white man sat on a stool behind a high, narrow desk, like a hybrid of a podium and a drafting table. A gooseneck lamp cast a dim glow of yellowed light on the pages before him. Though he glanced at the pages from time to time, he seemed to feel every word, even those that weren't his. She'd learned from Chad on the way over that his friend, a transplant from Kansas, loved Chicago authors and poets and wanted them to come alive for others as they had for him. So he'd started doing rooftop readings of their works with some of his own writing sprinkled in wherever and whenever he could. She had to admit that she was more moved now by the words she'd been forced to read over and over in school than she'd ever been before. The little man's passionate reading, underscored by the output of a jazz trio off to his side, poured out into the clear, crisp night as the glow from his lamp faded into the backdrop of the moon and the stars and the subtly shifting lights of the city skyline. She'd never experienced her city quite like this.

She absorbed the commingling of music and poetry and thought, "Zoey would love this." As a light wind filtered through the crowd, she shuddered a little. Automatically Chad removed his jacket and draped it across her bare shoulders, whispering, "Okay?" She nodded as the pang of memory hit her and she saw herself tucking Zoey into her work jacket two nights ago. Their almost kiss floated up in her consciousness, and she forced it to the back of her mind, wondering how long she would have to struggle to get over someone she had never even kissed.

Applause all around her jarred her from her musings, and she quickly began clapping, hoping Chad hadn't noticed she'd been off in space. He seemed oblivious as he leaned close and said in her ear, "What next?"

Warmed but unsettled by his nearness, she turned in her seat to face him and put a small distance between them. She hadn't decided when they were in the car if she should invite him to Ziggy's. She still wasn't certain, but the persistence of her feelings for Zoey made her lean toward spending more time with Chad to help her move on. "Do you need to see your friend?"

"I'll congratulate him on the way out. I'm sure he won't care. Besides, I'd rather spend my time with you." He laid his hand on hers, and it didn't bother her so she smiled and let it stay.

"Well, if you're okay with it, I'd like to meet up with the band. We're sort of precelebrating possibly being signed."

"That's incredible! Of course we'll go." His broad smile warmed her further. Rather than the smarmy creep she'd considered him, Chad was really a nice guy. They were hardly more than acquaintances, yet he seemed proud of her accomplishment. Maybe, given enough time, she could feel something for him. She was already enjoying his company more than she ever thought possible. He could be her ticket away from Zoey.

As they filed down the stairs and out onto the street, he placed a steadying hand on the small of her back, keeping it there for the short walk to the car. It felt warm and powerful, and she leaned in to him a little, seeking some comfort from his strong presence. When they reached the car, she removed his jacket and handed it back to him. "Thanks. It's a little warmer down here. I should be fine."

He took the jacket, asking, "Are you sure?" As he opened the car door for her, she nodded and got in. Fastening her seat belt, she noticed that the butterflies from earlier returned, and she wondered if that was a good sign.

At the bar half an hour later Chad was getting them drinks when she spotted Zoey. A stampede of elephants trampled the butterflies from the car, wreaking havoc on the thin veneer of assurance she'd developed throughout the evening. "Uh-oh," she sighed as Zoey headed for her.

Grabbing Jessie in a friendly embrace, Zoey spoke in her ear, "You look amazing. I love your dress." Even in heels, Jessie was still a few inches shorter than Zoey, whose warm breath curled around Jessie's ear like a kiss. She felt Zoey's warmth and the substance of her there in her arms, savoring her nearness while also kicking herself for making things harder.

Forcing herself, she stepped back, muttering, "Thanks. You look good too."

Though Zoey simply wore jeans and a cream V-neck sweater, she was stunning. For half a second Jessie allowed her eyes to take in the full view of cleavage presented by the vee of the sweater. A person could get lost in that narrow valley of flesh, and Jessie followed it to a logical, stimulating conclusion in her mind. Almost before she had time to chastise herself for acting like a pervert, Chad sidled up next to her, handed her a beer and placed his suddenly heavy hand around her waist.

Zoey's eyes widened, and she stammered a greeting, helping to clear the recent fog from Jessie's brain. "I'm sorry." She shook her head, laughing at herself and introduced the other two sides of her personal romantic triangle. Chad's weighty hand left her free floating for a moment as he reached to shake Zoey's hand and exchange the usual pleasantries.

"Nice to meet you."

"You too." Zoey shifted a little uncomfortably, wiping the hand she'd just given Chad on her jeans. "I should go back. The boys are playing pool, and if they ever finish, Carla and I get to play."

Before Jessie could protest, Zoey was gone. For the rest of the night, she saw Zoey only fleetingly between conversations and congratulations or as they passed on the way to and from the bar. Each time they spoke, Zoey was cordial but distant, but as the night wore on Chad grew less distant. His hands stayed on her almost constantly, touching an arm or hip, stressing the connection between them. And though she was never a fan of public affection, she kissed him a few times right in front of everyone. When their lips met the first time, a leaden iciness descended upon her stomach. Ignoring the warnings in her head and gut, her own more reserved nature and even her friends' not-so-subtle stares, she kissed him more fully, their tongues volleying. When she broke the kiss, feeling little more than disgust at her behavior, she opened her eyes to Zoey's stony gaze. As a smile of resignation passed Zoey's lips, she slowly turned away, adding to Jessie's trepidation. Each kiss she shared with Chad intensified her sense that something was wrong, while also seeming to intensify Chad's sense of something being right. After one particularly affectionate and unsettling kiss, Jessie excused herself to use the bathroom. Knowing her bandmates, she warned Chad not to let her friends get to him and headed upstairs to find peace in the toilet.

Most patrons seemed not to know about the upstairs bathroom at Ziggy's. It had taken Jessie two visits and the sheer desperation caused by a long line and an overfull bladder to send her to the mostly vacant second floor at all, but once she discovered it, she preferred it to the usually damp and crowded bathroom on the first floor. Its distance from the throng, increased slightly by a long, narrow corridor leading from the door to the stalls, sinks and mirror, deadened the noise of the bar, making thought and conversation a possibility, and its size meant that, even on nights when other women found their way there, she could maneuver around them to a sink or the mirror. Tonight as she turned the corner at the end of the little entryway, she saw Zoey at the far sink. Both she and her heart gave a little jump.

"Hey." Her shaky voice sounded strange to her ears. For the first time that night, they were alone.

"Hey," Zoey replied, still distant.

Jessie leaned against the wall, not wanting to go into a stall and risk Zoey leaving. Rather than the solitude she had come in search of, she suddenly wanted to be near Zoey. Evidently her plan had backfired miserably. Instead of shifting her desire, pitting Chad against Zoey actually intensified the attraction she felt for her best friend's girlfriend. With acute sadness and disgust she realized that she'd selfishly used a really nice man and that she was doomed.

Unsure of how to proceed, Jessie focused on small talk. "Nice place," she gestured to the plain white walls and checkered tile of the bathroom. Nothing extraordinary.

"Yeah." Silence again. What was going on with Zoey? Was she mad? Had Jessie upset her somehow? Jessie was about to ask when Zoey finally turned to face her. "So your date is cute."

"I guess so." Ashamed, she stared at her hands not wanting to look at Zoey or to face her own reflection in the mirror.

"You don't like him?" Jessie shrugged, a noncommittal bleat escaping from her throat, and Zoey stepped closer. "It seems like you really like him. And he's definitely interested in you." Her words were cold and hard, and she closed in on Jessie, standing inches away from her. Softening a bit she said, "But why wouldn't he be?"

Instantly thinking of a half a dozen reasons, Jessie found herself deplorable. Though she hadn't intended to hurt anyone, she would, at the very least, bruise Chad's ego when she refused a second date, which she had to do now that she recognized her mistake. On top of that she couldn't consider Neal's pain if he ever found out about her betrayal, contained though it was. And she still had the problem of her attraction to Zoey. Her eyes stung, and she heard, as if from a distance, "Please don't."

She had no idea if she or Zoey said it, but soon Zoey's arms were tightly around her. They were warm and secure, and her face was in Zoey's hair breathing in the smell of her shampoo and perfume. Zoey spoke softly in her ear, her voice warm and low. "Why are you crying? Oh, please don't cry."

Her misery slightly abated, Jessie turned her head to try to answer, and Zoey must have turned her head too. Their lips met, briefly, alarmingly, and they pulled away, each woman searching the other's eyes for a sign. The corner of Zoey's mouth twitched slightly upward, and Jessie felt as though she was swimming through molasses trying to get back to Zoey's mouth. Time slowed, and the air grew heavy as their lips met again, still hesitant and a little uncertain. Jessie thought it must be the sweetest kiss in the history of human affection. Then she felt Zoey's tongue flicker across her lips, and for a moment she enjoyed the soft, tickling sensation. Zoey whimpered, growing impatient, and Jessie opened her mouth to receive her. Endlessly their tongues met, caressing one another. Far better than any fantasy, this kiss woke all of Jessie's senses and set them on fire. She was drowning in the softness of Zoey's mouth, the taste of her warm and sweet and tinged with alcohol.

Jessie raised her hands, which she now noticed were trembling, to touch Zoey's soft hair. Running her fingers through the silken mass, she grabbed Zoey by the back of the head, pulling her closer in her suddenly fierce desire. She heard a muffled groan of pleasure, which sent her soaring higher as Zoey's hand lightly brushed her shoulder then worked its way slowly down her arm. Her attention divided between Zoey's mouth and her hands, Jessie thought she would die from the heightened and dueling sensations overwhelming her as Zoey's fingers trailed lightly over her skin. When Zoey finally reached Jessie's hand, their fingers automatically entwined, and Jessie's heart beat through her chest. She couldn't contain the guttural "Oh" that resonated in her throat, and their kissing grew deeper still.

Their free hands began to roam over one another's bodies. Jessie ran her fingers down the length of Zoey's torso, sending shivers, which ignited a cascade of trembling in her own body. Zoey's hand inched its way from Jessie's throat downward. Fiercely aroused, Jessie pulled Zoey closer, wanting to feel the heat and density of her, and another little moan passed between them. Just as Zoey's hand found its way down to Jessie's thigh, they heard the bathroom door open and women's voices close by. They leapt away from one another, hands separating and eyes focusing elsewhere as a pair of oblivious brunettes entered two of the stalls, still talking. Jessie, on the verge of tears again, whispered, "I'm sorry" before fleeing the bathroom.

CHAPTER NINE

Zoey gathered her wits the best she could with the mindless prattle echoing through the suddenly cavernous bathroom. Then she ventured back downstairs to her boyfriend. Though she tried to act normal, as if she hadn't just kissed her boyfriend's best friend, as if it hadn't been one of the best kisses she'd ever experienced, she failed miserably. Neal's gaze swept over her, and his brow furrowed.

"First Durango, now you. What happened? Did you two get into it or something?" He rubbed his hands over her arms affectionately, misinterpreting her still trembling body.

"What do you mean? What did she say to you?" Surely Jessie wouldn't have mentioned their activities, but she couldn't keep the nervous edge out of her voice.

"She didn't say anything. Her boyfriend told us they were leaving."

"He's not her boyfriend," she snapped before she could stop herself.

"Coulda fooled me. I've never seen Durango act that way with a guy before. I'd bet she's in for a fun night."

"Don't be a pig." She slapped his chest and, breaking his half embrace, reached for her drink. Irritated, she downed half her beer.

"Tell that to Chad," Neal snickered, and Sean, who stood nearby contemplating his next shot, giggled in response.

"I'm telling it to you." She bit off the words, unable to control herself. She only marginally registered Sean's muttered "Uh-oh" as he sidled away from Neal. It dawned on her that she was lashing out at Neal over her own inner turmoil, and she worked to regain a good mood.

Neal faced her directly, and for the first time in their relationship, she saw anger in his eyes. "Do you want to leave or something?" It was less a question than a command.

Breathing deeply and planting a smile on her face, she answered meekly, "I'm sorry I'm being a bitch. This is supposed to be your night, and I'm ruining it. I don't really know what came over me." She finished her beer. "But I'm over it." Neal's look of displeasure softened into his usual easy grin. "Next round's on me." She spoke over her shoulder on her way to the bar for more drinks.

After closing the bar, and long after they should have stopped drinking, they made their way drunkenly to Zoey's apartment, where Neal promptly passed out. Though she was still fevered by recurrent thoughts of her bathroom rendezvous with Jessie, she thought Neal's lack of consciousness was probably for the best. He was too drunk, and she'd just end up more frustrated than anything. Not that she wasn't frustrated now. She couldn't believe how worked up she was. What was it about Jessie that turned her into a quivering pile of hormones?

Hardly sober herself, she carefully undressed her blacked out boyfriend, then groaned at the mess she'd made of her life. Looking at Neal she felt affection and desire swirling around inside her. She cared about him a lot, and though she tended to be the least traditional of her sisters, she had found herself wondering more than once if Neal was The One. She could see herself marrying him in some small but fantastically booze-laden extravaganza and being happy once the hangover disappeared. Until tonight it had seemed possible that they would at least live together someday. Without the rest of the band, she hoped.

But when Jessie had walked into the bar tonight, something inside Zoey had shifted. It was like she had truly opened her eyes for the first time. Reflecting on her thoughts of that morning, she laughed bitterly at her naiveté. She'd been so sure of her purely platonic feelings toward Jessie, of how easy it would be to be Jessie's friend. She shook her head, then instantly regretted it. Gently settling herself on her side and planting her foot on the floor as an anchor, she closed her eyes to sleep. Fleeting images of Jessie—with that beefcake who'd better be keeping his hands off, and then with her, memories of soft lips and tender kisses that grew hungry—passed before her eyes before it all went black.

* * *

Back at home and in bed staring at the ceiling, Jessie wondered if she'd ever get a good night's sleep, not that she deserved it. But maybe it would help clear her head. Even as she reviewed the night in her mind, she grew upset by both the events and her reactions to them. The kiss, though it was wrong, made sense to her. She was unabashedly attracted to Zoey, a fact she'd firmly established this evening. Oddly, her attraction to Zoey didn't surprise her in the least. It's not like she was steadfastly heterosexual. Up to this point she hadn't been *any* sexual. And certainly she had appreciated the beauty of women before, like her seventh-grade algebra teacher Mrs. Moore. Math had never been so appealing. But the strength of the attraction, the seemingly uncontrollable urge to have this woman, startled her.

And what was Zoey feeling or thinking? Was she confused or guilt-ridden? Jessie hadn't stayed at the bar long enough to find out. After running from the bathroom she'd found Chad and demanded that they leave.

"I don't feel well," she'd lied. Underneath the guilt she soared with energy. But Chad, all concern and sweetness, had reacted immediately, escorting her from the bar and even saying goodbye to her friends for her. Thank god because she couldn't stand to look Neal in the eye. But the ride home had been torturous. Chad grew sympathetic, comforting her in her nonexistent illness. He'd even offered to help her inside and stay with her until she felt better, and when she politely declined he said he would call her tomorrow.

Tears threatened once more, so she studied her feet as she said, "I don't think we should see each other again, Chad." She risked a glance in his direction and regretted it instantly. His face was twisted in confusion.

"I don't get it. I thought it was going well."

"It was. But I'm just…it's me, Chad. I'm sorry."

"I waited so long for this night. I thought you'd never agree to go out with me, and when you did, I was so excited. I thought it would be so great." He sounded more sad than angry, which only made her feel worse. "When your friend Neal told me not to get my hopes up, I ignored him. I thought he was just being protective. But I guess he was right. Maybe you're just inaccessible."

Normally she would have gotten angry at Neal for interfering, but tonight it seemed like justice. Watching as Chad's taillights shrank in the distance, she wished that he and Neal were right about her inaccessibility.

And what would happen with Neal? Would Zoey tell him? Jessie didn't know if she hoped for or against that, but she figured it would be obvious soon enough what Zoey decided to do. She didn't relish the thought of that conversation but felt the prospect of Neal's anger was just punishment for her betrayal.

Still, in spite of the fact that her behavior this evening had been nothing but wrong—every aspect of it from using Chad to her disloyalty to and avoidance of Neal—she couldn't ignore the overwhelming feeling of rightness she had when kissing Zoey. Nothing in her life had ever been that perfect, not even playing drums, and she knew she would do it again if given the chance.

"I'm going to hell," she spoke to the darkness as Sheila E. curled up beside her head on the pillow. He placed a paw on her cheek and meowed a reply. Jessie reached over to touch his soft fur, and though she felt comforted by his warmth and light purr, she murmured, "You're no help" before falling into a fitful sleep.

* * *

Someone had a jackhammer to Zoey's head. After a second it stopped, but too soon it started up again. Tentatively opening one eye to find the culprit, Zoey squinted at the bright sunshine pouring through her bedroom window. The phone rang again, and cursing the early caller, she stumbled to get it.

"Mmmph," she grumbled into the receiver just before her voice mail would've picked up.

"Zoey?" The small voice on the other end sounded uncertain.

"Grace? It's so early." Zoey shuffled miserably over to the couch and curled herself under a blanket, grateful for the cushy support that kept her off the floor. Though the floor did look inviting.

"Uh, Zoey, it's eleven o'clock."

"Eleven? Shit. How'd that happen?"

"Late night?"

"The latest." Zoey's head fell into her hand, and she groaned again.

"Aren't people supposed to be too mature for that sort of thing once they turn thirty?"

"Uh-huh. Extenuating circumstances."

"So are you going to be able to make it today?"

"Today?" Zoey racked her aching brain for information. None came.

"Lunch with your sisters before shopping for bridesmaid dresses."

Zoey's stomach lurched at the thought of lunch, or any food, but she successfully suppressed her nausea. "I'll be there."

"Do you want to go together? It sounds like you need the support."

"Very funny. But yes. Give me half an hour?"

"I'll be here. And hey, maybe by then you'll be making big girl sentences."

"Don't count on it."

Hanging up, Zoey shuffled into the bathroom, nearly falling over Neal, who was retching spectacularly in the toilet. She would leave her spare keys for him so that he could lock the door behind him whenever he was well enough to leave.

Startled awake by the phone, Jessie glanced at her alarm clock as she dashed across her apartment to pick up before the call went to voice mail. The early hour coupled with the fact that she'd never given Zoey her number left Jessie with the disheartening awareness that it wouldn't be her calling to talk. But her momentary sadness lifted as she heard her mother's sweet voice on the other end.

"Good morning, *mija*," she cooed.

"Morning Mama."

"I'm sorry to call so early, but I wanted to catch you before you headed off on any adventures."

"I rarely have adventures at seven thirty on Sunday morning," she laughed with her mother. "What's up?"

"Nothing much. Your dad and I just missed you." Uh-oh. How long had it been since she'd gone home? She couldn't remember. "We were hoping that you were free today. Maybe you could come over."

It wasn't so much a request as a polite order, and Jessie briefly considered her plans for the day. Aside from band practice, which she figured the guys' certain hangovers would cancel, she was free. "I'll be there this afternoon."

"Great. We'll make dinner together."

"Sounds good, Mama."

Hanging up the phone Jessie realized she looked forward to spending time with her parents. The comforts of home might help settle her emotions. Certainly she wouldn't tell them what was going on, but just being with them, having fun, knowing they loved her, surely that would help.

"Just water. Please." Zoey's stomach churned at the stench of grease in the cheap diner where they gathered.

Grace smiled sympathetically and rubbed her big sister's back while Juliana and Laurel stared openly at Zoey.

"Don't say a word, Jules. I've held your hair out of puke too many times to take shit from you about this." Somehow she managed to fix a menacing expression on her face.

Juliana spread her hands in a gesture of innocence. "I'm just a little surprised. You're usually more in control."

"Last night was…weird." Feeling flushed and queasy again, Zoey sipped at her glass of water.

"What was so weird?" Though Laurel's question seemed innocent enough, Zoey suspected her sister would pick on her in her weakened state, so she answered carefully.

"We were celebrating." All of her sisters' eyes snapped in the direction of her hands, wrapped around the water glass, scanning her fingers for a ring. "God, you guys. I'm definitely not engaged." A collective, disheartened "Oh" surrounded her, and sighing in surprised relief, Zoey continued. "A small, local label is interested in Neal's band."

"Wow. You could be like Yoko Ono." Grace practically bounced out of her seat in her excitement.

Zoey blanched and cringed at the comparison. The Yoko association hit a little too close to home for Zoey given her potentially band-dividing activities last night. Before she could recover, Laurel blasted Grace over the comment.

"A Beatles comparison?"

"Well, excuse me, but the only other rock girlfriends I know of are Nancy, of 'Sid and' and Courtney Love, and I didn't think the heroin reference was appropriate, given Zoey's current state."

"Courtney Love was a wife and a musician in her own right," Laurel shot back.

"For that matter so was Yoko Ono, but you know the point I was making."

"Anyway," Zoey interrupted her sisters' sparring, which didn't help her pounding head, "the owner of the label is going to be at Double Door on Thursday to check them out. Oh," she cried in a sudden, painful burst of inspiration, "you guys should come with me. Help me cheer and save me from Maureen."

Juliana and Laurel both murmured mild interest, but Grace declined, citing her dissertation and minimal cash flow as reasons. Before Zoey could offer to pay or get a comp ticket from Neal, Juliana jumped in, "But that's not weird."

"What?" Zoey's mind was really not up to dealing with her sisters.

"You said last night was weird. That's not weird."

"Did I say that?" Zoey sighed internally at her unfortunate word choice.

"So what woke the booze hound?" Laurel again seemed innocent in her inquiry.

Zoey hung her head, not wanting to have this conversation but also not having the mental wherewithal to talk her way out of it. Finally she muttered to her lap. "I kissed someone else last night."

"You?"

"What!"

"Who?"

Their simultaneous, shrill cries converged on her. In the excited chatter that followed, their words overlapped one another's at top speeds. She couldn't focus on any one question or comment, and the waiter, bringing three plates of grease-reeking food and a carafe of water offered her no reprieve, for her sisters immediately dismissed him and looked to Zoey for answers. She poured more water for herself, trying to ignore them and act casual, but Laurel prodded impatiently, "Well?" As Zoey still said nothing, Laurel rolled her eyes exaggeratedly and said, "Details please."

Inhaling deeply, trying to find some calm within herself, Zoey related the story of her kiss with Jessie. "I don't really know what happened. We were talking privately, and something upset her—"

"Her? You kissed a girl!"

Zoey hissed at Laurel, "Do you want a megaphone? I don't think anyone in Lake Zurich heard you."

"Sorry," Laurel replied more meekly than Zoey thought possible.

"Anyway, I tried to comfort her, and the next thing I knew we were kissing."

"Wait," Laurel interrupted again, "are we talking about an innocent 'I'm so sorry you feel bad' peck, or—"

"Tongues were engaged. Hands roamed."

Her sisters let out another collective "Oh," and then Juliana asked, "I've always wondered about being with a woman. How was it?"

Swallowing hard Zoey remembered the kiss. The memory of sweetly soft lips that grew fierce with possession of hers flushed her cheeks. "Amazing," she sighed. "I've kissed a lot of people—"

"Among other things." Laurel just had to get a jab in.

Doing her best to ignore her younger sister, Zoey continued, "But this was, I don't know. It curled my toes and made my stomach flip. I think I felt it in my hair. It's like she touched every part of me with that kiss." Zoey sniffed, and then, seeing Juliana and Laurel staring at her, she blew her nose in a napkin and tried to play it off. "Yuck. I'm making *myself* sick."

Grace squeezed her hand and softly asked, "So what are you going to do now?"

"I don't know." Zoey sighed heavily. "Jessie ran out of the bar before we could talk, and I proceeded to drink my weight in whiskey."

"Jessie?" Juliana sounded stunned. "Jessie the drummer? Neal's friend-slash-housemate-slash-drummer? That Jessie?"

"Yes, that would be the one."

"So she is gay!"

Zoey gave her sister the most level stare she could manage. Softly she said, "And what does that make me?"

"Oh, right. But I am totally going on Thursday." Juliana practically salivated in anticipation of melodrama.

"Thank you for your support."

Around a mouthful of food Laurel said, "I really don't think it's such a big deal." Now all of the sisters stared at Laurel. "What?" Looking at Zoey, she spoke plainly, "Do you and Neal have some kind of exclusivity contract? We've already established that there's no ring."

"That's not how I work." Her sisters glared at her. "Usually."

"Why not? David and I both slept around before we moved in together. I never hit so close to home myself, but I don't see a problem as long as you're careful and honest. Besides Neal doesn't really look like the virtuous type. Too bad I didn't meet him before you did."

"Laurel!"

"He is cute. He seems a little too dirty for me," Grace interjected.

"Depends on your definition of dirty," Zoey spoke before thinking.

"Oooh, intriguing," Grace replied.

"Don't worry, Z. I don't find him attractive at all. But I can't wait to see the drummer. Oh, I wonder who you'll bring to the wedding."

"Jules!"

"As if you're so pure and virginal." Laurel barely concealed her disdain for Zoey's parochial attitude. "You had sex before any of the rest of us."

Grace seemed shocked, as if this was the first time she'd heard this, but Zoey didn't have the energy to coddle her. "It's not my fault that I'm older than you two and that Juliana waited so damn long to give it up. Aside from the characters on *The Facts of Life*, what kind of freak waits until she's almost twenty to have sex?"

"I think you should talk to both of them," Laurel brought their focus back to Zoey's confusing love life. "See where you stand. Who knows? Maybe you're in for a really fun time."

"I'm not," Zoey answered emphatically before draining her water glass. "But I will think about things when my brain works again." She refilled her glass and drank it down again. "I don't want to talk about it any more though. Can we move on please?"

They all agreed, but before they changed the subject Grace said to Laurel and Juliana, "I expect a full report about Thursday night."

Zoey laughed and shook her head gently as they began discussing the wedding.

A physically small woman—she was just over five feet tall and less than one hundred pounds—Silvia Durango seemed larger than life to anyone who knew her. Her students understood that Señora Durango was tough but fair, and her classroom had the fewest disciplinary issues of any in the school. Everyone knew Sra. Durango expected excellence, respect and politeness from her students, and those who doubted her reputation rarely needed more than a flash from her fiery eyes to settle them back into model behavior. As a teacher she was formidable, but as a mother she was a force of nature.

Throughout their lives each of Silvia's children had been both blessed and cursed by her love and ferocity. She had raised them to always be well-mannered and courteous, and she tolerated poor behavior at home even less than in the classroom. However, on the rare occasions that her children got in trouble outside the home, she defended them tooth and nail. Once they got home, though, they wished she'd never found out about their indiscretions. But along with iron discipline, Marco and Jessie received even more relentless love and compassion, so much so that, upon leaving home as adults, both children wept like infants for their mother's loving arms. During her time in Alaska, Jessie received weekly letters from her mother full of encouragement and pride. Those letters, more than her own stubbornness, compelled Jessie to withstand the lack of companionship or comfort and the labor she found wholly unenjoyable. She refused to disappoint her mother and came home only after Silvia hinted, through her own desire to see her daughter, that it would be okay if Jessie quit. Jessie kept the letters, and from time to time she pulled them out to remind herself of just how much she was capable of enduring.

It was this that Jessie considered as she climbed her parents' porch steps, and either because she'd been watching or because she still always seemed to know what her kids were up to, Silvia threw open the door before Jessie even had a chance to reach for it.

Mother and daughter greeted one another in a warm embrace, and Jessie asked, "Where's Dad?"

"He went to the office—he swears just for a couple of hours. Tax season, you know."

As Silvia shepherded Jessie fully into the house then led her daughter to the kitchen table where they could sit and talk, Jessie noticed shafts of white shooting like bolts of permanent lightning through her mother's long braid. She wondered when her mother had gotten old. In the kitchen Silvia poured coffee and produced a plate of freshly made cookies that Jessie happily sank her teeth into. For several minutes they exchanged neighborhood gossip and small talk. But after some time Silvia reached across the table for Jessie's hand.

"You look terrible, *mija. ¿Qué te ocurre?*"

Surprised but comforted by her mother's perceptiveness and no-nonsense concern, Jessie smiled. "Nothing's the matter, Mama. I'm just tired. I haven't been sleeping much lately, but I'll be okay."

Silvia continued to hold her daughter's hand, gently rubbing it with her small, strong fingers. She held Jessie's gaze as well, looking into her eyes, questioning with her own. Jessie felt her resolve to keep quiet begin to crumble, and she quickly looked away.

"What's keeping you up at night? Is it those boys you live with?"

When Jessie first moved into the house in Pilsen, she had assured her parents, and later Marco, of the purely platonic nature of her living arrangements. Still the Durangos had bristled at the thought of their daughter living with three men.

Over time they had come to know Sean, Paul and especially Neal, and now they cared for them like family. But they still half-jokingly assumed that any trouble Jessie encountered must be the result of her living with those boys.

"No Mama," Jessie replied softly. Afraid to let her mind wander too close to Zoey, she offered no alternate reason for her lack of sleep.

"Well then? What is it?"

Jessie nibbled the edge of a cookie to buy time. After she finished two, she still didn't answer.

"*Mija*, I know there's something bothering you. I can tell by those little lines between your eyebrows. Ever since you were a baby, whenever you got upset, you'd scrunch your face up and get those lines." Jessie smiled halfheartedly as Silvia's small hand gently stroked her cheek. "Maybe if you tell me what it is, I might be able to help you fix the problem."

Jessie looked from the table to her lap and then studied the tiny fissures in the tile floor for a time before finally staring at the wall behind her mother's head and speaking so softly that she almost didn't hear herself, "I think I'm in love."

Silvia laughed gently. "Poor baby. That's horrible."

"Mama, it is! It hurts, and I hate myself for feeling this way, and I want to stop, but I can't. I've tried, and I can't." Big tears ran slowly down Jessie's cheeks, and she drew a ragged breath before dropping her head in her hands and sobbing.

Silvia moved behind Jessie and tenderly stroked her daughter's hair and back. "Shh, Jessie. Tell me, what's the problem with being in love?"

"The problem isn't being in love. It's that I can't be with— this person can't love me back."

Silvia's protective side flared as she huffed, "And just why wouldn't this mystery person want to be with my beautiful daughter? Is he blind or stupid?"

"Neither. I'm a third wheel."

"Oh. He's already in a relationship?"

"Yeah," Jessie cleared her throat a little. "With Neal."

Her mother's hands stilled on her back. "What?"

Jessie turned in her chair to face her mother. She'd never lied to her before, not even when she'd stolen candy from the corner store and faced the most serious trouble of her five-year-old life. She decided not to begin now. "Mama, I'm in love with a woman."

Silvia sat down heavily, looking old and perplexed. She folded her hands in her tiny lap and took a deep breath while Jessie waited to know her thoughts. Long ago she'd learned to let her mother process information fully before expecting a reaction. Pestering her usually pushed her into a negative response borne of a lack of time to consider the situation fully. Excruciating though it was, Jessie knew that waiting for Silvia to speak would be far better than asking questions about her feelings or talking about how wonderful it would be to have a lesbian daughter.

After a very long ten minutes, Silvia exhaled slowly and loudly and said, "Have you ever had a blood orange?"

Questioning her mother's grip on reality, Jessie answered cautiously, "Sure. Lots of times. Why?"

Silvia took her daughter's hands in her own tiny ones, looking at them as she spoke. "I had one yesterday. It was so sweet and delicious. Thing is, I thought I'd grabbed just a regular orange until I'd peeled it and went to take a bite. I wasn't even paying attention until I saw rubies and garnets where there should have been amber and gold. It was such a surprise. Not in a good way, not in a bad way, just different. You're like that, Jessie. You always surprise me."

Silvia's eyes drifted up to Jessie's, locking on them as she continued, "I've been very lucky. I've always known what I wanted, and I've usually gotten it. But you keep searching for what you want. You look everywhere, no stone unturned, and your father and I have supported your questioning, even if we didn't like the decisions you made, like not going to college. What we want for you, even more than we wanted you to get an education or to have a safe, respectable career, is happiness. I wasn't expecting your search to take you in this direction, but if it will make you happy, I'll support you in this too."

"You're not upset?"

"I'm not ecstatic, and it's certainly not what I would have picked for you." Jessie's heart and body sank as her mother's words hit her. Silvia cupped her daughter's chin, lifting her face up to make eye contact again. "But if this will make you happy, *mija*, then I can accept it. I'm just not sure that this is making you happy. Convince me. Why is this woman so special?"

With a hopeful heart, Jessie opened up about Zoey. "Well, she reminds me a little of you actually."

"Is she Mexican?" Silvia seemed encouraged by this possibility.

"No Mama. She's a white girl named Zoey. I call her '*guera*,' and she laughs—she has a great laugh that goes from this tiny giggle to a huge cackle without warning." Her involuntary reflection that Neal had gushed just like this not long ago gave Jessie momentary pause. Sighing, she continued, "She's a college professor, and when she talks about her students, her voice fills with delight and frustration, and her eyes dance. She loves it. She was probably born to do it. Like you. And she's smart and funny and tall. She's almost as tall as Neal, but she's prettier. Mama, she's beautiful."

"Does she know how you feel?"

"Probably. We kissed last night." Her mother's eyes grew twice in size and locked on her, making Jessie's cheeks red and warm in embarrassed shame. She knew her mother held fidelity in high regard, and because she hated to disappoint her, Jessie tried to explain the circumstances surrounding the kiss, but her mother wouldn't hear it.

"What about Neal? Does he know?"

"I don't think so. He got home when I was leaving, and other than a nasty hangover, he seemed normal. He says hello, by the way."

Silvia smiled but remained focused on the conversation. "Have you talked to Zoey?"

"No. I ran away from her."

"Oh, honey. You have to talk to her."

"I know. It's just so hard."

"You've never run from a challenge before."

"Yeah, but—"

"No but's, *mija*. You've never held anything back, and even when that meant a lot of pain for you, you always refused to give anything less. This is the same. You have to approach this situation courageously, openly and honestly. With Neal, with Zoey, and with yourself. You have to figure out what you want and go after it." She gave Jessie's limp hand another little squeeze. "But you also have to be willing to sacrifice. No matter what, you're going to lose something in this situation."

"I know." She hung her head considering the possible loss she faced. Zoey or Neal might never talk to her again. Neither prospect filled her with joy.

"Talk to Zoey. See how she feels. Maybe the decision will already be made for you. Whatever happens, though, you must be honest. Someone's going to get hurt here, and lies will only make the pain worse."

Jessie nodded solemnly, tears ready to fall yet again.

"I love you, Jessie, no matter what." With that the tears ran down Jessie's cheeks, and she hugged her mother tightly.

"Thank you Mama."

Shortly after that her father's key scraped in the lock, and the three of them spent the rest of the afternoon talking and laughing together, Antonio and Jessie getting in Silvia's way as she cooked. Despite Silvia's reverence for honesty, she opted not to tell Jessie's father about the situation. Silvia said it would only worry him, and the best course of action would be to wait until it was absolutely necessary to inform Antonio Durango of his only daughter's unconventional romance. So they just enjoyed each other's company until well into the evening. Jessie told them about the possible deal with Dino and, wanting their support, invited them to the show on Thursday, even leaving her comp tickets as incentive. But she knew they likely wouldn't make it. They encouraged her ambitions wholeheartedly, but the Durangos maintained a strict nine o'clock bedtime, a curfew which she now threatened to break for them.

As they said their goodbyes, Jessie's parents loaded her down with leftovers for those boys, and Silvia, hugging her daughter tightly, said, "You remember what we talked about, Jessie."

"I will, Mama." She walked to her truck, arranged the food on the seat next to her and, pulling slowly away, wondered if she had the courage to listen to her mother's advice.

CHAPTER TEN

Having only a couple of morning classes on Tuesdays and Thursdays, Zoey devoted most of those days to office hours and grading. This Tuesday, sitting at her desk face-to-face with the revisions that had started trickling in, Zoey couldn't make herself read them. Several times she reached for her purple pen—red left too many of the essays looking gory and blood-stained—but almost as soon as her fingers wrapped around it, they slackened again, and she set the pen back down, wrapped up in thought. It had been three days since she and Jessie had kissed, and though memories of the event plagued her, she still hadn't figured out what to do. Avoiding Jessie (and Neal) had worked so far, but eventually she'd have to bite the bullet. Their big show was Thursday night, and ready to face them or not, she'd promised to go.

A knock on her door jarred her from her thoughts, and she looked up to see Nora, usually one of her best students, standing in the doorway. In the past weeks Nora had been absent more often than not, and though Zoey thought it odd, she refused to pry. It was ultimately none of her business. In her hands Nora clutched the essay Zoey had returned the day before, a week later than the rest of the class due to Nora's recent absences.

"Have a seat, Nora."

The young girl perched nervously on the edge of the chair next to Zoey's desk. Instead of her usual impeccable appearance, Nora wore pajama pants and a Bulls sweatshirt, and she'd covered her close-cropped hair with an old bandana. Zoey found her student's current unkempt state troubling. After a painfully silent moment, Nora held the paper out to Zoey and said helplessly, "I've never failed anything before, Professor Carmichael. Ever." Her lips quivered, and her voice shook as tears welled in her big eyes then spilled over onto her brown skin.

"So what happened?" Zoey resisted the urge to place a comforting hand on her student's arm. These days even innocent touching could be easily misconstrued.

"Personal stuff." Nora seemed shy, uncertain, a drastic contrast to her usual in-class personality.

"Can you tell me about it?" As a rule Zoey kept herself separate from her students' private lives. They held no bearing on the classroom, and it was easier to award grades based on performance if her personal feelings for a student didn't get in the way. But in extreme circumstances, she couldn't maintain that barrier.

Aside from a few reticent sniffs, Nora stayed quiet for a few moments. When Zoey gently nudged a box of tissue toward her, Nora blew her nose then softly said, "My gramma died."

At times like this, in the face of suffering and loss, Zoey felt a rare thankfulness that she'd never known her own grandparents. Her father had been orphaned as a boy, left to the care of a cold government for two years before an older sibling took over his upbringing. Her mother's parents, though still alive, had visited from Ireland only once, when Zoey was ten. They'd been kind and friendly enough but had seemed like strangers, talking in that same funny tongue as her mother, and she'd been indifferent to their presence and departure. Often in her years she'd felt a sense of lack but also confusion and relief as she'd watched her friends grieve the loss of their grandparents. She'd felt it when Jessie spoke of her grandfather, and she felt it again now.

"I'm so sorry to hear that, Nora."

The girl wiped away fresh tears. "She helped raise me. I haven't really been thinking about school very much, and with the funeral and everything, I didn't get to the library to do the research. I'm sorry."

"Oh, Nora, why didn't you tell me? I would have given you an extension."

For half a second after she spoke, Zoey wondered if she was being played with. Today's students had no reservations about using long-dead relatives as excuses. Often they even killed off perfectly healthy parents and grandparents to get an extension or a pass on an assignment. But Zoey remembered Jessie's tears for her lost grandfather and how she longed to comfort her, and she sensed that the loss before her was just as potent.

As Nora wiped giant tears from her chipmunk cheeks with another tissue, Zoey grabbed a pad of paper and pen and started making notes, speaking as she wrote. "Here are a couple of good, basic sources on Steinbeck. Start with these. They'll give you some solid background, but more importantly they'll point you to more specific sources. You can take an extra week to get this done."

"Really?" Zoey nodded, and for the first time Nora's face brightened. "Oh my god, thank you, Professor Carmichael. I'll go to the library right now." She stood up to leave.

"Good. And Nora?"

"Yes?"

"If you have any trouble, come see me. We'll work something out."

"I will Professor Carmichael. Thank you so much."

Watching her student race down the hallway, Zoey sighed to herself, "I'm getting too soft for this job." Then she turned back to the ungraded revisions before her and thought about Jessie.

* * *

For Jessie the week passed in a blur. Both Marco and Neal worked her endlessly, and though she welcomed the near constant activity, she missed having any time to herself. She wanted to heed her mother's advice and really contemplate her situation, the possible outcomes of it and which of those she could best live with, but at the end of each night she trudged up the stairs to her apartment too exhausted to do little more than feed Sheila E. and fall into bed. Most nights she even forgot to feed herself.

By Thursday morning she'd given up hope of figuring anything out until after the show. She couldn't guess what her reaction would be when faced with Zoey, who'd been conspicuously absent from the house since Saturday night. Afraid to arouse suspicion in Neal but even more scared that she'd driven Zoey away, Jessie had casually questioned Neal on Tuesday night after practice.

"Where's Zoey been lately?"

"Oh, she says she's got a ton of papers to grade. She's trying to get them done so she can come to the show on Thursday."

"Cool." She thought her voice had sounded shaky, but if it was Neal hadn't noticed.

"Yeah. I've been thinking about the set list for Thursday, and I think we should play her song."

"Really? I don't know if we've got it down yet."

"Are you kidding? It sounded perfect tonight. And I want her to hear it for real."

His emphasis on this last point held a world of meaning for her, but of course she'd agreed with him—arguing would draw his attention to where she least wanted it to go. But now on top of seeing Zoey for the first time since they'd kissed, she would be playing her a heartfelt love song in front of a mass of people. Granted, no one would know that it was heartfelt from her as well as Neal, but that thought didn't settle her nerves any.

As nine o'clock, the scheduled start of their set, inched ever closer, she found herself growing more on edge. She'd been so skittish at work, fumbling tools and parts and nearly dropping Marco's favorite coffee mug, that he'd sent her home early. Though she planned on napping before the show, once her head hit the pillow her mind began racing at a thousand miles an hour, manufacturing new worries in addition to those she already had regarding Dino and Zoey. So instead of getting much-needed rest, Jessie found herself packing up gear. Consulting a mental checklist, she went over their equipment three times and still felt uncomfortable. Glancing at her watch, however, she convinced herself that the boys would soon be home to help her remember what she forgot, so she headed back upstairs to shower and dress.

Naturally she labored over what to wear—she wanted to look rock and roll, but not unapproachably so. Plus she worried that she should offset the guys' jeans and T-shirt approach to fashion while still looking as if she belonged. There was another, more compelling reason she wanted to look good, but she turned her thoughts away from that. Half an hour later and deep into the recesses of her closet, she finally decided that comfort would be her best friend on a night like this, and she donned soft old jeans and a simple white tank top under a gauzy black cotton pullover. Though the black complemented her coloring, she would almost definitely take off that shirt, light though it was, once she heated up onstage. She left her hair down, its thick waves framing her face but likely to look a little wild as she played. Dressed and ready to go, she now had nothing to keep her mind off Zoey.

Zoey stood at the convergence of North, Damen and Milwaukee avenues, waiting for her sisters. Since Juliana insisted on driving, there was no telling which direction they'd come from, so Zoey periodically glanced up and down all three streets. They'd promised to work on Grace's resolve, and she hoped they'd convinced her, though in her heart she knew her little sister wouldn't come.

Cursing her sisters for making her wait alone, she scanned the area for anyone she knew. Though she still wasn't sure she was ready to face Neal or Jessie, she couldn't help the hopeful, nervous flutter in her stomach whenever she saw a tall, lanky man or a short Latina woman approaching. The resulting disappointment and relief she felt each time the fake Neal and Jessie passed her by prompted her to wonder, as she had all week, what she should do.

She'd tried to consider her feelings and weigh her options logically, but unexpected and unsought memories of that kiss broke into her consciousness at the most inopportune moments—while she lectured, in a meeting with her department chair, during a phone call with her mother. It was disturbing.

After the call with her mother, she'd seriously considered what her parents' reaction would be if she told them she had feelings for a woman. Her father would likely be unfazed, as usual, but her mother was a different story. She had made her extreme displeasure known when Laurel and David had decided to live together. Zoey suspected that placating her mother was the impetus behind Dave's surprising proposal last October, and though she was happy for her sister—hideous bridesmaid dress notwithstanding—it didn't bode well for her current situation. If Fiona Carmichael couldn't handle a little hetero shacking up, what would she say about her second born delving into lesbianism?

If that was even what she wanted. She cared about Neal. They had fun together, and aside from his occasional immaturity, he was a really great guy. She dreaded the idea of hurting him, but there was something undeniable between her and Jessie.

"What am I going to do?" she sighed as she spotted Juliana and Laurel heading toward her on Milwaukee.

"No Grace?" she asked when they got near. Her stomach in fresh knots, she wanted the comforting presence of her baby sister near her, something to even out the influence of the two harpies she led into the venue.

"She's too focused on schoolwork, like someone else we could mention." Zoey had used her job as an excuse not to talk to her sisters or Neal. She didn't want to face any of them or their questions.

Frowning, Zoey ignored Laurel's comment and ordered them drinks. They were a little early, yet the place was filling up. As she handed her sisters their beers, she scanned the crowd for Neal or Jessie. Seeing neither, she turned her attention back to her sisters.

"Sure you should be doing that?" Juliana gestured toward Zoey's drink.

"I'll be okay if I stick to beer." She took a defiant swallow and, feeling her nervousness subside slightly, realized she'd have to be very careful not to succumb to the temptations of liquid courage.

"So what are we in for tonight?"

Zoey wasn't sure if Laurel was asking about the bands or her personal life, but not being prepared to answer to the second of those, she focused on the first.

"If it's anything like last time, we'll have to endure some truly awful music before we get to Nuclear Boots. Conversation will be next to impossible, but it's fun to watch the crowd." Unconsciously, her gaze returned there, scanning for Neal and Jessie.

"And will Nuclear Boots be truly awful as well?"

"Don't worry Jules. They're actually quite good. They practice every day." Distracted, still searching the mass of people, Zoey added, "I think."

"Because they have to or because they're dedicated to their craft?" Laurel began looking at the growing crowd as well.

"The latter. I was surprised. Neal can actually sing, although I think he sometimes tries not to sound good."

"And the rest of the band?"

Zoey knew what Juliana was asking, but she played dumb.

"Sean and Paul both play well, at least as far as I can tell."

Exasperated, Juliana asked sharply, "What about Jessie?"

Zoey's stomach flipped at the mention of Jessie's name. She still couldn't find her in the crowd, but the knowledge that they'd eventually have to face one another filled her with excited dread, and she drank more beer before giving up her search and answering her sister.

"Jessie," she sighed, unable to control the quaver in her voice, "is amazing. She's powerful and focused and absolutely joyful. It's amazing to watch her, and, well, you'll see." Embarrassed by her sisters' knowing smirks at what sounded to her own ears like the ranting of a schoolgirl with a crush, Zoey again looked away to find Jessie. To fill the dead air between her and them she added shyly, "She's been playing since she was ten."

Before her sisters could get in any comments, the first group took the stage and began their auditory assault. Several minutes into the set, when it seemed that the band was starting the same decidedly bad song for the third time in a row, Zoey felt a strong hand on her hip, and in the second before she felt scratchy kisses on her neck, her mind went to Jessie. Surprised by her momentary disappointment she turned to greet Neal, who thankfully offered her a beer.

Self-conscious as Juliana and Laurel both smirked again behind the cheap brew Neal had brought to replace their empties, Zoey kissed Neal deeply. He stayed through most of the rest of the first band's performance, shouting brief comments to Zoey and her sisters, but mostly holding Zoey tightly to himself. Utterly confused, Zoey felt good in his arms.

When the first band announced their last song (which sounded to Zoey just like all the other songs they'd already played), Neal took his leave, shouting, "We're up next." And Zoey was left alone with her sisters. Though she knew she shouldn't, she headed to the bar for more drinks to avoid any conversation with them, even letting others go ahead of her to kill more time. She returned to Laurel and Juliana just as Nuclear Boots walked onstage.

Before they started playing, Laurel leaned over and said, "That's Jessie?"

Not wanting to tear her eyes away from Jessie, who looked better than Zoey remembered, Zoey simply nodded and then laughed heartily when Juliana commented, "She's definitely not ugly."

Laurel added, "I can see why you'd be tempted to switch teams."

Then the music began. Just like last time, Zoey was impressed by their talent. They played wonderfully, and Jessie was, if possible, even more incredible than the first time Zoey had seen her. She had that same focused determination, but her glee was even more evident from the grin on her face. When Jessie removed her top shirt between two songs, tossing it to the side of the stage, Juliana whistled and screamed Jessie's name. Zoey elbowed her older sister in the ribs, but was relieved to see Jessie laughing. For the duration of the set Zoey watched Jessie, doing her best to tune out everyone else around her, especially her sisters. Taken aback when Neal dedicated a love song to her, she grew even more rattled by her sisters' screams and looks full of meaning. Somehow she tuned them out again and stayed focused on Jessie until, too soon, they started packing up their gear. Anxiously, she waited for an opportunity to talk to Jessie, and she submitted herself to Juliana and Laurel's good-humored ridicule.

Jessie's nervousness increased, heightening with the passing of each minute and reaching its apex as she walked onstage just after nine. She had sought Zoey out beforehand, thinking it would settle her nerves to get their initial meeting out of the way, but it was to no avail. Though they'd played Double Door a few times in the past, the crowd seemed enormous as she gazed out from behind her drums. But once she picked up her sticks and began to play, a calm washed over her. Her body moved with fluid precision that filled her with elation. Normally focused and expressionless as she played, she couldn't contain the joyful grin that spread across her face, and she even laughed when she removed her shirt between songs and heard a whistle followed by an enthusiastic female voice shouting her name.

The band, as a whole, played flawlessly, a fact emphasized by the cheers reverberating through the building. The crowd, though often standoffish at Double Door, even edged near the stage, dancing a little and sometimes singing along. Before they started "Crushed," the song Neal had written for Zoey and insisted on playing, he actually dedicated the song to her.

Despite the small chorus of screaming females who responded, Jessie groaned inwardly. Otherwise they completed their set seamlessly. It might have been their best show.

While they broke down their equipment, Jessie noticed a small, skinny man with thinning hair in a ponytail and a loud silk shirt approach the area to the side of the stage where they stashed their instruments. In his left hand he held a mixed drink, in his right, a fat, thankfully unlit, cigar.

"Neal?" he questioned in a gruff baritone, shifting his cigar to his mouth and holding out his hand.

Neal spun in the direction of the voice. "Dino?"

"Nice to meet you." He pumped Neal's hand twice then grabbed his cigar from between his lips.

"You too." Neal stretched himself to his full height, towering over Dino. "What'd you think?"

Artless, Jessie thought, shaking her head a little. Seeing that Amazing Technicolor, the next band on the bill, was itching to set up, Jessie dashed back onstage to finish clearing her equipment from the stage, missing Dino's response. As she labored over her cymbals and, now, all of Neal's stuff, she watched the two men talking. Neal smiled and nodded vigorously several times, and as both men laughed, Jessie wished she knew how to read lips. Dino finally handed Neal a business card, shook his hand again and walked away. Jessie thought she heard him say, "See you next week," as he passed by. She leapt off the stage and grabbed Neal.

"Well?"

Neal's smile split his face in two as he said, "We're supposed to go to the studio on Thursday."

Jessie screamed in her excitement, a high, ear-splitting shriek that drew stares from those around her. She didn't care. This was the first time any label had shown any interest in any band she'd ever been a part of, and she wasn't about to let decorum or social poise stand in the way of celebrating her dream. The boys seemed equally elated, smiling and laughing as they finished packing up their equipment.

At the bar she bought them all celebratory drinks, and after Sean, Paul and Neal drifted off to talk to fans and friends and with the heat of the alcohol surging through her, she spotted Zoey. She stood twenty feet away with two slightly shorter women, one a redhead, the other a dirty blonde, talking animatedly. Savoring the perfection of her day so far, she allowed herself, unbeknownst to the other woman, to take in the full, glorious picture of Zoey. Her well-fit blue jeans rode low on her enticing hips and hugged all the right places from her strong thighs all the way down. Instead of her usual running shoes, she had on scuffed boots, and her pink scoop-neck top clung attractively to her chest, at least what wasn't exposed by the cut of the shirt. In one hand she held a beer bottle loosely by the neck, and occasionally as she spoke to her friends she ran her free hand through her soft blond hair, lifting it from her graceful neck then letting it fall back in sensual waves. The rest of the time, when she wasn't emphasizing a point in her conversation with a touch or a gesture, she hooked her thumb in her pocket, inadvertently and deliciously tugging at the waistline of her jeans. She and her friends, leaning in to talk over the noise, touched easily, and Jessie envied their casual closeness. She watched as the redhead spoke directly in Zoey's ear then laughed grandly as Zoey, grinning and playful, punched her arm. Meanwhile the blonde made eye contact with Jessie, smiled, grabbed Zoey's arm and pointed. Instantly mortified, Jessie froze, wondering what Zoey would do. She nervously ran her hand through her hair as Zoey turned to where her friend had pointed. Their eyes locked, and time stopped when Zoey smiled and waved at her to come over. Holding a finger up to signal that she'd be there in a minute, Jessie turned to the bar and ordered a shot and another beer. A moment later, lubricated but trembling all over, she headed across the bar.

Zoey greeted her in a lingering hug, whispering in her ear, "You were wonderful, as usual." Jessie, enjoying the torment of Zoey's hot breath tickling her ear, sighed in blissful agony before Zoey broke the embrace then introduced her to the other women. "I want you to meet my sisters, Juliana," she pointed to the redhead, "and Laurel," the blonde.

As they shook hands, Laurel cried, "You're tiny! I can't believe you're so little." Jessie, trying to be polite for Zoey, merely nodded, but Laurel compounded her error when she attempted to clarify her comment. "I'm sorry. It's just that you played so, um, loudly. You sounded bigger." She made a dismissive facial gesture as Zoey looked apologetically at Jessie.

"Proving once again that size doesn't matter," Jessie interjected, raising Laurel's eyebrows and eliciting laughter from the other two sisters. As their conversation lulled, Jessie fell back on her stock comment, "Thanks for coming out."

Juliana spoke in a rich, low voice, almost as sultry as Zoey's, "I'm glad we did." After a moment's hesitation, she added, "It's our first time."

"Well, you picked a good one to start with." Turning to speak directly to Zoey, Jessie excitedly blurted out, "We're headed into the studio on Thursday!"

"Oh my god! Congratulations!" Zoey wrapped her in another embrace, and Jessie murmured a soft thanks in her ear.

"I'm not surprised," Laurel chimed in, compelling them to separate and focus on her. "You're absolutely amazing." She threw special emphasis on the last word, and Jessie smiled broadly and thanked her.

"We're just sorry that Grace couldn't be here for this too," Juliana jumped in. "She's writing her dissertation, and we can't get her to come out and play no matter how compelling the circumstances." Juliana and Laurel shared a knowing smile as Zoey glared at her sisters.

Obviously missing something and growing uneasy, Jessie tried to excuse herself, but Laurel spoke up, "Zoey hasn't stopped telling us how amazing you are, so we had to come and see for ourselves. That's the word you kept using, right Zoey? *Amazing.*"

Zoey made no verbal reply, but the fire in her eyes could have reduced a person to ash.

Suddenly feeling like she was under a microscope, Jessie said as politely as possible, "And what do you think?"

"Well, of course we don't have all the experience with you that Zoey has." Zoey's jaw tightened as she stared at Juliana, who blithely continued, "but so far so good." Again Laurel and Juliana smirked while Zoey's eyes blazed.

Looking from one sister to the next, Jessie felt distinctly uncomfortable and, needing to extricate herself from the situation, said, "Well, I'm glad you liked the show. But if you'll excuse me, I see someone I need to talk to. It was nice meeting you." Before they could respond, she bolted, making it halfway to the exit before she felt a hand on her arm, tugging at her, compelling her to stop.

"Jessie, wait. I'm sorry."

"For what?" She spoke more harshly than she intended.

For a long time Zoey didn't reply. Her hand slipped down Jessie's arm and took her eager hand, their fingers automatically entwining as they had on Saturday. Her heart fluttering and crashing against her ribs, Jessie's gaze drifted from their hands, brown and white perfectly intermingled, up to the vibrant green of Zoey's eyes. Finally Zoey's eyes pulled away from Jessie. Looking at the scuffed, beer-soaked floor she said, almost shyly, "My sisters were rude."

"Look, I don't care about that. I don't care about anything but—just let me go, okay?"

Slowly Zoey dropped Jessie's hand, but the warmth of her touch radiated for several moments as she stared into Zoey's eyes. Wondering how the elation of a few short minutes before had turned so quickly to despair, Jessie spun on her heel and headed out onto the street for air.

CHAPTER ELEVEN

"I heard the lurid *National Enquirer* account yesterday. What's the *Tribune* version of Thursday night?"

"Oh god, Grace," Zoey sighed into the phone. "What did they tell you?"

"Pretty much what you'd expect, high drama and the like. Pared down, they both agree that you've made a fine mess for yourself and that you've got it bad for the drummer, who, according to Juliana, looks tasty. Laurel says that Jessie lives up to the accolade but that she scares too easily. Whatever that means."

"That means they teamed up and attacked her with that uber-polite thing they do."

"I'm sorry, Zo."

"I am too, though I can't say that I'm surprised."

"So what are you going to do?"

"I wish I knew." She'd been in a state of perpetual confusion since Thursday night. Unsure of where things stood with Jessie, she didn't even know if she could bear finding out. But things with Neal continued barreling along in spite of her uncertainty. On Thursday night, as she'd lain in his arms feeling unsatisfied and oddly guilty after sex, he'd pulled her close to him, said, "Love you," and kissed her forehead. The revelation, a first for their relationship, startled Zoey. Stunned and even more guilt-ridden, she'd whispered, "You too." Looking to alleviate some of her guilt, she'd kissed him with an intensity she didn't really feel, duping him into elation that he'd probably be better off not feeling for her. She'd never felt more reprehensible in her entire life.

Back in the present her sister was saying, "Well, do you care about Neal?"

"Yes."

"And what about Jessie? How do you feel about her?"

Zoey breathed heavily, considering the tangled mess of her emotions before answering. "I feel nervous and excited and scared. I get all worked up and jittery, and then I don't know what to do or say. It's kind of like being in high school."

"Do you care about her?" Grace gently prodded.

Again Zoey paused before answering. "Well, I've been brooding about her for days. Here it is, the first truly beautiful Saturday of the year. I could be out doing anything, but instead I'm holed up in my dark apartment, in my pajamas, talking about a woman who makes me crazy. So what do you think? Do I care about her?"

"Sure sounds that way," came Grace's soft response. "Sorry Zo."

"But I'm not positive that that's not just some sort of spillover from what I feel physically. Grace, I've never felt such an intense physical pull toward someone. I want to devour her."

When Grace stayed quiet for a time, Zoey worried that she'd been too frank for her baby sister, but Grace's voice crashed in on her thoughts. "Well, I'm no expert on romance. I mean, I've had precisely two long-term relationships, both of which failed because I put school first. So don't feel obliged to listen to me. But I think you already know what you want. You just have to do something about it."

As soon as Grace said it, Zoey knew she was right. "When did you get so insightful?"

"It comes with watching all of your big sisters make so many mistakes."

"Thanks, that's reassuring," Zoey responded. Sighing softly she added, "I think you're right. I just wish I knew what to do."

"Go for a run, figure out what you want to say and then talk to her, Zo. Right now, that's all you can do."

* * *

The days following the show, Jessie rode a wave of conflicted emotions, one moment elated at the band's success, the next falling into desolation over the hopelessness of her situation with Zoey. On Friday, when she told her brother the good news, he congratulated her and gave her all of Thursday off. Naturally he assumed the tears building on her lower lids throughout the day were those of joy, and sometimes they were. She was repeatedly struck by their amazing fortune. Certainly other bands working just as hard and with just as much talent had fallen prey to the wretched nature of the music industry, bitterness and lost dreams consuming ideals and individuals and leaving a stultifying hollowness in their wake. But her thoughts about the band always ventured to Neal, how he'd fought for her and made her a part of this dream come true, and now she was willing to turn on him for a fluttering heart, weak knees and meltingly soft lips. Her thoughts and emotions tormented her, but she saw no way out.

On Friday afternoon when she told her parents about their record deal, her mother praised her in an excited, repetitious, frenzied mix of Spanish and English that culminated in an invitation for the whole band and their girlfriends to come to dinner on Sunday.

"I'll cook all day," she exclaimed excitedly. Thinking aloud, she muttered, "I guess I'll have to go to Mass on Saturday night so that I'll have more time on Sunday."

"Mama, are you sure that's a good idea?"

"Well, I prefer church on Sundays, but this is a special occasion."

"No, Mama, I mean inviting all the girlfriends. That includes—"

"Oh. Zoey. You haven't talked to her, I take it."

"Not really." She added quickly, "I haven't had a whole lot of time."

"I see." There was a lengthy pause during which Jessie heard only her mother's heavy, thought-laden breath. "Well, I guess you'll have to decide who receives the invitation, but I'm extending it to everyone."

"I'll figure out who's coming and let you know tomorrow, okay?"

"All right, but not too late, honey. I have to shop."

She hung up the phone feeling more confused and at odds than before, and talking to Sheila E. didn't help her sort anything out. During practice she decided not to decide. Let fate handle everything. Maybe no one would be able to make it. So after practice as Paul lovingly put away his favorite guitar and Neal stretched out on the couch and Sean popped open another beer, she casually announced, "My mom invited everyone to dinner on Sunday to celebrate the thing with Dino. You don't have to come if you've got plans, but she'll be cooking all day."

"You don't have to ask me twice," Neal answered immediately.

"That sucks," Paul blurted out and then clarified, "I have to work all weekend, or there's no hope of me getting Thursday off."

"I'm supposed to hang with Maureen," said Sean.

Before she knew what she was saying, she added, "Mom said that everyone includes girlfriends."

Sean, ever the romantic, happily agreed to make it "the cheapest date ever," and Neal thought that Zoey would love some of Silvia's home cooking. Fate seemed to have made its decision.

She worried all night that she had made a mistake, that she wouldn't be able to make it through a meal with Zoey, especially with Neal sitting close by. Her concern grew the next day when

Sean announced that he and Maureen wouldn't be at dinner after all.

"After using way too many synonyms for stupid, Maureen reminded me that we're going to her niece's baptism tomorrow, and since Maureen's the godmother, we can't skip it," Sean grumbled.

"I'll bring you some leftovers," Jessie sympathized with him while panicking internally. Her only hope of surviving the day and her role as onlooker to Zoey's happiness had been the promising distraction of other people. Now she wouldn't even have that, and just when the situation seemed like it couldn't get more hopeless, she realized that her mom would scrutinize Zoey throughout dinner, looking for fatal flaws or clues of Zoey's worthiness.

Normally a cathartic cleaner, Jessie mounted an attack on any dirt lurking in her living space, but by midafternoon, though her apartment was immaculate, her anxiety level hadn't budged. She refused to clean the guys' space—not enough Lysol in the world—but beating on her drums for a while might prove therapeutic. Paul was working, and Neal and Sean had just ventured out to a Cubs game, so for the first time in a long time, she could just play what she felt.

Her drums took a good pummeling as she unleashed her inner riot grrl, and she began to feel relaxed, at home. Though most people would disagree, Jessie found the sound of drums soothing, especially when she was responsible for the racket. This time was no exception, and she welcomed the glorious peace of noise. Until the phone rang.

At first she ignored it. It was the downstairs phone, which meant it was for one of the boys. But whoever was calling was very persistent, and they refused to leave a message and leave her alone. The machine picked up, and a minute later the ringing resumed. After several minutes, her concentration broken and her blissful relaxation replaced by irritable edginess, she stomped over to the phone.

"Yeah," she growled brusquely into the receiver.

"Hi," came Zoey's shy response.

Her mood turning slightly, Jessie spoke more kindly. "Neal's not here."

"I know."

Irritation returning, Jessie grew curt, "Then what do you want?"

"I, uh, I'm not sure." She sounded hurt and vulnerable. Jessie wanted to reach out to her, but she didn't know what to say. "I'm sorry," Zoey whispered quickly before hanging up.

Jessie stared at the now-silent phone. "Me too."

CHAPTER TWELVE

When she'd thought about it while running, it had seemed so easy, and in the shower after pounding the pavement for an hour, she'd felt certain it would work. But now, clutching the lifeless phone in her still trembling hand—an unsettling tremor that had started when she'd picked up the phone and had mounted each time she dialed—now she allowed herself to feel a little battered. "Well that didn't go over well," she said to the silent room, wondering yet again if this was worth all the work and turmoil.

She was tempted, not for the first time, to walk away from the whole sordid mess, to let go of these feelings and forget Jessie Durango and that kiss and just move forward with her life with Neal. She didn't need this confusion and aggravation. But the fact that, in a week, she had done little more than remember that kiss and dwell on her confusion told her that forgetting wasn't really an option. She had to talk to Jessie to find some order in her life.

Not willing to brave the phone again, Zoey considered what to do next. Given the emotional turbulence of the past week, putting off the discussion seemed like a very bad idea, and obviously the conversation would have to be in person. Though they would see each other the next day, Zoey didn't believe that dinner at the Durango household with Neal looking on was an appropriate forum for confessing her confused attraction. Realizing what she had to do, Zoey grabbed her keys and, before she could chicken out, headed out the door.

* * *

An hour after the disastrous phone call with Zoey and fresh from a soothing shower that, though it provided ample time for thought, left her certain only of her uncertainty, Jessie sat on her couch trying to read but unable to focus. Putting the book down, she considered what she might have with Zoey, if Zoey even felt the same way about her. Her body tingled, and her breath grew shallow at the thought of intimacy with her. Her heart expanded as she envisioned the two of them together long into the future. She thought she could be completely happy with Zoey.

On the other hand, she had built a strong friendship with Neal over the last four years. He'd become almost like a brother to her, and they confided in one another and comforted each other whenever necessary, though that comfort typically flowed from Neal to Jessie as one more guy proved himself to be just another jerk looking to get laid. Neal's typical lack of emotional investment in relationships offered him a unique perspective on Jessie's dating woes, but it also meant that Jessie almost never needed to console him. This time, however, he would need it and certainly wouldn't turn to her, the cause of his heartache, for solace. On top of that, the band was just starting to take off after years of hard work. She surely couldn't stay in the band if she betrayed Neal. How could she turn her back on her dream? The situation was impossible.

Sitting in her gradually darkening living room, a mix of her favorite emotionally tormented music from The Smiths and The Cure blasting from her stereo as conflicting thoughts and emotions waged war within her, she jumped as the phone rang next to her head. Turning her music down, she picked up the phone.

After enduring the perilous world of public transportation and the hazards of her own doubtful mind, Zoey stood in front of the little house in Pilsen, totally lost. Twice on her journey she'd started to turn back home, but before she'd gotten very far the thought of her baby sister laughing at her for acting like an idiot had put her back on track. But now that she stood fifteen feet from the door to what she wanted, fear gripped her and she couldn't compel herself to act.

Suddenly aware of eyes on her, she looked around to see Jessie's next-door neighbor, outside enjoying the warm weather, looking at her quizzically from her front porch. A small boy sat beside her, disinterestedly bouncing a rubber ball off the door. Feeling foolish, she smiled at them and moved toward the front door, and though she knocked before giving herself the chance to think about what she was doing, her knock went unanswered.

"Maybe she's not home," she thought, though as the faint sound of Morrissey, lamenting some tragedy or other, filtered down from above, she knew that Jessie had to be in her apartment. A curious mixture of relief and sadness within her, she turned from the door and saw the old oak she'd climbed once before. "You're crazy," she told herself as her eyes darted back and forth between the front door and the tree. Her heart pounding in her chest, she heard the blood rushing in her ears. Once again gathering her courage, she muttered, "It's now or never," and smiling at Jessie's neighbors, she strode over to the oak to begin her cautious ascent.

"Jessie, did you forget to call, or were you waiting until the last possible moment to tell me how many people are coming?"

"God, I'm sorry, Mama. I've been really busy today, and it just slipped my mind."

"Uh-huh." Silvia's disappointment was evident in those two terse syllables. "Did you even tell anyone about dinner?"

"Yes, I did," Jessie answered sullenly before nightmare visions of what tomorrow had in store for her engrossed her thoughts.

"And am I supposed to read your mind, or will you actually let me know how many people I'll be feeding tomorrow?"

"Sorry Mama. Sean and Paul can't make it, so I promised to bring them care packages." As she spoke, Jessie thought she heard something thud dimly outside but assumed it was either a strong wind battering the trees or the rotten kid next door playing ball against their house again. "That means it's just me, Neal and Zoey. Plus you and Dad."

"Are you okay with that?"

"I guess I'll have to—" A knock at the door to her porch drew her attention away from her conversation. "Hold on a second. Someone's at the door." Totally uncertain of what to expect, Jessie threw open the door to see Zoey standing before her on the roof, her face a beautiful mixture of confusion, anger and determination.

"I have to go, Mama. I'll see you tomorrow." Jessie hung up without saying goodbye and stood aside to let Zoey in. Their eyes remained focused on each other as they silently entered her apartment and Jessie closed the door. Several feet separated them, and neither woman spoke as they stood staring at each other. Finally Zoey broke the silence.

"I don't know what to do. Ever since we kissed, that's all I think about. I can't concentrate on anything except you and your lips and kissing you again."

Her whole body shaking, Jessie crossed the distance between them and grabbed Zoey's hands. She didn't realize until she tried to speak that she'd been holding her breath, so she said only "You too?" before her mouth was on Zoey's, warm softness welcoming her home.

Their kisses rapidly grew in intensity as hands traveled through hair and down limbs, seeking solidity, proof that this was real rather than fantasy. Somewhere in the back of her mind, Jessie heard Robert Smith singing that he'd waited hours for this, and the appropriateness of the song registered briefly as Jessie's mouth left Zoey's to kiss her neck, her tongue lightly traveling from Zoey's earlobe down to the hollow at the base of her throat. Zoey shivered, a throaty, grunting "Mmm" seeping from her before she grabbed Jessie's arms and, with surprising force, pushed her against the door behind her. Pressing her thigh between Jessie's legs, Zoey kissed her fiercely before her mouth left Jessie's to kiss her neck and ears and shoulders. Heady with pleasure, Jessie struggled to emerge from the spell cast by Zoey's mouth. She finally asserted herself and, pulling Zoey's face back up to her own, kissed her forcefully. As Jessie's hands moved down Zoey's body, she felt tiny tremors in the woman who pressed against her. Hesitantly, Jessie trailed her hand just inside the waist of Zoey's jeans, tickling just above the slight, enticing swell of her hips.

Pulling back Zoey looked at Jessie, her expression thick with desire. She raised her eyebrows in a question that Jessie, entranced, answered with the barest of nods. Without warning Zoey pulled Jessie from the door, steered her to the bed and sat her down. Wordlessly she pulled Jessie's T-shirt over her head, revealing small breasts, their brown nipples already hard. Breathing shallowly, she kicked off her shoes then removed her own shirt, flinging it aside, but as she reached to unhook her bra, Jessie grabbed her hands, pulling Zoey down astride her and kissing her roughly. Jessie's hands and mouth began tenderly caressing the ample flesh she'd thought about so often. Unable to control herself, she lightly bit Zoey's nipple through her bra, feeling it swell and harden as a soft murmur of pleasure escaped from Zoey's throat. In a trance, Jessie reached around Zoey to unhook her bra, releasing full breasts with firm, pink nipples. Slowly, delicately, she touched the rich flesh, first with her fingers and then hungrily with her mouth, eliciting another moan from Zoey.

Suddenly overcome with emotion Jessie grabbed Zoey, pulling her tightly to her, unwilling to let her go as Zoey kissed Jessie's head and softly stroked her hair, running fingers damp from Jessie's still wet hair lightly over her back and arms.

Reluctantly Jessie loosened her embrace as Zoey gently pushed herself from Jessie to stand at the edge of the bed. Jessie planted soft kisses along the taut muscles of Zoey's abdomen as tiny sounds of pleasure escaped from the other woman's throat. Emboldened by Zoey's responses, Jessie began unbuttoning Zoey's jeans and slowly working them over her hips, revealing the barest slip of lacy black underwear. It was her turn to groan as her arms grew weak and Zoey took over, removing the rest of her clothes and Jessie's as well. She then pushed Jessie down on the mattress and, straddling her, kissed her fiercely.

Automatically they began moving together in a rhythm of their own making. Jessie's whole body tuned to Zoey, and feeling more light tremors she traced her fingers down the length of Zoey's torso, evoking a cascade of shivers and another little moan. Her hands lingered on Zoey's breasts for some time, enjoying the weight and pliancy of them. Then her mouth took over as she slowly ran her hands down Zoey's body and over the soft skin of her strong thighs, and hearing a ragged, "Please Jessie," she allowed her hand to settle in the heat between Zoey's legs. Moaning herself as Zoey's rhythmic grinding grew in urgency, Jessie slipped a tentative finger within Zoey. The sharp intake of breath of the woman above her indicated Zoey's pleasure as she rose up and writhed above Jessie, and another deeper groan escaped as Jessie's other hand began its own explorations of Zoey's core. Too soon Zoey's movement stilled as her muscles tensed and, crying out, she climaxed and fell forward onto the body beneath her. Jessie felt fading contractions for some time as they lay entwined, one hand still within Zoey while the other stroked her back.

Soon she felt light kisses on her ear and along her neck, which turned to playful biting as Zoey's hand touched Jessie's breast for the first time. The kisses and bites slowly descended until Zoey's warm sweet mouth was on Jessie's breasts, first one, then the other, kissing her way in slow circles to Jessie's rock-hard nipple, gently biting it in conjunction with the slow kneading of her hand. Jessie didn't think she could take much more as Zoey's mouth traveled back and forth between the heightened nerves of her small breasts, and just as she was ready to cry out or explode, Zoey's mouth left her chest entirely, traveling lightly along her body. Her moist, warm tongue seemed to cover every inch of Jessie, leaving traces of moisture on the soft skin of her arms and legs, even her navel. She gradually worked her way down and back up Jessie's body, and as her mouth savored Jessie's neck and shoulders, Zoey's hand began the same slow exploration. Tickling and teasing, Zoey's hand trailed its way down Jessie's compact torso, finally settling between her legs. Her fingers glided over Jessie's throbbing center, and Jessie groaned, a deep, animal sound, then begged, "Kiss me." Zoey's mouth returned to hers, biting Jessie's lower lip then caressing her tongue with her own as her strong, sure fingers stroked in a rhythm that matched the undulation of Jessie's hips. Quivering with the pleasure of her heightened sensations, Jessie spread her legs wide, and urging Zoey on, she thrust her hips once, twice and then groaned in exultation as she wrapped her legs around Zoey, trapping her against her.

Calm and sated, Zoey rolled on her side and spoke in a languorous, peaceful tone. "Mmm, I wasn't expecting that."

Jessie snuggled into Zoey, lightly running a finger up and down her arm. "What were you expecting?"

"Honestly I just came here to talk." They both laughed. "Are you usually so…assertive?"

"No. This is my first time." She placed gentle kisses along Zoey's collarbone.

"Do you expect me to believe that you've never lured someone into your bed by playing hard to get before?" Zoey, incredulous, stirred as Jessie continued caressing her.

"No, I'm serious. This is my very first time."

Zoey sat up. "Wait. You mean your first time at all? As in, I'm your first lover?"

Jessie sat up too and nodded, smiling sweetly at Zoey and at the idea of having a lover.

"Wow. A virgin." They sat silently for a time, gazing at each other in the twilight of Jessie's apartment as Zoey contemplated what she'd just learned. "Don't take this the wrong way, but how is it possible that you've never had sex before?"

Jessie looked shyly away. Hesitantly she explained, "In high school I pretty much drove my boyfriend over the edge. He always wanted to, but it never felt right, and I got hurt by him. Since then I've had a couple close calls. I mean, there have been guys who wanted to, but it takes more than him remembering my name through dinner for me to offer up dessert. I guess," she finished lamely, "I was just waiting for the right person to come along."

Zoey took Jessie's hand, smiling. "How long were you with him, your boyfriend?"

"A little over two years," Jessie responded crisply, sounding a little bitter.

"We haven't known each other very long at all," Zoey spoke with soft wonder.

Kissing Zoey's palm lightly before bringing it to her own cheek, Jessie said with finality, "What can I say? When it's right, it's right."

Zoey traced Jessie's lips with her finger, a stirring of desire shifting her focus as Jessie took her finger into her mouth, sucking and tasting before slowly releasing it. Snapping back suddenly Zoey said, "You know, you don't act like a virgin."

"Well, I've flown solo a few times."

"Thank God," Zoey uttered.

"What does that mean?" Jessie asked. She seemed shy and nervous.

"Well," Zoey started, thinking of the best way to explain her reaction to Jessie. "Your first time playing the drums, was it in front of an audience?"

"No, I had to practice first. Oh, are you saying I need practice?" Jessie's worry was evident.

"Need? No, but if you want to practice, I'm all yours," Zoey said. Their lips met in a quick, rough exchange before Zoey pushed Jessie onto her back. Jessie murmured soft sounds of pleasure as Zoey's kisses moved to her neck and down her body. She again covered Jessie's breasts and stomach with kisses, lingering over each body part on her slow descent. Jessie whimpered as Zoey's tongue tickled inside her thighs. A surprised "Oh" left her throat as Zoey's tongue found the ache between her legs, then her "ohs" joined the muffled sounds of Zoey's delight. With each stroke of Zoey's tongue, Jessie's trembling increased, and she opened herself fully to the wonder of Zoey's mouth. Her own senses on fire, Zoey imagined the waves of sensation washing over Jessie, increasing in intensity until, overcome, she thrust her hips and cried out. Reluctantly Zoey relinquished her position and worked her way up Jessie's slight, trembling body.

Gradually each woman's breathing slowed and, wrapped in each other's arms, bestowing occasional, sweet kisses upon one another, whispering soft endearments, they fell into contented sleep.

Enveloped in darkness and wrapped in Zoey's warm body, Jessie woke from the first sound sleep she'd had in over a week. Glancing at her clock, she was surprised to find that it was just after midnight. Refreshed and rested as if she'd been sleeping for two days, she carefully turned to look at Zoey, and for a time she gazed at the sleep-softened features of the woman next to her. As Zoey's chest rose and fell in the rhythmic cadence of breathing, Jessie reached a cautious hand to touch soft honey-blond hair. She let its silken softness cascade through her fingers, aching to kiss the delicate place where hair met skin, and as she pressed her naked body against Zoey's, draping a protective and possessive arm across her, she felt a peaceful contentment within herself. "This," she realized with sublime clarity, "is what I want." Kissing Zoey's small, round shoulder, she whispered into the darkness, "I love you," and fell into a euphoric slumber.

CHAPTER THIRTEEN

In the soft light of early morning Zoey's eyes fluttered gently open. Taking in her surroundings, remembering the night before, she smiled involuntarily. She felt elated, effervescent and peaceful all at once. Her mind at ease, she stretched expansively then looked at the woman next to her and smiled more fully. When she'd answered the door, Jessie had been startled and confused yet pleased, but now with her thick dark hair framing her sleep-softened features, her face revealed a peaceful contentment equal to Zoey's. Jessie looked like an innocent child, and remembering last night's brief conversation, Zoey shuddered at the depth of Jessie's innocence.

Having been sexually active for over half her life and in and out of more relationships than she cared to count, Zoey's experience, a matter about which she'd never before felt shame, now seemed somehow problematic to her. She had fallen into bed so quickly in the past, deluding herself, believing in love that quickly devolved into one-sided longing or complicated bitterness. With Neal she'd somehow avoided that. They had developed a strong friendship as well as a physical closeness. She'd thought their relationship was working well until Jessie swooped in with her passion and playful humor. And that body. Fully clothed Jessie was an attractive woman, but, good Lord, if any man in Chicago suspected what she kept hidden beneath the jeans and T-shirts, Zoey guessed that Jessie wouldn't have been a virgin last night. Some libertine, like Neal, would have talked his way in.

But, Zoey reflected, she hadn't done that. Somehow, without intending it, they had both just let each other in. And now, in spite of what she'd thought about Neal, the magnitude of her feelings for Jessie compared to everything that had preceded this moment assured her of the correctness, the truth of her emotions. The force of that assurance scared her.

More frightening, though, was the knowledge that Jessie's discovery was completely different from her own. She knew Jessie's miniscule sexual history, what with being it and all, but she couldn't help but wonder about Jessie's romantic experiences and what that meant for them. Now that Jessie had unloosed her sexual side, what would prevent her from exploring her other options? After her own initial disastrous foray into sex, Zoey herself had explored quite a bit. In the face of that possibility, she didn't know that she could hold on to Jessie now, and the thought of losing what she'd just discovered she needed terrified her.

In a panic Zoey left the bed and began dressing. As she did she told herself over and over that Jessie was too honest, too good, too sensitive and caring to walk away from her in search of new experiences, more satisfaction. The more she told herself this, the less she believed it, and the more the urge to flee took hold. Before she ventured onto the roof and back down the tree, she scribbled a note on a pad of paper she'd found on Jessie's counter, placed it on her pillow and touched the soft black hair framing Jessie's face. Then she was gone.

During the short cab ride home she second-guessed her hasty departure. Though she was now hopelessly lost in Jessie, she had no idea what Jessie might be feeling, and because she was such a chicken she had no way of finding out. Had she stayed, she could have talked it out, learned her fate and accepted it. She could have fought for what she wanted rather than running scared from it. Nearing home, other thoughts crashed in on her. At some point she would have to face Neal and own up to her inappropriate behavior. She knew he cared for her deeply, that anyone with the swaggering bravado he had wouldn't easily show his softer side. She knew that his declaration the other night had been both honest and undeniable for him, making her infidelity that much worse. He would be crushed when she told him. She knew because she had lived through such a betrayal herself and had never considered that she might be the one to cause someone else that pain. Now that she had done the up-to-now unthinkable, her heart grew heavy.

* * *

In the morning Jessie woke alone. For a moment she thought she'd dreamt the whole exchange, but her nudity and exultation and a handwritten note on her pillow convinced her otherwise. Picking up the note, she read, "Jessie, I thought I should leave early. Maybe we can talk later today?" She'd simply signed it "Z" and had written her phone number at the bottom of the soft-edged paper. Disappointed but understanding, Jessie got out of bed feeling radiant and giddy. Tucking the note in the pages of a book of poetry, she considered without care what a cliché she was since she was sure she must actually be glowing.

She'd slept much later than she intended and had to hurry to get ready and squeeze in band practice before heading over to her parents' house. She scooped up Sheila E., gave him a quick, unwanted kiss on the head and sent him scurrying away from her before jumping in the shower. Unable to stop smiling, she laughed at her foolishness but kept right on smiling as she dressed and made the bed with Sheila's help. After straightening the tangle of sheets, she actually sniffed her pillows, inhaling the scent of Zoey.

At noon she left her room, and it wasn't until she went downstairs and saw Neal in the kitchen that the full impact of what she'd done last night hit her. She'd slept with Zoey. Neal's Zoey. And now she had to spend the day with both of them pretending that nothing had happened when all she wanted to do was drag Zoey back into bed with her and hold her forever.

Her heart fell, and her involuntary grin faded as Neal said, "Mornin', sunshine. You're awfully chipper."

"I, uh, slept really well, I guess."

"I sure didn't. After the game we went out drinking. I'm so freakin' tired."

"Hung over?" She asked, noticing his red-rimmed eyes and feeling even sorrier for him, but at least she knew he hadn't come home and heard her and Zoey's lovemaking.

"Not too bad. What did you do last night?"

Hating herself, she answered truthfully, "I just stayed in my room, went to bed early."

"You're such a good girl." He took a giant gulp of coffee before lumbering into their rehearsal space.

Skulking along behind him, she saw her mother's warnings about the pain of deceit materializing. But what could she do now?

"I took your advice, sort of." Zoey had dialed Grace's number as soon as she closed her apartment door behind her, not even glancing at the clock to see if it was a decent hour.

"Explain please." Grace yawned as she spoke, but Zoey didn't have time to feel bad. How often had she looked, sounded and felt over fatigued when working on her own Ph.D.? Grace would live.

"I went to Jessie's house—"

"Which is also Neal's house."

"Yes. Thank you for the reminder," Zoey snapped. "I went to talk to Jessie."

"And? How did it go?"

"Well, we didn't so much talk as have sex."

"You what?" Grace shrieked. "That was *not* my advice."

"I know!" Zoey cried. "It wasn't supposed to happen. It just did."

"I guess you know now how you both feel," Grace offered hopefully. When Zoey didn't say anything for several seconds, Grace asked, "There's more to this story, isn't there?"

"I bolted this morning before she woke up," Zoey admitted.

"God Z! You didn't say anything to her? You just banged her and left?"

Grace's crass wording didn't help Zoey feel any better about her behavior. Defensively, she stated, "I left her a note."

"Oh, a note. That will make her feel good." Grace's sarcasm was making Zoey question the wisdom of turning to her baby sister for help. "A 'Dear John' message, or more of a 'Darling Nikki' scribbling?"

"'Darling Nikki'?"

"That exceptionally dirty Prince song. She leaves him a note that says, 'Call me up whenever you wanna—'"

"Got it. Thanks," Zoey cut her off. "I told her that we need to talk. We're supposed to see each other today."

"Once again I advise you to talk to her. For real this time. You'll never know what this is, where you stand, if you don't discuss it."

"You're right, Gracie. I just wish I wasn't terrified."

The ride to her parents' house set the tone for the rest of the day—guilt-tinged confusion and longing. On the brief drive to Zoey's place, Neal chattered excitedly about the record deal and Zoey and the Cubs' prospects for the season, saying the same thing he and every other Cubs fan said during the spring: "This will be the year!" Of course Jessie knew it wouldn't be—it never was—but envied him his faith anyway. Still she wondered which disappointment would hit him harder, the Cubs' inevitable losing season or what she and Zoey had done together. She dimly hoped Neal would never find out about what had happened last night, but as with the Cubs' prospects for the season, she suspected that hope wouldn't materialize.

When they pulled up in front of Zoey's apartment building, she was waiting outside. Jessie's pulse quickened at the sight of her. She turned her head away to hide her flushed cheeks and broad grin from Neal, but she needn't have bothered as he noticed nothing except Zoey.

"Have you ever seen anything so beautiful?" Neal uttered before he hopped out of the truck.

"No," whispered Jessie. "No, I haven't."

"Hey babe," he said, and Jessie cringed as he kissed Zoey deeply. Though Zoey ended the kiss quickly, Jessie still felt ill. Zoey held him at bay and, smiling a little sadly, returned his hello. When she turned her attention to the familiar pickup truck and said, "Hi," her voice sounded calm, but the intimacy of the eye contact she shared with Jessie before she slid toward her across the worn cloth seat betrayed her. She was just as nervous and excited as Jessie, and seemingly in league with Zoey's emotions, Jessie's stomach fluttered and flipped wildly. She merely nodded hello, not trusting her voice. Zoey settled herself in the angular position she'd used her first time in Jessie's truck, but now she intentionally pressed herself against Jessie, making her squirm with desire and anguish. Still, Jessie returned the concealed embrace and took full advantage by brushing the back of her hand against Zoey's thigh every time she shifted gears. Wanting desperately to rest her hand on Zoey's thigh, to trace the inseam of her jeans from her knee all the way up, she kept it instead on the gearshift, clutching it tightly in her torment.

Neal, however, appeared oblivious as he recapped the same game highlights he'd already shared with Jessie. Zoey seemed about as uninterested as Jessie had been, and the fact that Neal failed to notice this helped Jessie convince herself that she deserved Zoey more than Neal did. As she drove she began a list of justifications in her head, and she had compiled quite a collection—Neal could have anyone, he and Zoey had nothing but height in common—before she realized that Neal had stopped talking about the stupid Cubs.

"You know, they hated me at first, but after Jessie explained that we weren't dating anymore, we were just friends, they warmed up to me. Especially her mom."

"You guys dated?" Zoey seemed stunned.

"For about a minute," Jessie answered quickly.

"That's just too weird."

"What's weird about it?" Neal cut in. "Jessie's a total hottie, and," he grinned with broad confidence, "women find me irresistible."

"Don't be so sure," Jessie replied dryly, feeling cruel as the words left her mouth and Zoey nudged her gently.

"Ouch Durango. Well, I know at least one who does." He threw his arm around Zoey and pulled her to him, planting a sloppy kiss on her cheek even as she pulled away slightly. His hurt puppy expression registered his concern, but they had arrived at the Durango house, leaving him no opportunity to question Zoey's reaction.

Silvia and Antonio met them at the door, greeting them warmly, and as usual, Neal lifted tiny Silvia off the ground in his hearty embrace. She chastised him playfully as he cried fondly, "Mama Durango!"

"Neal's the only person that can get away with that," Jessie explained to Zoey. "If anyone else, even my brother, tossed Silvia Durango around like a rag doll, there'd be hell to pay."

Silvia slapped at Jessie for her language, and Zoey laughed and held her hand out to Jessie's mother. After polite introductions Silvia directed Jessie to help her in the kitchen while Antonio made their guests comfortable.

"Can I help?" Zoey was all smiles, earning points with Jessie's mother even as Silvia told her to sit down and enjoy being a guest.

Though she was reluctant to leave Zoey, Jessie knew better than to argue and resigned herself to her role as dutiful daughter.

CHAPTER FOURTEEN

Frustrated at being so close to Jessie without being able to really be close to her, Zoey did her best to chat and socialize with Neal and Antonio. Still, a recurrent stream of irritated-sounding Spanish coming from the other room kept turning Zoey's mind back to Jessie.

She smiled politely and listened halfheartedly as Neal and Jessie's dad argued good-naturedly about the Sox versus the Cubs, all the while straining to make out Jessie's voice in the conversation in the kitchen. Why she bothered she didn't know. Even if she had been practical enough to study Spanish in school instead of succumbing to the romantic appeal of French, it was more than likely that those language skills would have atrophied from disuse just as her French skills had. Besides that, Jessie and her mother spoke much too quickly for her untrained ears to discern anything beyond the basic sound of another language. Even the occasional burst of English didn't make things any clearer for Zoey. But hearing Jessie's voice, no matter what it said, made Zoey's stomach flip, and like the first time she'd heard Jessie speak in Spanish, Zoey was mesmerized. She grew as restless in her excitement to be near Jessie as she was uneasy in her betrayal of Neal. The unsettling mix of emotions within her put her on edge, and sitting next to Neal, who touched her easily and often and smiled so sweetly at her, only made her want to run away from the whole mess.

She sought some ruse to see Jessie alone, but her mind had never been less cooperative. Just when she thought she'd scream from the tension and the difficulty of maintaining such a placid façade, an idea, far from brilliant but not exactly feeble, made its way to her. After making her excuses to the men, she ventured into the kitchen where Jessie and Silvia, all smiles and laughter, continued their rapid-fire bilingual discourse.

With more confidence than she felt, Zoey addressed Jessie's mother. "Mrs. Durango, may I borrow your daughter for a while? I'm hoping to get a look at the rest of your beautiful home."

"Call me Silvia, please. And you'd be doing me a favor if you took her." Silvia laughed then threw out one last comment in Spanish to Jessie, who rolled her eyes before leaving the room with Zoey.

Jessie escorted Zoey through the lower levels of the house, showing her each of the rooms without interest or enthusiasm. Zoey barely registered anything beyond her nearness to Jessie. But on the top floor, away from everyone else, Zoey grabbed Jessie and pulled her close, hugging her from behind, savoring her smell, her softness and the warmth of Jessie's body so close to her.

"I'm finding it difficult to be near you without touching you." Zoey spoke softly, thickly, and Jessie turned to face her. Zoey was struck then by the honesty, the vulnerability in Jessie's soft brown eyes. It seemed like she really could trust Jessie with her heart. She asked in a whisper, "Which one of these doors leads to your room?"

The corner of Jessie's mouth quirked up before she took Zoey's hand and led her to the last door at the end of the hallway. Once inside Zoey said, "So this is where you grew up?"

"Yep." They both took in their surroundings. Zoey noted with pleasure the deep, dark purple of the walls, at least she liked what she could see peeking out from behind the pictures and posters of bands and soccer players that hung at drastic angles. The main rule of Jessie's youthful decorating seemed to be a complete rejection of straight lines, right angles or anything level.

A small bed, looking entirely too princessy to have ever belonged to Jessie, sat neglected under a window on the far wall. "My mom did this," Jessie said, fingering the frilly white cover and laughing. "So not my style."

Opposite the bed, a white dresser stood against the wall, and on it rested several artifacts of Jessie's formative years. The room seemed a shrine to Jessie's youth, and Zoey wanted to linger there and study these mementos, to learn about the woman at her side. Among the pieces were a number of framed photos of Jessie and her friends in school. She saw a bright-eyed, chubby-cheeked girl in pigtails smiling expansively as her companion stuck her tongue out. Zoey couldn't tell at first which of the girls was Jessie, but as she reached out to grab the photo and get a closer look, Jessie said, "Oh no you don't," and spun her away from the display.

Struck by Jessie's beauty and the privacy they now shared, Zoey brought her mouth to Jessie's, kissing her feverishly. Her hands began to roam over Jessie's body when, to Zoey's surprise and torment, Jessie abruptly ended their kiss. "We shouldn't be doing this. Not here, not now," she said and cast a troubled glance in the direction of the floor. Gently she pushed Zoey from her and added, "I missed you this morning."

"God, I hated to leave. I wish I'd stayed. I almost turned around to come back to you." Zoey moved closer to Jessie and reached for her again.

Resolute, Jessie sidestepped Zoey's attempted embrace and sat on the bed. "Why did you leave?"

Zoey exhaled slowly and sank onto the bed beside Jessie. "Because I panicked." She took Jessie's hand in her own, a reassurance. "Last night was incredible. It was perfect, maybe the best night of my life. But in the morning, the repercussions of what happened crashed down on me."

"Neal."

Zoey nodded, her mouth a tight line. "I had so many questions and concerns bouncing around in my mind, cluttering my thoughts, and watching you sleep was not helping me sort them out."

Jessie squeezed Zoey's hand. "Makes sense."

"We really need to talk, but not here, not now," she echoed Jessie's earlier statement. They gazed at each other for several minutes, before Zoey broke the trance. "I suppose we should go back downstairs. I don't want to upset your mom. She seems like a very serious woman."

"That's putting it mildly. She's ferocious."

"What did she say to you downstairs?"

Jessie hesitated before answering. "She told me to talk to you."

"About what?" Zoey's expression was quizzical.

"Please don't be mad at me." Zoey's stomach grew heavy as she considered the possibilities implied in Jessie's preemptive plea for forgiveness. "I told my mom about you. I mean, about how I feel about you." Zoey's eyes enlarged drastically. "It was last weekend after we kissed. I was going nuts, and I needed to talk to someone. I couldn't talk to Neal, obviously, and she always knows when I'm upset. She just pried it out of me. I'm sorry."

"Wow. That's awkward, but," she paused, standing up and looking at the hardwood floor, "I guess I understand. After all, I did the same thing with my sisters."

"You didn't."

"I did."

"That's why they were so weird the other night?"

"'Fraid so. I'm sorry."

"It's all right. But my mother's right. We do need to talk. About a lot of stuff."

"I know." Zoey ran a hand through Jessie's dark hair, fingering the ends, taking in its weight and texture. "Can you come over tonight?"

"Yes. After I drop Neal off and feed Sheila, I'll come back to your place." Zoey's heart fell a little as her thoughts turned to Neal, but there under the surface of her guilt, an overwhelming happiness filled her core.

On her way back to Zoey's after dropping Neal off, Jessie reflected that dinner had gone surprisingly well. She'd been a nervous, guilty mess before they all sat down to eat, a circumstance not helped by her mother's interference. Once she'd dragged Jessie into the kitchen, Silvia had begun an onslaught of aggravated Spanish.

"Have you talked to her yet?"

"Not exactly."

"When are you going to?"

"I don't know, Mama. Things are complicated right now."

"Well, they're going to get a lot more complicated if you don't talk to her. Hand me a spoon."

Jessie picked up a utensil and passed it to her mother. "I promise I will talk to her soon." Silvia set down the meat tenderizer Jessie had offered her and got her own spoon before slapping Jessie's hand away from the tortilla she was picking at. "I have been thinking about things. I know what I want now."

Silvia continued her activities, working around Jessie, who provided little actual assistance. "And what is that?"

"I want her." Silvia's rigid posture fell a little, and she sighed. "If she feels for me even half of what I feel for her, I could be happy for the rest of my life, Mama. And I think she might."

Silvia stopped cooking. "Talk to her. Be sure. If she does care for you, I will welcome her in my family. But you have to tell Neal, and don't you dare hurt that poor boy."

"I won't, Mama." She hugged her mother tightly, hoping that she wasn't lying. And after another half hour of less serious conversation and getting in her mother's way, Jessie was rescued by Zoey's request for a tour of the house.

After that things had seemed easier. The food had, of course, been delicious. As usual when she entertained, Silvia made enough food to satisfy a small village for a week. In addition to pozole, enchiladas and tamales, she also prepared a pot roast, mashed potatoes and two lasagnas (one with meat and one vegetarian). Jessie had no idea where her mother found the time and energy to create such monumental, delicious feasts.

Everyone had seemed to get along wonderfully as well. The conversation had flowed easily throughout dinner, and toward the end of the meal, Jessie's father, more animated than she'd seen in some time—probably thanks to the tequila he and Neal had shared before dinner—had told funny stories about his childhood. Most of them Jessie had heard several times before, but since they were also about her Papa Nestor, she gladly listened again. However, once he ventured into stories of her childhood, Jessie had to stop him.

"Dad, I'm sure no one cares what I was like in kindergarten." Neal instantly voiced his disagreement, and a hand squeezing her knee under the table told her she was wrong. Certain her face flushed from Zoey's touch, she'd feigned embarrassment and began clearing the table as her father resumed his story.

Over dessert Zoey and Silvia had engaged in a lengthy conversation about education throughout which Zoey's knee pressed firmly against Jessie's. Jessie could tell by her mother's voice and expressions that, though she searched for flaws in Zoey, she was impressed by this woman who had captivated her daughter.

When they'd finally left, Neal shook Antonio's hand and gave Silvia another boisterous hug, saying *"Gracias"* in an oddly meek voice. The only time Jessie ever saw Neal without confidence was when he spoke Spanish to her mother. He became awkward and self-conscious, but because it pleased Silvia that he tried, he always made an effort, however small.

Zoey too had offered sincere thanks. "You have a beautiful home. Thank you for making me feel so welcome here."

"It was a pleasure. You're welcome any time, *mija*." Jessie shook her head in wonder as the two most important women in her life embraced.

Then, as she had bid farewell to her parents, she hugged her mother tightly, whispering a heartfelt, "Thank you, Mama," in her ear.

It had been awkward when, in front of Zoey's building, Neal had shut the passenger door behind them both and said through the open window to Jessie, "I think I'll see you tomorrow, Durango." Instantly Jessie felt panicked, guilty and a little ill, a feeling that didn't subside as Zoey spoke up. "I'm sorry, Neal, I can't tonight. I've got some important things to take care of." Then she'd kissed his cheek lightly and sent him miserably back to the truck. When his back was to her, she signaled to Jessie a confirmation of their earlier plan.

Parking down the street from Zoey's building, fear mounted in her stomach as she considered the possibilities of her impending conversation with Zoey. Though she felt almost certain that Zoey cared for her, the small chance that she was wrong terrified Jessie. Her hand shaking, Jessie hit the buzzer labeled "Carmichael." Right away Zoey's voice crackled through the speaker. "Jessie?" She buzzed her in almost before Jessie answered.

Mounting the stairs, Jessie heard a door open above her. Looking up to the second-floor landing she saw Zoey smiling down at her, and she ran up the last few stairs to get to her.

"Hey you." Zoey enfolded Jessie in an embrace right there in the hallway, and Jessie nuzzled her face into Zoey's neck, inhaling her familiar scent.

"Hi." Then Zoey took her by the hand and led her inside.

Zoey's apartment, a cozy one bedroom, immediately felt inviting to Jessie, who made herself comfortable on a long, soft couch, and as Zoey disappeared into the kitchen, she familiarized herself with her surroundings. Aside from the couch, there were a few other pieces of furniture in the room. One chair sat at a right angle to the couch. In front of both of them was a low coffee table almost entirely free of the clutter of daily living. In fact the only untidy aspect of Zoey's home seemed to be an overflowing bookshelf that spilled its contents onto the floor in front of it. Zoey appeared to have as many books as Jessie had records, CDs and tapes, and they looked just as loved.

Zoey had brightened the walls, in the standard Apartment Beige, with a few pieces of colorful artwork. Jessie found out later that they were the creations of Zoey's sister Juliana. Across the room from her, Jessie noticed a narrow table full of framed pictures, and she crossed over to examine them. There were several with Zoey and one or more of her sisters and a few of her sisters by themselves. Alongside those photos Jessie saw Zoey's parents' wedding picture. Her father grinned broadly, and looking at Zoey's mother, Jessie knew why. Mrs. Carmichael was a striking woman with the same sparkling eyes as Zoey. Jessie picked up a picture of all of the Carmichaels together, noting the similarities between Grace, the sister she hadn't met, and Zoey. Though Grace was smaller, she was easily as lovely as her big sister.

She called out to Zoey, "Is everyone in your family beautiful? Or do you have an ugly cousin hidden away somewhere?"

"Oh, all the cousins are ugly. We don't even invite them to family functions anymore." Zoey appeared at Jessie's side and placed a bottle of beer in her hand.

"Thanks." As they sipped their drinks, an awkward silence passed between them. After some time Jessie said, "One of us should probably talk if that's what we're here to do."

Zoey merely nodded, a vulnerable look clouding her expression.

"I've never been in a situation like this before," Jessie began hesitantly. "I don't really know how to do this."

"Me either, but I do have to say something." She took a deep breath as Jessie looked at her expectantly. "You shared something very intimate and honest with me last night, and I want to be honest with you too."

"Okay." In her nervousness Jessie couldn't imagine what Zoey might be about to tell her.

"I'm sure you've figured out that I'm not a virgin."

"Right."

"In fact, I'm pretty far removed from virginity." She smiled weakly, as if she'd tried to make a joke that failed to go over. "God. This is harder than I thought. I've never felt the need to confess to anyone I've slept with before."

"You don't have to, Zoey. It doesn't—"

"I do. I want you to know who I am, what you're getting into, and this is a part of it." She took a long drink. Jessie had forgotten she even held her own beer. "I lost my virginity when I was fourteen. Aside from a few brief periods of chastity, I've been sexually active ever since then. Very active. I've had a lot of partners, Jessie. I wouldn't call myself a slut—for a number of reasons—but I'm no prude either." She shrugged and sighed. "I'm not ashamed of my past, but it's very different from yours."

"I appreciate you telling me, Zoey, but it doesn't matter. Knowing that doesn't change anything." She set her beer down and paused for a full, long minute, gathering her words and her courage. Finally, she looked directly into Zoey's eyes, speaking from her heart. "I think about you all the time when I'm not with you. When I'm fixing a car or making music, sometimes it's like I'm not even there, my mind is so much with you." Zoey smiled softly. "And when I am with you I just want to hold you close to me. My hands—" she held them out in front of her, briefly glancing at them as she would an unfamiliar object "—my heart—" her hands fluttered near her chest "—my everything aches for you. I want to smell your hair and kiss your fingers and do all those other silly little things that I never imagined I'd do with anyone. Zoey, I love you."

Suddenly embarrassed and terrified, Jessie looked away, her hands hanging limp at her sides. Zoey gently took Jessie's still shaking hands in hers and led her slowly, carefully back to the couch. Each elongated second of silence that passed convinced Jessie that she'd been a fool. She should have talked to her, like her mother said, before going to bed with her. But now everything was complicated and confusing, and Zoey had tried to explain that it was just another sexual encounter to her, but stupidly Jessie had hoped for what she wanted instead of listening to what was being said. Now she'd ruined their relationship with her outpouring of emotions. Mortified, she continued battering herself with her thoughts when Zoey's hand came to her chin, lifting Jessie's face to her own and kissing her lightly on the mouth.

"You really are amazing, you know. I've never met anyone quite like you, so passionate and brave and honest." As Zoey continued rattling off Jessie's finer attributes, Jessie's worry increased. She couldn't help but notice that Zoey hadn't said that she felt the same, and she waited for the "but" to come. "It feels so good to be with you, like something I've been missing but didn't even know it." She grabbed Jessie's hands. "I can't imagine my life without you."

Jessie's fear compounded her uncertainty. She couldn't fully focus on what Zoey said, and she didn't know whether to take Zoey's words as a declaration of love or a gentle letdown. "What does that mean?" She stared into Zoey's eyes, searching them for meaning.

"Jessie, more than I've ever wanted anything, I want you to be a part of my life."

Her brain stubbornly refused to believe what she thought she heard, and still needing assurance, Jessie asked, "In what way?"

Laughing softly and smiling a little, Zoey said, "I'll take you any way I can get you, but I'd prefer if we were a couple."

"Really?"

"Yes really."

Jessie offered a silent prayer of thanks before kissing Zoey fully, languorously. But they still had another issue to discuss, and it was too easy to lose herself in Zoey. Forcing herself to end the kiss, Jessie asked, "What about Neal?"

"Oh God. Neal." Zoey dropped her head into her hands and sighed heavily. "I don't know what to do about Neal."

"You have to talk to him."

"I know. It's just going to be so hard. It's going to hurt him, and I don't want to be the person to cause that pain. He'll hate me, and he'll be right."

"We could tell him together if you want."

"No!" Zoey was adamant. "I don't want to drag you into this."

"I'm already in it, Zoey. Sort of playing an instrumental role."

"But if I tell him alone, he doesn't have to know about this."

Jessie opened her mouth to argue but stopped, a thought crashing in on her. Losing Zoey would be hard enough on

Neal, but telling him that he'd lost her to his best friend seemed unnecessarily cruel. And she considered further, if Neal didn't know, she could stay in the band.

"Plus it's such a bad time right now. I've got so much going on at work. I have to prepare for finals and grade about a bazillion assignments and work on the syllabus for my summer class. There's just so much to do, and I don't want to do anything but be with you." Her eyes bored into Jessie's, and Jessie's heart swelled nearly to its breaking point at the sight of distress in Zoey's eyes. "Can't we just have this to ourselves for now? Can't we just be together and not worry about anything else, just for a little while longer?"

Jessie thought of her mother's calls for honesty, and her own heart felt stifled at the idea of lying. Neal deserved the truth rather than being strung along. But there in Zoey's eyes was an anguish she couldn't abide, a torment she'd do anything to ease, and though she knew it was wrong, she assented.

"Shh honey. It's okay." She cradled Zoey in her arms, kissing her head and stroking her hair. "You can wait. Just promise me you won't wait too long, okay?"

Zoey returned Jessie's embrace and sighed her relief. "I promise I'll tell him as soon as I can." Shyly Zoey looked to the floor. "I know you two are close. Will you swear not to say anything to him until I have a chance to tell him?"

Again Jessie felt conflicted, but she nodded. "Of course. I promise."

Zoey grabbed Jessie's hands. "Thank you for understanding."

Jessie's lips touched the tender place just under Zoey's eyes, tasting the salt of tears almost shed. "You're welcome, *guera*." Zoey's mouth came to Jessie's, biting and kissing the full lips that eagerly met her own. They kissed for some time there on the couch, Jessie pushing Zoey onto her back and moving on top of her. Jessie's tongue traced the delicate curves and folds of Zoey's ear before moving down her neck to the hollow at the base of her throat. She felt tiny vibrations against her lips as Zoey purred her enjoyment then said huskily, "Wouldn't the bed be more comfortable?"

Gradually they made their way to the bedroom, their bodies in constant contact as they moved. Side by side, they kissed slowly and with slight touches stroked one another's hair and arms. Occasionally Jessie's hands would find their way beneath Zoey's shirt, teasing and savoring the feel of soft skin against her fingers. She could feel the effects of her touch in Zoey's trembling body, but she restrained herself, lingering over their lovemaking and enjoying the acute closeness they shared. Unlike her previous night with Zoey, Jessie felt no compulsion to hurry. There was no pent-up and urgent yearning for release. She could take her time exploring and teasing, slowly building arousal until it crested, sweeping them both along in a consuming wave of passion.

After Jessie's exhaustingly satisfying climax, Zoey pulled her lips almost painfully away from her lover's body. "Can I ask you something?"

Out of breath, she panted her reply. "Anything." But momentarily she blocked any questions with her kisses.

And for a time Zoey was content to be distracted, but finally she ended the exchange and spoke. "Your mom called me '*mija*' tonight."

"I can't believe you're thinking about my mother right now."

"I'm sorry, but I just keep wondering what it means."

"It means she likes you."

"I kind of figured that out on my own. What does it really mean?"

Jessie propped herself up on her elbow and gazed into Zoey's eyes. "If I tell you, can we stop talking about my mom?" Zoey nodded her agreement, and Jessie continued, "Do you know any Spanish at all?"

"Not really." Zoey frowned apologetically. "But I love to hear you speak it, and I want to learn."

Pleased, Jessie kissed Zoey before explaining. "Here's your first lesson. '*Mi hija*' means my daughter. If you run that together, you get '*mija*.'"

"So she called me her daughter?"

"Well, *mija* can mean that, or it can just be a term of endearment. Like my brother calls me *mija*, but no matter how much he tries to act like my father, I will never be his daughter."

Zoey's expression changed from curiosity to wonder. "That's so sweet." Then a naughty gleam flashed in her devilish green eyes. "Of course, when she said it, I'm sure she had no idea that I'd be ravaging her real daughter, but still, it's sweet."

"Yes it is. Now can we forget about my mom? It's a little hard to concentrate on your body and what I want to do to it with Silvia in the room." Jessie's eager mouth came to Zoey's breast.

"You're insatiable! I think I've created a monster."

Jessie lifted her head. "You have." Her mouth melted into Zoey's in a sweet, lingering kiss that shifted their focus back to each other, where it remained through the night.

CHAPTER FIFTEEN

The insistent buzz of the alarm jarred Zoey from a deep sleep. Morning had come around too fast, and for the first time since she began teaching, she was tempted to cancel her classes and play hooky. At the very least she wanted to hit the snooze button and cuddle back into the warmth of Jessie's sleeping body. But as they'd lain in an exhausted, radiant embrace some time after midnight, Jessie had been emphatic about getting up at five. Zoey glanced at the clock again—two minutes after five—and turned gently over, taking a moment to look at Jessie's naked body, so compact and perfect there in her bed, and remembering their night together.

"I love you." She'd spoken so clearly, so earnestly, expecting nothing in return. She hadn't said it to get Zoey into bed, nor had she bared her emotions grudgingly or halfheartedly as Neal and others had. "Love you," though a big step for Neal, was not the same as "I love you." It removed the personal connection and replaced it with fear and protection, neither of which were a part of Jessie's declaration. But even in the face of Jessie's certainty, Zoey had been too afraid of her own emotions to fully expose herself.

She spooned Jessie's body and gently lifted the thick, dark hair from her neck, clearing the way for her lips and tongue. Her fingers trailed lightly up Jessie's arm to her shoulder then down across her chest. Brushing her lips against Jessie's ear, Zoey whispered, "Good morning."

Jessie stretched against Zoey's body before craning her head for a kiss. A minute later she focused her heavy-lidded eyes on Zoey's and asked, "Can I wake up like this every day?"

Zoey's heart ached at the sweetness of the moment. She answered, "Yes please," before Jessie got up and began searching for her clothes.

"Are you sure you want to do that?"

Jessie smiled at her. "People will look at me funny if I go outside naked."

"You don't have to go outside. You could stay here." Feeling awkward, she said, "We could spend the day together."

"*Querida*," Jessie sighed as she crawled back across the bed to Zoey. She kissed her for several minutes before whispering, "If I could make money loving you, I would be a very wealthy young woman. But," she pressed her lips against Zoey's forehead briefly, "I have to go to work."

"You work for your brother," Zoey pouted. "Doesn't that get you anything?"

"Yeah," she laughed. "It gets me extra harassment if I try to take advantage." Jessie went in for another kiss, but Zoey, still pouting, stuck her bottom lip out. "*Guera*, I can come back tonight after practice."

"Fine," Zoey relented, offering her mouth up to Jessie's. "But I want you here right after. No dawdling."

"We won't even do any slow songs. I promise."

Ridiculously happy, Jessie left Zoey's shortly after five so that she could return home to shower and tend to a sulky Sheila E. before heading to work. She felt a twinge of guilt over Neal, who snored away in his room oblivious to her duplicity. She hoped that Zoey would tell him something soon.

At the shop, Marco worked her like a mule, allowing her to forget about Neal but also preventing her from losing herself in thoughts of Zoey. After a full, hard day under her brother's intense supervision, she returned home to clean up and appease Sheila until band practice, giving Zoey time to grade papers or run or even sleep before Jessie came over immediately after practice as promised.

When she arrived, though she'd been blissful all day long, for a moment after being buzzed in, panic washed over Jessie. Frightened that Zoey had come to her senses and changed her mind, Jessie trudged up the stairs hopeful that she worried over nothing, yet dreading the possible blow to come. But when Jessie reached the second-floor landing, Zoey stood in the hallway, as she had the previous night, ready to wrap her arms around Jessie and pull her inside, leaving all her fears on the other side of the door.

Over dinner, a light veggie stir-fry that Zoey prepared, they talked about their days. Zoey unloaded about her most frustrating students, the ones who waited until the last few weeks of the semester to care about their grades, and Jessie gabbed about Marco and the band (while carefully avoiding any direct mention of Neal). When Jessie was in the middle of a story about a particularly irritating customer, Zoey's phone rang. She glanced at it briefly and set it aside without answering.

"You could've gotten that. I'm not saying anything important." Though she enjoyed being the center of Zoey's attention, Jessie didn't want to monopolize her to the point of coming between Zoey and her friends and family.

"It's okay." Zoey returned to her seat across the little kitchen table from Jessie. "I didn't feel like talking."

"Why not?" Jessie asked, thinking she knew the answer but still curious.

"It's not your concern," Zoey answered curtly, and an uneasy silence descended.

Piqued by Zoey's shortness, Jessie carried her half-full plate over to the garbage can, dumped its contents and then began washing dishes, hoping the activity would dispel her frustration and doubt and maybe help clear the air. After several moments she felt Zoey's arms around her waist, and she leaned back into the warmth of Zoey, gratefully welcoming the taller woman's chin resting upon her head.

"I'm sorry I snapped." She kissed Jessie's neck, a gentle, apologetic peck that, nevertheless, stirred Jessie.

Eager to forgive, forget and move on, Jessie reached one soapy arm behind her to pull Zoey even closer. She felt like, even if she were inside of Zoey's skin, she wouldn't be close enough to her. She didn't dare ask who called, but Zoey seemed to sense the question in her mind.

"It was Neal." Zoey stepped away from Jessie to sit down again, and Jessie felt as if the wind had been knocked out of her. "Last night he called before you got here. He said he knew I was busy but that he really wanted to talk."

"And?" Jessie turned and leaned back against the counter, a dish towel in her hands. She gazed at Zoey with concern and curiosity.

"And I told him we'd talk today, but I forgot to call him back."

"You didn't call him?" Jessie's voice conveyed her disbelief, and Zoey merely shook her head, her eyes clouding as her lower lip found its way between her teeth. "He's going to be pissed."

"I know. But I had zero free time at work, and when I got home I was so anxious for you to get here that I had to do something to pass the time. So I ran eight miles, and then I smelled like an armpit, so I had to clean up before I started cooking, and then you buzzed." She spread her hands out before her in a gesture of innocence. "I didn't have the chance." Zoey's face was a mask of consternation, her lips trembling and her eyes bright.

Jessie inhaled deeply, a complex blend of conflicting emotions warring within her. Initially she'd felt elated that she was the focal point of Zoey's attention, but sadness and guilt over Neal's ousting from that position, and her large role in that circumstance, quickly surpassed her immediate joy. Just as suddenly, her mind returned to Zoey. Her obvious distress over Neal affected Jessie more than any other concern. She couldn't stand to see Zoey upset.

Dropping her dish towel on the counter, Jessie crossed the bit of space between herself and Zoey and knelt before her. Holding Zoey's face gently in her hands, Jessie spoke in soft, soothing tones, "Don't get so upset, honey. It'll be okay."

"I just feel so horrible. Not that you have any reason to believe me, but I'm not usually so inconsiderate." Her hand swiped a tear from her cheek.

"So you'll call him back and talk to him."

"And crush him."

"Probably. But," she continued, trying to convince herself as much as Zoey, "Neal's a big boy. He'll get over it."

"I hope so."

"I know so." She smiled with a conviction she didn't feel.

Zoey stood up, and pulling Jessie up next to her, she sniffed apprehensively. "Can I wait until tomorrow to call him?"

"Anything you want, *querida*." Jessie placed a gentle, reassuring kiss on Zoey's lips, and as Zoey returned the affection, they forgot about dinner and the dishes and Neal. Arm in arm, they made their way to the bedroom.

CHAPTER SIXTEEN

Tuesday began in much the same way as the previous day, with Jessie up and out early to start her backbreaking day. But she floated through the tiring hours, high on thoughts of Zoey. A few momentary pangs clouded her happiness when she considered Zoey's certain discomfort during her impending conversation with Neal, but soon that would be behind them. The thought of being with Zoey without feeling guilt over Neal sent her soaring again.

Late in the morning, Marco, apparently ascribing his sister's good mood to her record deal, approached her and asked over the lifeless engine of a Taurus, "What time on Thursday?"

"For what?" Jessie didn't look up from her work.

"For what? For your big recording session, that's what."

"Oh, that. Ten o'clock, I think."

"You think?" He practically shrieked in his disbelief. "What's going on with you?"

"Nothing." She glanced at him briefly before turning her attention back to the invalid vehicle before her. "What do you mean?"

"You're acting happy and weird, but it's not about the band. So what gives?" Marco leaned into her work space, obscuring her light. Still, she tried to remain focused on the task at hand.

His towering presence made her uneasy. "Can't I just be happy?" she asked in the direction of the fan belt.

"This is different."

Jessie finally stopped her work and looked at him. She wanted to share her joy with him, but concern over his reaction gave her pause. Her big brother's love and approval meant the world to her, and though she wouldn't stop seeing Zoey to appease him, she dreaded his rejection. Having Marco call her a horrible name or turn his until now always supportive back on her would be a knife in her heart. Finally, though, she reflected on her mother's admonishments to be honest, and she threw caution to the wind, saying simply, "I'm in love."

Now Marco paused. She could see him grappling with this information, his expressions morphing as he shifted into protective mode. From nowhere he asked, "With Chad?" His question felt like an accusation.

Stupefied, Jessie asked, "Chad?"

Suddenly, sharply, he grabbed her by the arm and dragged her into his office. After closing the door, he hissed, "I know you went on a date with him."

"So? I've gone on dates with lots of people."

"But I've seen how he looks at you."

Wrenching herself away from him, she barked, "And how is that?"

"Like he's a prisoner on death row and you're his last meal."

Exasperated, Jessie threw her arms in the air. "So what if he does? So what if I let him have his way with me?"

"I'll kill him."

"You're insane!"

"I'm your brother."

"I'm twenty-seven years old, Marco. Don't you think I'm old enough to make my own decisions about my love life?"

"No way. It's my job to protect you."

"From what, Marco? From sex? From love?"

"From guys like that jerk you met in high school." Marco's face exposed his tormented rage. He'd never forgotten how Andy had slipped under his radar and hurt his baby sister, and since then he scrutinized every guy that came close to Jessie with a menacing attentiveness.

Overcome with love for her brother, Jessie hugged him. "Oh Marco. Not all men are like him." She kissed his scruffy cheek before adding, "Besides, it's not a man I'm in love with."

Marco had been squeezing her tightly, but after her revelation, his grip loosened and he held her at arm's length, examining her, his expression a picture of gentle bewilderment. Though his face showed no anger or revulsion, the uncertainty contained in his silence threatened her with its unpredictability. Anxious, she awaited his reaction.

He grunted "Huh" several excruciating times before finally forming words, and when he did speak, his voice was that of a confused child. "You're a lez?"

Stung a little by his word choice, Jessie stepped back and squared her shoulders before answering, "I guess so."

Marco grunted a few more·"Huhs" and leaned his weight against his desk, slouching a little in a rare departure from his usual ramrod posture. Scratching his scalp, he said, "I guess it makes sense. I just thought I taught you to be tough, that that's why you like cars and all that. But, I guess, if you're a lez, you're supposed to do that stuff."

"Would you stop saying 'lez'? It's not about that. And it's not about my job, or any job I had before now, or even the fact that I could kick your ass right now."

"I'm sorry." He hung his head a little, and almost shyly he asked, "What is it about?"

Realizing that Marco hadn't meant to offend or hurt her, that he wasn't angry at all but just wanted to understand, she backed down. "I guess it's about how she makes me feel." Marco's expression showed his alarm. "Don't be a pig, *gordo*. I'm not talking about sex." He visibly relaxed, and for a time she considered how best to explain it to him. Finally she continued, "Do you remember that summer we went to Mexico with Papa Nestor?"

"Yeah, we drove all the way in that old truck of his. It took forever." Marco smiled in his fond memory of their *abuelo*. "And he dragged us all over town, introducing us to his brothers and sisters and all of their kids."

"There were so many people. I didn't think there was anyone in the whole village we weren't related to."

"Do you remember how happy he was to be home?" Marco said nothing but nodded reverently. "That's how Zoey makes me feel. Like I'm home."

Marco remained silent, absorbing and digesting this new information. He scratched his head again and cracked his knuckles, then scratched his arms and the backs of his hands before running his palms over his face. Jessie thought he might say something then, but he ran through this sequence of events twice more before he responded to her outpouring. And when he did talk, she could have kissed him. "So you know I have to meet her, make sure she's right for you, right?"

She hugged him again and said, "Ah *gordo*, she's perfect for me. But I will arrange a meeting."

"Good." He squeezed her to him once more. "Now let's get back out to the garage before Junior and Eddie decide to take a vacation too." And, careful not to show too much affection for one another, Jessie and Marco made their way back to the broken-down autos that awaited resuscitation at their hands.

Intent on keeping her promise to Jessie, Zoey dialed Neal's work number as soon as she got into her office on Tuesday morning.

"Neal, it's me," she broke in on his sterile office greeting. Her nerves a wreck, she couldn't endure the delay of politeness.

"Hey, babe," he replied cheerfully. "You had me worried." He sounded concerned, not angry. That was going to make things harder.

"I'm sorry I've been MIA. I, uh, got really involved in what I was doing, and by the time I finished it was too late to call." That wasn't really a lie, so why did she feel so guilty?

"No problem, babe. But I'm kinda puttin' out some fires here. Could we maybe do lunch?"

It would be kinder to tell him in person than over the phone, and then she'd only ruin half his day instead of the whole thing. "Sure," she answered. "Just stop by my office when you're ready."

She hung up and got to work distancing herself mentally from the unpleasant task awaiting her. The campus was unusually quiet, allowing her to grade several revisions and put together most of her American Lit final before Neal's sharp knock startled her, making her jump in her seat.

"Sorry. I didn't mean to scare you. Ready to go?"

"Yes," she said, saving her work before looking up to see him watching her. His smile was light and happy, and in his professional attire, he looked good, a cleaned-up scruffy. It was as if he was trying to make it as difficult as possible for her. "What should we eat?"

"Could you do a little Mexican?"

If you only knew, she thought guiltily before answering, "Definitely." Feeling like the set-up for some cosmic joke, she followed him out the door.

Sitting across from Neal at the Mexican restaurant two blocks from school, Zoey occupied herself with perusing the menu, trying to work on her courage. She'd been tempted to help that along with a margarita. However, even though she wouldn't be teaching after lunch, she still had work to do that wouldn't be improved by alcohol and emotional instability. She sipped forlornly at her water.

Wanting to delay hurting him as long as possible, Zoey convinced herself that she should at least let Neal enjoy part of his meal before she broke the news to him. But as soon as Neal took a bite of an enchilada, she heard herself saying, "We need to talk."

He nodded vigorously as he chewed. "Yeah," he said after swallowing. "I had it all set in my head, what I would say to you. It was beautiful too, would've made great lyrics. But of course I don't remember any of it." He shrugged almost meekly before adding, "I'm sorry, Zoey."

"For what?" Befuddled, Zoey could think of no offense Neal had committed, but as she stared at him, his face a confusingly sweet composite of desire and affection, her own sins came crashing in on her. She grew warm and uncomfortable under his unwavering gaze.

"For Sunday," he offered. "You weren't very, um, affectionate."

"I'm sorry about that, Neal."

"No. Don't be." Her confusion must have registered on her face because he took her hand and smiled crookedly at her. "I mean, at first I was hurt, but then I figured it out."

"You did?" She couldn't keep the panic from her voice. Just what had he figured out? Did he know about her and Jessie? If so, why was he being so nice? God, she hoped he didn't suggest a three-way.

"Yeah. It was 'cause of Durango." Her heart pounded, her ears rang and she was sure all the color drained from her face, but she could make no sound. "I guess you were shy in front of her, or embarrassed or something since you're sort of friends."

"We are growing close," she offered, bewildered by Neal and his misplaced sensitivity. Why couldn't he take pity on her and just be a jerk?

"Good. I really want you guys to like each other." She looked away in shame that he misinterpreted. "You don't need to worry about Jessie, though. She knows me well enough to have figured out that we're having sex. She won't think less of you for it. I promise."

"Great," Zoey said a little sadly, knowing she couldn't tell him now. She couldn't bring herself to repay his consideration and kindness—undeserved and misplaced though they were— with betrayal and heartbreak—also undeserved. She'd have to disappoint Jessie for another day. Turning her attention to her untouched food, she really wished she'd gotten a margarita.

* * *

The Taurus repaired and its owner called, Jessie went to lunch feeling elated. The almost perfect weather summoned her outside to a nearby park, where she sat and contemplated her life. The conversation with Marco had been unexpected but wonderful. Though she hadn't started her day thinking that she would out herself to her brother, the outcome couldn't have been better. Before that morning she hadn't even considered telling him and certainly hadn't allowed herself to think about his likely reaction. Now she chided herself for not having more faith in her big brother, who was really just a lovable oaf. She knew that he would take to Zoey, just like their mother had.

That morning before work, Silvia had called Jessie. She couldn't ignore Jessie's obvious happiness and agreed that it was time to fill Antonio in on the subject, but she grew angry with her daughter when she learned that Neal still remained in the dark. Jessie had tried to keep the conversation away from Neal, but Silvia's near-maternal affection for him manifested itself in an unnatural concern for his well-being in this situation.

"Don't you think he should know at least as soon as your father?" she'd said, and knowing Zoey's plan for the day, Jessie had assured her mother that he would know soon. "I'm happy that you're happy, *mija*," she had told Jessie before ending the call.

Jessie didn't worry at all about her father's reaction. She knew that he loved her no matter what. He might be surprised, but he wouldn't be angry. Soon her whole family would know that she was in love with a woman, and none of them would really care. On top of that, the band was headed into a real recording studio for a real record label. Winning the lottery might come close to feeling this good, but Jessie doubted it.

Still, her life wasn't perfect yet. Like her mother, Jessie was concerned about Neal. She hated the thought that the source of her happiness would be the cause of misery for him, and she prayed that Zoey would let him down easy. Given her history, Zoey must have broken up with guys before. Surely she'd found a way to be gentle about it. Then after Neal had time to heal, after he started dating someone else (which wouldn't take much time considering Neal's dating habits), maybe Jessie could tell him about her relationship with Zoey. Not when and how it started, certainly (that would cause him unnecessary pain), but she longed to share her joy with the one important person in her life who still remained in the dark. It wouldn't be long now, she told herself, and if she waited until Zoey was just another of his many exes, he might actually be happy for them.

Buoyed by that optimistic and willful delusion, Jessie felt the need to celebrate, publicly, with Zoey. An idea occurred to her, and she headed back inside to spend the rest of her lunch break researching her idea and making phone calls.

* * *

After her disastrous lunch outing with Neal, Zoey wanted to retreat to the comfort of Jessie. She started to call her but stopped mid-dial when she considered Jessie's likely disappointment over her continued failure at breaking up with Neal. How could she explain it in a way that didn't make her look selfish and inconsiderate? As she sat pondering her options and completely ignoring the pile of essays on her desk waiting for her input, her cell phone rang.

"I was just thinking about you," she cooed into the phone.

"Really? What were you thinking?" Jessie asked.

"Nothing I can discuss in public," Zoey answered.

"Maybe I should call back later."

"Why don't you just come over later?" Zoey grew coquettish.

"That's actually why I called," Jessie sounded a little nervous, which made Zoey a little nervous.

"I'm still going to see you tonight, right?" Zoey couldn't keep the whine from her voice.

"Of course, *guera*. But I was wondering if, instead of staying in, maybe you'd like to go out."

"Jessie Durango, are you asking me on a date?"

"I am." Jessie's voice quivered a little, but she quickly recovered. "Are you interested?"

"Well, I have to check my schedule, but I'll pencil you in."

"What an honor."

Zoey's mood changed again as she said, "Our first official date. Where are you going to take me?"

"It's a surprise."

"Oooh," she purred. "Good move. I like surprises."

"Well, I think you'll really like this one," Jessie said.

They continued talking for a short time longer, swapping tales of worst first dates. Zoey easily took the cake with the story of a man who brought her to a cheap motel and told her that if she was good he'd buy her dinner.

"Well, there goes my surprise," Jessie laughed.

CHAPTER SEVENTEEN

Zoey's delight was evident when Jessie escorted her onto the same old South Loop rooftop she'd visited with Chad. The night, clear and warm, seemed perfect as they found seats just the right distance from the band with equally good views of the podium and the city. As Jessie had hoped, Zoey loved it. She knew many of the poems by heart, but seemed eager to revisit them after hearing the little man from Kansas, and she couldn't wait to dive into the works she hadn't heard before. It was as if a whole new literary world was opened up to her, and she thanked Jessie for exposing her to it.

"It's so beautiful. How did you find this?" Her voice was filled with wonder as they stood near the edge of the roof, sipping wine and looking out over the city they'd just heard immortalized by some of the most talented writers in American history.

Jessie, who didn't care for wine, sloshed hers around in its plastic cup more than she drank it. She wouldn't have gotten it at all, but the only other option was diet soda. Not looking at Zoey she said, "Chad brought me here."

"You recycled a date?" Zoey stared at her, an incredulous smirk on her face.

"I suppose I did." Jessie shrugged her shoulders. "But I just knew you would love it, and I wanted to share this with you. I didn't think you'd care."

"You're right. I don't. I'm too happy to be here with you." She squeezed Jessie's hand before Colin, the little man from Kansas, came over to thank them for coming.

Zoey took the opportunity to pick his brain about his performance. She asked so many questions that Jessie thought he must surely be annoyed, but he answered all of them as ardently as she asked them. Jessie began to feel like an outsider or an orphan in one of those hokey Christmas movies pressing her face up against the window of some beautiful family scene. There she was, a mechanic who had gone no further than high school, skirting the fringes of intellectualism. Not that she felt stupid, just out of place and a little jealous. But as she watched Zoey engaging with this man about the thing that moved her as much as she was moved by music, she found her reservations melting. She'd long since lost the thread of the conversation, focusing instead on the whole of Zoey. Her dress—the first Jessie had seen her in—captured her beauty and accentuated the grace of her long, lean, muscular limbs, and Jessie found herself floating along on the sound of Zoey's impassioned voice as she watched her interactions. It wasn't until she felt Zoey's hand on her arm and heard her say, "Thank you, but we're together," that she refocused her attention. Realizing that Colin had been hitting on Zoey right there in front of her, she glared at him openly. Shortly after that he excused himself, and Zoey asked if she was ready to leave.

As Jessie drove them to a little Italian restaurant buried in Uptown, Zoey apologized for the scene with Colin on the roof.

Though the situation bothered Jessie, Zoey's unhesitant pronouncement of their relationship pleased her more, so she said, "I guess it just comes with the territory. I'll have to find a way to adjust to loving a beautiful, brilliant woman."

Zoey slid across the seat and nuzzled Jessie's ear. Aided by the fact that Jessie also wore a dress, Zoey slowly raked her fingers over Jessie's bare thigh and whispered in her ear, "Are you sure you're hungry?"

Grateful for the red light that allowed her to stop before she crashed her truck, Jessie grabbed Zoey's hand and, after kissing her hard, said, "Just let me take you to dinner, okay?"

Facing forward and folding her hands in her lap, Zoey said sulkily, "Okay."

Once they were seated in the restaurant, Jessie felt vindicated for her resolve. Judging by Zoey's smile as she gazed around the dimly lit, intimate dining room, she was pleased.

"It's so cozy in here," Zoey said.

"I know, and they've got great food."

"Did Chad take you here too?" Her teasing barely covered the note of bitterness in her voice.

"I'm not that blatant. It was a totally different guy." Zoey's eyes grew larger in her astonishment, and Jessie relented. "I'm kidding. My *tia* knows the owners."

"Oh. Good. I don't want to share anything about you with that guy."

"Are you jealous?" Jessie took a sip of her water to hide her satisfied smile.

"Yes." Zoey's voice grew hard-edged and angry. "The instant I saw that pile of steroids put his hand on you, I wanted to punch him in his perfectly chiseled face."

"Are you serious?" Jessie couldn't hide her shock.

"Oh, and when he kissed you! I almost broke my pool cue across his head."

"I had no idea." Though totally surprised by this side of Zoey, Jessie found certain aspects of that night falling into place. Zoey's coldness, the distance she kept, it made sense now, and it made Jessie feel strangely happy to know that she hadn't been the only one struggling with her desire. "You don't need to worry, you know. No one could affect me like you do."

"Good," Zoey responded, blushing a little. She narrowed her eyes as she added, "But remember, I'm not above resorting to violence when necessary."

Jessie laughed with Zoey, thinking that she had far more reason to worry than Zoey ever would—after all, it was only their first date and Zoey was already fending off the advances of strange men. She just couldn't offer Zoey the kind of visible attachment that Neal or any man could, and the thought worried her. Still, she pushed all such ideas from her mind, opting to focus only on Zoey and their time together.

* * *

On the drive back to her apartment after dinner, Zoey planted herself in the middle of the bench seat, curling herself against Jessie's body as she steered the pickup south through the city. A feeling of complete contentment filled her, and she didn't even mind when Jessie inquired, sounding only slightly parental, "Did you call Neal today?"

"We had lunch together, actually." Traffic was getting ugly, so she sat up and buckled her seat belt.

"Really? How'd it go?"

"It was weird. He wanted to apologize to me."

"For what?"

"For being so forward on Sunday. He thought he'd embarrassed me by acting like that in front of you, since we're friends."

"Oh."

"Yeah. He thought that was why I was standoffish. He was so sweet and considerate and worried. And I just sat there looking at this man that I really cared for, that I still do care for, and all I could do was accept his apology. I couldn't tell him."

"I see," Jessie said before snapping her jaw shut.

Zoey turned in her seat to look at Jessie and saw the muscles along her lover's jaw working in anger or disappointment or both. She reached out and rested her hand on Jessie's arm, saying with conviction, "I'm going to tell him."

Sullen, Jessie replied, "I know."

She repeated herself more gently as Zoey ran her hand up Jessie's arm to her shoulder, which she squeezed, and then continued moving it down Jessie's side, finally letting it rest on her thigh. Zoey saw Jessie's expression relax into an easy grin.

When Jessie pulled up in front of Zoey's building, Zoey declared, "This has been the most wonderful first date. Thank you."

"Does it have to be over already?" Jessie asked as she maneuvered into a parking spot.

"Well, you're coming in, right?"

"Are you inviting me in?"

"Of course." Zoey opened her door, and they walked to her building.

As they mounted the stairs to the second floor, Jessie said, "I didn't want to be like motel guy. I mean, this *is* our first date."

"Well," Zoey responded playfully, "I'm not usually so brazen, but since we've already slept together about a thousand times, I'll make an exception." She stopped at the first landing and pinned Jessie to the wall with kisses, which Jessie seemed happy to receive until one of Zoey's neighbors unlocked his door. Before he emerged, they scampered up the remaining stairs to Zoey's apartment where Jessie made it increasingly difficult for Zoey to unlock her door by stretching herself to kiss Zoey's neck and shoulders.

Once the door opened and they were safely inside, Jessie asked nonchalantly, "Did I ever tell you that I went to school for massage therapy?" Zoey raised an eyebrow in her curiosity. "I didn't pursue it as a career, so I've never really tested my skills, but do you want to see what I remember?"

"Oh, you're good," Zoey said as they wound their way into the bedroom.

"I haven't even touched you yet."

Zoey stopped her in the doorway to the bedroom. Holding her hands and staring at her intently, she said in all seriousness, "Yes you have."

Some time later, Zoey laid her head on Jessie's stomach, listening to all the sounds of life behind the wall of skin and muscle. Jessie ran her fingers through Zoey's hair while Zoey's hand traced an intricate pattern on the soft skin of Jessie's leg. Softly Jessie asked, "When did you know?"

"Know what?" Zoey lifted her head to look at Jessie.

"That you wanted to be with me."

Zoey remained silent for a while, contemplating their history. "Well, I know that I was drawn to you almost immediately. At first I told myself that it was because you were so nice to me and seemed genuinely interested in what I was talking about. And you were funny and didn't seem to buy into Neal's projected self-image. It was refreshing. I thought that, finally, I'd met a friend of Neal's that I could stand and that you'd be fun to hang out with. This was all in the truck on the way to your show, by the way."

"That was a fifteen-minute ride," Jessie said as she shifted her position.

Scooting up to the head of the bed, Zoey placed an arm around Jessie, who rested her head on Zoey's shoulder. Needing to feel Jessie's skin and substance, Zoey ran her hand over her torso in a slow, constant motion as she continued.

"I think too much. Anyway, when I saw you play, something shifted. I know I should have been all moon-eyed and transfixed by Neal, but I just couldn't stop watching you. You probably aren't aware, but when you play, you get this intense look on your face. It's like…ferocious bliss. And the way you move is so effortless but visceral and forceful, and so feminine too. It was very powerful—I told you I'm a big feminist, right? It was just beautiful, and I was hooked. I decided I had to get close to you, so I approached you as soon as you were done. I didn't even look for Neal first. I wanted to get to know you, which is not one of my strengths, and I don't know how it happened, but I started flirting with you. And it felt comfortable and right. Especially after you got so worked up about female musicians." Zoey looked away, blushing. "Somehow I lost control of myself, though. I turned into a high school cheerleader going after the quarterback. It's a little embarrassing."

"It wasn't that bad," Jessie reassured her.

"Come on! I was all over you, touching you and leaning in close to talk, and then coming by the house so much after that. It was gross." Zoey took her arm back and sat up straight to tell the rest of her story. "But when we almost kissed that night after the poetry reading, I got scared. I thought I'd given you the wrong impression—although I don't know what other impression you were supposed to get. But I decided to tone it down a bit and just be friendly, which was harder than I thought it would be."

"Were you still sleeping with Neal then?"

"Oh yeah. Even more than before I met you. I was always ready to go, and you know Neal." Jessie just nodded. She didn't look like she really wanted to hear any of this. "It's funny, but I didn't realize the true nature of the feelings I had for you until I saw you with that lunkhead. Chad." Zoey rolled her eyes in disgust at the thought of him. "Then it was like a cartoon lightbulb went on over my head. I felt so stupid for not understanding earlier that I was totally attracted to you. But what could I do at that point?"

"Make out with me in a public bathroom while our dates played pool downstairs?"

"I didn't hear any complaints from you."

"And you're not going to."

"What about you? When did you know?"

Jessie grinned. "Oh, I'm still not sure."

Zoey popped her with a pillow, saying, "Don't be a jerk. I was honest with you."

"Okay, okay. It was a lot like what you went through. At first I thought I liked you so much because you were so important to Neal. And I was really happy for him that he'd found someone worthwhile to fall for." Zoey smiled, pleased. "But I was awfully giddy, and I just couldn't explain that. Until you tried to kiss me."

"Me?"

"Yes you. Luring me in with that 'I'm so cold' routine. Where is my coat, by the way?" Jessie laughed as Zoey hit her again with the pillow.

"You're not getting your coat back."

"Why not?"

"Because it's warm and comfy."

"I know. That's why I want it."

"But I look kind of cute and butch in it."

"So do I."

"I'm sure, but I like having it because it smells like you."

Zoey smiled, and Jessie sighed in delighted resignation. "Fine. I'll have Marco order a new one for me. But if people start calling you Jessie, it's not my fault."

An impish smirk erased the innocence from Zoey's features as she replied, "I'll just say he's my boyfriend."

Jessie's expression was wide-eyed and wounded as she said, "You better not."

"I wouldn't. I'll tell them it belongs to my hot Latina lover, who happens to be the drummer for Nuclear Boots, and then screaming hordes of fans will try to rip the coat from my body just to have a piece of Jessie Durango."

"That sounds better."

"Don't you even care that I could be hurt in the fracas?"

"If you'd just give me my coat, I wouldn't have to worry about your safety."

"You're not getting your coat back," Zoey stated firmly before kissing Jessie to stop any further arguments. Her devious strategy worked.

CHAPTER EIGHTEEN

Jessie soared through her workday again on Wednesday. Her happiness over Zoey and her excitement about the band's impending trip to the studio sent her flying so high that eight hours of manual labor seemed to pass in no time at all. After work, band practice passed just as quickly. The boys shared her good mood, and she enjoyed the levity and camaraderie of a great practice before dashing out the door to see Zoey.

As was becoming their habit, Jessie met Zoey on the second-floor landing. After a lingering greeting, Zoey's face took on a worried expression. Her eyebrows furrowed, and she looked anxious.

"What's wrong?"

"I did something stupid." Jessie, in a daze, stared at her silently, her head swimming with horrible speculation about what Zoey might have done. Zoey scrunched her face and bit her lip before spitting out, "I just got off the phone with my mom. I sort of told her that you'd fix my dad's car tonight."

"That's it?"

"Yes. You're not mad?"

"Well, I can think of a few things I'd rather do tonight, but as long as it's nothing major I can take care of it."

"Really? Even after you've spent the whole day fixing cars?" Jessie nodded. "Come here," Zoey said, pulling Jessie close to her. "You're wonderful."

Jessie smiled and said, "Let's go. Maybe I'll finish fast."

"You'd better," Zoey replied as she followed Jessie out the door.

Out on the street in front of the Carmichaels' apartment, Jessie listened as Zoey's father, Martin, described the symptoms his Malibu exhibited: fluctuating brightness of his headlights, a grinding noise and what he called "a weak engine." With Zoey and Martin watching intently, Jessie tested a few things before coming up with a diagnosis.

"The bearings on your alternator are shot," she spoke matter-of-factly.

Martin, looking confused and concerned, scratched his graying beard but said nothing.

Zoey jumped in and asked, "What does that mean?"

"It means we need to replace it."

"Ugh. Is that expensive?"

Jessie saw Zoey's anxiety over her working-class parents' pocketbook, so she attempted to ease both of the Carmichaels' minds. "It shouldn't be too bad. Depending on where I get one, you're looking at a couple hundred." Martin gave a low whistle, so she added, "You can buy a rebuilt alternator and save some money that way, but I wouldn't be able to get that tonight."

"How long would that take?" Martin asked cautiously.

"I could probably get one in a day or two. I know a reliable guy."

"But I really need to get to work tomorrow," he said as much to himself as to Jessie.

"Well, as long as you didn't turn on any unnecessary accessories to drain it, you could limp along on the battery's reserve for a little while."

"That doesn't sound very safe, Daddy." Zoey turned her attention back to Jessie. "And if we get a new one?"

"In that case I could do it tonight, and you'd save money on the free labor."

Martin spent a few minutes deliberating before announcing, "Oh, hell. Let's do the thing tonight."

After getting what she needed from an auto parts store in Edgewater, Jessie worked quickly and efficiently to fix Martin's car while Zoey held a flashlight and Martin stood by asking numerous questions. Once the car was up and running, Jessie performed a cursory inspection of the rest of the vehicle. Giving it a clean bill of health, she suggested that Mr. Carmichael bring the car to the garage for a more thorough examination and a tune-up. He'd have to pay for parts, but labor would be free. Obviously embarrassed by his lack of mechanical prowess, Zoey's father initially declined to take her up on her generosity, instead offering Jessie cash (which she steadfastly refused) and apologies for dragging her out of her house. Jessie brushed his concerns aside, saying that dinner would make them even. Then she spent what remained of the evening enjoying the hospitality of Martin and Fiona Carmichael as well as getting to know Zoey's baby sister Grace, who was there for one of the many free meals she mooched from her parents.

And though Fiona, a thin, attractive woman of average height, was no Silvia Durango in the kitchen, she held her own, serving up generous portions of an entirely vegetarian meal in honor of Zoey and "our tiny heroine." Jessie, usually defensive about her size, didn't even mind Mrs. Carmichael's nickname for her. In fact, Fiona's funny little accent, with its lilting musicality gave her every utterance a magical quality, so much so that, when she ordered Zoey and Grace to clean up the dinner mess, Jessie had leapt up to help them because it sounded more like a delightful adventure than a chore.

"Now, now, Jessie," Fiona had said firmly, "you've already worked for your supper. Let these two earn their keep while we get to know one another better. Martin will freshen our drinks, and we'll settle into the living room for a nice chat, then." She encircled Jessie's slight shoulders with one long arm, steering her past the kitchen and saying, "Tell me, Jessie, how does a little thing such as yourself fare in the world of automotive repair?"

As their voices trailed off, Zoey balked at subjecting Jessie to her parents without supervision. Who knew what damage Fiona could do by the time the dishes were done? After a few minutes of indecision, Zoey turned to the kitchen sink to face Grace, who'd gathered all of the dishes together, staring openly and smirking at her.

"What?" Zoey began filling the sink with scalding water, the only acceptable temperature for washing dishes in Fiona Carmichael's kitchen.

"Just that Laurel and Jules were right," Grace replied, still grinning.

"About what?"

"The drummer." Grace grabbed a steaming plate from Zoey's hand to dry it. "You're in love with her."

"I am." Zoey smiled in spite of herself. "Is it really that obvious?"

"To me, yes. I saw how you looked at her at dinner, how you watched her fixing Dad's car."

"Do you think Mom and Dad noticed?" A ribbon of laughter made its way from the other room.

"You're probably safe. I'm not sure Mom's brain thinks that way, and I doubt Dad will care. Are you going to tell them?"

"That I'm having mind-blowing sex with a woman every night? I thought I'd skip it."

"No, stupid. That you're in love with a woman."

"I haven't even told Jessie yet."

"You haven't?" Zoey shook her head as she rinsed silverware. "Why not?"

"For one thing, it's been less than a week."

"So? I bet she's told you."

"She's a lot braver than I am."

"You're scared?"

"Grace, I'm terrified. It's only been a few days, and I'm already so lost in her that I don't know what I'll do if she leaves." Zoey's vision blurred with tears she didn't want to shed, and she sniffed loudly before she felt Grace's hand on her shoulder.

"God, Zo. I haven't seen you so worked up about someone since you were fourteen."

"And you know how well that worked out."

"I think you might be comparing assholes and oranges here. Jake was a jerk, but I like Jessie. She's nice, and she looks at you like the world doesn't exist unless you're in it. You deserve someone like that, and she deserves to know how you feel."

"I know she does, but I just keep thinking that maybe if I hold something back, she won't be able to hurt me as much."

"You know you're being an idiot, right? Maybe if you keep holding back, you're going to push her away. Have some faith. In both of you."

"You're right, which is just creepy. My baby sister should not be giving me advice on love."

"Fine, but you might want to hurry up with these dishes so you can save your girlfriend from her future in-laws."

In complete agreement, Zoey turned her attention back to the mess of the kitchen, working quickly to get back to Jessie. Once the dishes were done, the sisters joined the conversation in the living room, steering it away from stories of Zoey's misspent youth.

CHAPTER NINETEEN

The next day at school, a revitalized Zoey challenged herself and her students to go beyond their comfort levels. The schedule for the day included poetry she'd lovingly labored over as a student, and as she urged and encouraged her own students, their uncharacteristically eager participation thrilled her. They grappled for and found meaning in the dense verse of Plath, Sexton and Rich, and the class session ended too quickly, leaving her frustrated and eager for their next meeting. She met with the same success in each class and after her office hours, left campus feeling rejuvenated.

At home, still exhilarated by the response of her students and her thoughts of Jessie, she found herself chatting with her mother. Fiona had called to thank Zoey for bringing Jessie over to fix the car. That business tended to, she continued the conversation.

"How is your young man?" Fiona asked in that tone that expressed extreme displeasure through the outward politeness of the question. Zoey had never met anyone outside of her family who could be so courteously unpleasant.

"He's fine, I suppose, but he's not really my young man anymore. I started seeing someone else."

"Oh you did, did you?" Her mother's delight a little too evident, she asked, "And what's this one like? Not another musician, I hope."

"Well, actually yes. But I'm pretty sure you'll get along," Zoey said coyly, trying to delay the inevitable with subtleties and vagueness.

"So you've been endowed with psychic powers now, have you?"

"No Mom." Zoey swallowed hard. "You've already met… her."

The line went completely silent and stayed that way for so long that Zoey asked, "Mom? Are you still there?"

"Yes, Zoey Colleen Carmichael, I'm still here, despite your efforts to put me in an early grave."

"Mom, it's—"

"You're in a relationship that goes against God's law, are you not?"

"From your perspective, yes."

"My perspective, she says. My perspective," Fiona muttered to herself before turning her attention back to Zoey. "Have you talked to a priest?"

"I don't think Hail Marys are going to change this, Mom. I'm in love." The silence threatened her again. "This is a good thing."

"How can you believe that?" Despite her words, Fiona's voice had lost some of its harshness.

"Mom," Zoey spoke with surprising calm. "Jessie is the kindest, most generous, most honest person I've ever known. She loves me like Dad loves you. I just don't see how that's wrong." Fiona grew silent again, and Zoey knew she'd scored a point by bringing in her father, a confirmed agnostic whom Fiona's entire family had looked down upon. She still received Christmas cards from distant relatives addressed to Fiona O'Connor, despite her thirty-five-year marriage. The quiet stretched out for several more minutes.

"Mom," Zoey said softly. "Are you okay with this?"

"No," Fiona answered bluntly, crushing Zoey a little. "I'd prefer if you stopped what you're doing."

"Mom, I—"

"But you're a strong-willed, pigheaded woman, so I don't expect that you will."

"No, I won't."

"Well then, I'll leave you to your conscience."

"What does that mean?" Zoey grew cold with uncertainty.

"It means I won't waste my breath telling you what's right."

"You're not disowning me, are you?"

Fiona cackled into the phone. "Oh child, if I didn't disown you for all the sex you've had up to now, why on earth would I disown you for this?"

Floored, Zoey was too stunned to answer. "And," Fiona continued, "your father would never let me do that, not even if you were cavorting with Satan himself."

"That's comforting."

"Now you bring this young lady over for dinner so we can properly get to know her. Next week."

"I'll see."

"That wasn't a request, young lady. I have to make dinner for your father and tell him what his daughter is up to. Were there any more of God's laws you've been ignoring, love?"

And like that it was over. She told her mother she was in a homosexual relationship, and the world hadn't imploded. Still out of sorts and disappointed, she donned her running gear and headed out the door to clear her head.

Though Jessie had begun her day on Thursday in an unparalleled state of elation, by the afternoon she felt broken and hopeless. When they finally, thankfully left the studio, Jessie drove Neal home, fed her cat and ran out the door. Alone in her truck as she fled to the safety and comfort of Zoey's arms, the tears she'd managed to suppress all day flowed freely. She didn't stop crying until she arrived at Zoey's apartment building. She trudged to the door, wiping her tear-dampened face with her sleeve, but before she rang Zoey's buzzer for entry, she heard her name being called.

"Jessie? I wasn't expecting you so early." Zoey, who was just returning from a run, wrapped her arms tightly around her lover, but when she saw Jessie's crestfallen expression, she dragged her into the apartment and demanded to know what was wrong.

"I just had the worst day of my life." Flopping down on the couch, Jessie threw her arm across her eyes, a long, weary sigh escaping from her.

Zoey perched next to Jessie on the couch and took her hands so that she could look in her eyes. "What happened?"

"Do you know what a click track is?" Zoey, obviously confused, shook her head, so Jessie filled her in on the details of her day in the studio.

They'd all been anxious at home, fidgeting and jittery, getting in each other's way, so they had decided to screw the image of them as cool, casual rock stars and had shown up a little early. Still, Dino had immediately produced what seemed like thousands of sheets of paper for them to read and sign. Though Jessie knew she should examine any paperwork before she put her signature on it, she'd been so anxious to start playing that she'd accepted Dino's assurances that it was just a "standard recording contract" and forgot about it. When they'd finally finished the boring prelude to recording and she'd gotten into the actual studio, she'd had to slip on headphones and play using a click track, a sort of electronic metronome standard in the recording industry. Though she understood Dino's reasoning— there were a lot of technical editing and mixing procedures that depended upon a consistent beat—Jessie had never played with any sort of metronome because she'd never needed one. She was the metronome.

But because of the weirdness of an outside beat in her ears, on her first few attempts at playing with the click track, she'd played like a spastic teen in a third-rate garage band. She'd dropped beats and missed fills. She just couldn't match her playing to the damn metronome. After several tries Dino had grown frustrated, growled at her to step aside and put in his studio drummer, Billy Stewart, who'd sat right down and played the song like he'd written it. Meanwhile she'd waited on the sidelines feeling stupid and utterly useless, especially when Dino conferred with Neal behind closed doors. Their talk, which was no doubt about her, did not go well, judging by Neal's stony silence on the ride home. The worst part, though, was that Dino had expected her to fail because it certainly wasn't free to keep a studio drummer hanging around just in case.

"So now I have to learn how to play using a stupid click track, and I have to do it soon. I won't be replaced. I won't." She pounded her fist against her thigh in her anger and frustration.

Zoey grabbed her hand and squeezed it, saying, "They can't replace you. You're the best part of the band."

Jessie laughed bitterly. "Neal is a good-looking, soon-to-be-single sex machine. Commercially speaking he's the best part of the band."

"Still, why would they replace you?"

"It happens all the time. Drummers are expendable. Just throw someone else with sticks in there to hit things. No one will know the difference, right? Christ, even Sleater-Kinney went through something like four drummers before they found Janet Weiss." Zoey's blank expression said that she had no idea what Jessie was talking about, and Jessie let out an exasperated whimper. "Never mind. We'll work on your musical education later. Did I ever tell you about Huey Lewis?"

"As in 'And the News'?"

Jessie nodded.

"No. What about him?"

"I heard this story when I was a kid, and even though I never got into his music, I gained a lot of respect for him."

"What did he do?"

Jessie sat up straight, imbuing her story with an energy she had not shown since walking through Zoey's door. "His band got a recording contract, and it was a big one, not like Dino's operation. Of course they were excited. I mean, that's the dream. But when they went to record, the studio execs wanted him to ditch his drummer and replace him with one of their studio guys. They kept riding him about it. They were relentless."

"Did he give in?"

"No, he didn't. The guy was one of his best friends and a good drummer, so he held his ground. His loyalty cost them the recording contract, and they spent ten more years playing bars and dealing with garbage before they got another deal. But he hung on to his drummer."

"That's fantastic."

"I know. It always impressed me." Jessie relaxed a bit, sinking back into the couch. "When I told Neal that story, he said that it wasn't true, but he swore he'd do that for me. He said he'd rather be in the best band in obscurity with me than a successful band without me. And I believe he really would have sacrificed himself like that." She glanced away from Zoey. "Until now."

"Because of us?"

Jessie nodded. "When he finds out he's not going to want me anywhere near him or the band. He's going to hate me. And I can't blame him. He really cares for you, and this is going to hurt him so much."

Zoey folded her hands in her lap. Almost inaudibly she whispered, "I know."

"He needs to know soon."

"You're right." Zoey picked at a hangnail on her thumb. "But if I tell him now, you're out of a job."

"And a house." Jessie slumped forward, dropping her head into her hands. "Why does this have to be so hard?"

Zoey took Jessie into her arms, and they sat in silence for a long time. From time to time Zoey administered soothing kisses on Jessie's forehead or cheek. Finally she offered some hope. "When do you go back to the studio?"

"Tuesday. Dino's going to be out of town until then, and he runs a very hands-on operation."

"Well, that's four whole days. So why don't you practice with the metronome thing—"

"Click track."

"Practice with the click track until Dino gets back. Then you'll show him that you are the best drummer in the world."

"What about Neal?"

"Give me a little more time to figure something out, but don't you worry about him."

Jessie hesitated. She knew she could master the click track. She could do anything musically. But could she leave Zoey so soon? Did she even want to be without Zoey? "I'll really have to focus. I won't be able to come over very much."

Zoey smiled thinly. "I know, but it's only a little while. We'll have plenty of time after this." Zoey kissed her gently. "But you don't get to start until tomorrow. Tonight you're all mine."

"I'm always all yours. But you have a deal."

Later, as they lay in bed together out of breath and perspiring, Zoey gazed at the woman beside her. Jessie's eyes, puffy from crying, drifted closed as she fell softly asleep. Childlike and vulnerable, she was beautiful, and Zoey's chest constricted in love. She loved every inch of Jessie and had tried to express as much physically. She was still too frightened to say the words, but with every kiss, every touch, she communicated her intense love. Even now, drained from her amorous assault on Jessie, Zoey's heart beat so hard she was sure Jessie could see it or even feel it as she curled herself into the warmth of Jessie's slumbering body.

Facing the next four days without Jessie, Zoey wanted to stay in bed with her all night, stockpiling a reserve of affection and intimacy to get her through the lonely days ahead. But she knew that they needed to feed appetites other than the sexual. Her run, followed by her activities with Jessie, had left Zoey ravenous, not to mention a little ripe. She needed to freshen up and find something to eat, no easy feat given the current bare state of her cupboards. After planting a delicate kiss on Jessie's cheek, Zoey padded off to the bathroom.

Wanting to get back to Jessie as quickly as possible, Zoey took only ten minutes in the shower. Still, as she dried herself off, a naked and bleary-eyed Jessie shuffled sleepily into the bathroom. "Why didn't you wake me? I could have joined you."

"I'm sorry, honey. I thought you could use the sleep." Zoey planted a quick kiss on Jessie's forehead. "I didn't use up all the hot water, so if you want to shower, you can. My hair care products are your hair care products."

Saying that it might help her wake up a bit, Jessie thanked Zoey with a kiss.

"I'm going to find us something to eat," Zoey said as Jessie stepped into the shower.

Rooting around the kitchen and wondering if they'd be better off ordering takeout, Zoey heard a key scraping in the lock of her front door. She could think of no one other than her landlord who had a key to her home, and as the door slowly opened, panic washed over her, immobilizing her. When she saw Neal staring at her, she remembered leaving her spare keys for him, and as she watched the blank canvas of his face grow aghast, she saw the scene through his eyes and instantly felt a sick shame.

She pictured herself, wet-haired and wearing nothing but a robe so sheer she might as well have been naked, standing in the darkened apartment. She saw the clothes—too many for just one person—that she and Jessie had shed earlier, strewn about the floor in an obvious path to the bedroom. She heard the unmistakable sound of someone showering and sent a small prayer of thanks that Jessie wasn't singing in there. She knew what Neal must be thinking. There was nothing else he possibly could be thinking, yet some small part of her held onto the hope that the situation wasn't as bad as it seemed.

"Neal! What are you doing here?" She clutched at her robe in a vain effort to feel less revealed.

"I came to talk to you. I didn't know you were busy. Again."

"So you just dropped in unannounced," she offered weakly. She couldn't even muster any indignance at his unwelcome intrusion into her home.

"Well, I tried knocking, but I guess you were too busy screwing whoever's in the bathroom to hear me."

Stung by his words, unable to deny them, Zoey remained silent.

"I'm such an idiot." He coughed out the words in his anger and sadness.

Zoey, still shocked that this was happening, couldn't think of what to say to him. She prayed that he would leave before Jessie exited the bathroom and made everything worse.

"I guess Durango was right about you. She warned me, and I told her she was wrong."

"Excuse me? She *warned* you about me?" Zoey felt certain that she had misheard Neal, that he had misspoken.

"She said that I shouldn't trust someone like you, that you'd do to me what you did to Brian."

"Someone like me?" Zoey couldn't believe what she was hearing. Surely there was some mistake. "What the hell does that mean?"

"You're the one with the Ph.D. and the multiple sex partners. What do you think it means?" His derisive jeer hit its mark. Zoey was too stung to do more than glare at him as he continued, "How many dates did it take for you to hop into bed with Mr. Clean in there?"

She heard the smack of skin against skin, felt a sting in her hand and realized that she had actually slapped him. Before she had the satisfaction of kicking him out, he threw her keys to the floor and stormed out the door, leaving her momentarily alone in her rage and disbelief.

"I feel so much better now." Jessie emerged from the bathroom wrapped in a towel. Refreshed, hungry and blissfully unaware that anything had happened to alter her happiness, she asked, "Did you find anything to eat?"

Zoey made no reply, and Jessie found her sitting on her couch in the darkened living room, staring silently ahead of her. "What's wrong?" Jessie knelt before Zoey and grabbed her hands.

Out of nowhere, she asked, "What was your first impression of me?"

Dimly aware that something was amiss but clueless as to what that something might be, Jessie answered uncertainly, "I thought you were really tall." Zoey's expression, one Jessie was sure had terrified more than a few students, indicated that her attempt to lighten the mood had failed.

"Is that all?" Aside from glaring at Jessie, Zoey hadn't moved, but now she rose, stalked over to the light switch and abruptly blasted them with harsh light from the overhead fixture.

In the light, Jessie more clearly saw anguish in Zoey's expression. She moved to hold Zoey, to soothe her, but Zoey sidestepped her advance. Jessie's embrace rebuffed, she cocked her head in confusion. "You're angry. Did something happen while I was in the bathroom?"

"Neal stopped by." Jessie felt her eyes widen and her jaw drop at Zoey's announcement. "It's safe to say that he and I are no longer a couple." Jessie didn't know how to react. She really wanted to rejoice that the lies and sneaking around were over, but knowing that there was more to the story, she stood in stupefied silence waiting for Zoey to fill her in.

"He said some rather interesting things to me, and now I would really like to know what you told him about me."

"Oh no." Now understanding the drastic change in Zoey's mood, Jessie sensed that the world was crumbling around her, falling away bit by bit and leaving her with nothing to stand on. She swallowed hard and answered, "I told him that you were nice enough."

"And that I'm a whore," Zoey stated matter-of-factly and folded her arms across her chest.

"I never said that."

"Don't lie to me, Jessie." She now loomed over Jessie in her anger, and her voice held no warmth.

"I'm not lying," Jessie wailed. "Not that it should make a difference to you."

"Meaning?"

"Meaning this relationship has been nothing but lies since it began. What's one more in the mix?" Jessie's own anger rose, blotting out the guilt and fear she had felt moments before. Remembering her near nudity and wanting the dignity of more than a towel as covering, she grabbed her clothes off the floor and began putting them on.

"I never lied to you, Jessie," Zoey shot back.

"No, but you somehow convinced me that lying to everyone else would be for the best, but it wasn't. It was just the most convenient for you."

"What are you saying?"

"I don't know. Maybe you didn't want to break up with Neal because you didn't want to hurt him, or maybe you wanted to keep him around just in case." Having said it Jessie realized that her concern for honesty and her best friend's feelings, though genuine, just masked her own insecurities. Now these doubts seemed to dictate her speech and emotions.

"In case what?"

"The novelty wears off."

"What are you talking about?" Zoey gasped in her shock.

"Well, you jumped from that guy you were dating to Neal and then from Neal to me, but you haven't told anyone. Neal still wouldn't know if he hadn't barged in here. So are you just using me until something better comes along? Do I mean anything to you, or is this just some fun to pass the time until you find something kinkier?"

Clearly stunned by this accusation Zoey's jaw dropped, but she remained silent. Wrapped up in her own fear and fury, Jessie misread Zoey's silence. "Is that it? You're just collecting weird sexual encounters? You said yourself you're no prude."

Her eyes flashing, Zoey stared at Jessie. Her jaw tightened, her nostrils flared, and Jessie noticed the white patches on Zoey's knuckles as she clenched her fists at her sides. She seethed with anger that, unfortunately, Jessie chose to ignore.

"Maybe you should fuck Sean and Paul too. Put the whole band in your scrapbook."

"You need to leave." Zoey stormed to the door, her long legs covering the distance in a few swift strides. Not fully comprehending what was happening or how the situation had turned on her, Jessie stood rigidly in Zoey's living room, her leaden feet riveted firmly to the floor.

Zoey threw the door open, reiterating her demand, "Get out now." The violent indignation expressed in those three words turned Jessie's veins to ice, and in that instant her fear overtook her, completely obliterating her anger. She didn't dare look at Zoey, nor did she risk standing there long enough to incite another chilling eviction. Instead she ran out the door wondering, "What have I done?" Before she reached the first step, the door slammed behind her, a sharp crack of finality reverberating through the building.

CHAPTER TWENTY

At the sound of her alarm the next morning, Jessie made no move to get out of bed. Instead, she called her brother to let him know she wouldn't be at work. She offered no explanation and didn't care if he was upset with her. She had never called in sick to any job ever, not even when she actually was ill, and she felt entitled to one day off to lick her many wounds.

Plagued by her warring emotions, Jessie had slept intermittently all night, and now, still unable to sleep, she stayed in bed with Sheila, listening as the boys moved around downstairs. Eventually they headed off to work, and the house fell silent, leaving Jessie with nothing to distract her from her thoughts.

At first, her rage had fueled a running commentary in her head that, in turn, further fueled her anger. As she stared at her ceiling, her fury bounced back and forth between herself and Zoey like a ping-pong ball. Initially she seethed at Zoey for her selfish behavior. She'd treated both Jessie and Neal carelessly, stringing them both along with lies, which seemed to be Zoey's specialty. She had been lying to everyone from the beginning and had convinced Jessie to go against her more honest nature with hardly a qualm. Immediately she'd drawn Jessie into the deceit on which she, apparently, thrived. Reluctantly Jessie reminded herself that she was as much to blame. After all, she'd willingly believed Zoey and thrown her own morality overboard on the strength of one night of sex.

Even Neal, the only person who should have remained blameless in the whole messy episode, had fallen victim to Jessie's unfocused anger. If he hadn't barged in on them, she thought, or if he had just kept his mouth shut, then Jessie would still be with Zoey. But, Jessie admonished herself, if she had never offered Neal her honest but ill-informed opinion of Zoey, then Zoey wouldn't have a perfectly good reason to hate her.

By noon Jessie had spent too much time in bed wallowing in her own misery. The situation with Zoey seemed impossible to sort out, and she still had another problem to deal with. She had to master playing with the click track, or at least improve enough that Dino would not replace her when they returned to the studio in four days. She needed to quit moping and get to work.

After a lingering shower, a weary and heartsick Jessie visited a music store and, intending to build herself a homemade click track, bought an electric metronome. She probably could have gone to her old teacher's studio to practice or even to Dino's, she imagined, but she was embarrassed, and the thought of entering Dino's studio unprepared filled her with dread. Besides, she planned on practicing until she fell over just to get it right, and having her bed two flights up instead of a drive away seemed ideal. So with her purchases in her arms and her self-worth in pieces around her, Jessie crept up the stairs to her apartment and set about rigging up her improvised machine. After band practice she'd see if it worked.

However, when she went back downstairs, ready to rehearse, she instantly felt Sean, Paul and Neal's discomfort over the events of the day before. She'd been spanked in front of them, her musical abilities called into question by Dino, and though she hadn't cried or caused a scene, they knew she'd been angered and embarrassed. Aside from an occasional rough rehearsal, Jessie's talents as a musician had never before been doubted. She was an incredible drummer, and everyone knew it. Until now.

And now they were all acting weird. The air in the room felt thick and heavy. Whenever she glanced Paul's way, his eyes immediately drifted to his guitar or his amp or his shoes, and he wouldn't look back until he thought she'd shifted her focus. On top of that Neal hugged her—a gesture he usually reserved for times of extreme heartache—then walked her to her drums, gently depositing her there before gingerly walking away. The worst part, though, was Sean. Not one snide comment slipped past his lips, and he actually smiled at her, a sheepish, almost apologetic twitch of his lips. They acted like she'd been diagnosed with some wasting disease or was suddenly made of glass. It was worse than Dino's scorn, and she snapped.

"Would you quit acting like fucking idiots?" They exchanged hesitant glances with one another, none of them willing to be the first to speak. "Yesterday sucked. I'm aware of that. But if we could just get on with practice, regular practice, then I can work on fixing the problem. If you're just going to stand around staring at me like frightened cows, then you need to get out of my way so I can work on this alone!"

She stared at them, daring them to challenge her. One by one each man nodded his intention to move on. Just before they began to play, Sean said in a voice tinged with humor and a little fear, "'Frightened cows?'"

She laughed with him, the discomfort in the room dissipating already. "Shut up. It makes sense in Spanish," she lied.

From there practice went smoothly. They even started work on a new song, a drum-heavy, pulse-pounding number they thought Dino would really like. Practice went well, and for at least an hour, Jessie managed to avoid dwelling on her troubles, but as the boys drifted from the room, Jessie's thoughts turned back to Zoey. She was tempted to call her and beg for forgiveness, to hear her voice and feel like her world hadn't ended. Only her fear of Zoey's rejection kept Jessie in her seat. She resolved to master the click track and fix the one area of her life that she knew she could repair.

Riding the crest of her anger, Zoey made it almost halfway through the following morning before tears threatened. Standing in front of her poetry students, forty glassy eyes focused on her in various degrees of interest as she elaborated on the heartbreaking wretchedness of Dickinson's "The Heart Asks Pleasure—First," she heard her own voice quavering and felt heat behind her eyelids. Sipping from her cup of abominable vending machine coffee to buy time while she tried to calm herself, she lamented the unfortunate synchronicity of her syllabus and her heartbreak. Why couldn't they be looking at nature poetry or war themes? Because fate picked the night before their exploration of the most powerfully heartbroken poet in American and possibly all of literary history to send her relationship into a tailspin, that's why.

Maybe Jessie had a point about Zoey's secrecy, but just because Zoey hadn't shouted her love from the rooftops didn't mean it didn't exist. Jessie's attack—and her doubts—were inexcusable. If she loved Zoey as much as she claimed, shouldn't Jessie just understand intuitively what Zoey couldn't say? Should it really—

"Uh, Professor Carmichael? Are you okay?"

"I'm fine. Sorry. Sometimes I just get so moved by Dickinson."

Hoping her students bought her story, Zoey worked twice as hard to stay focused on her class, and though she had no repeat episodes of drifting into space, she still felt lifeless, detached from her work and her students. She plodded through her remaining classes in much the same way before seeking the reprieve of solitude in her office.

She checked her office and cell phones for messages from Jessie, to no avail. It had been over seventeen hours since they fought (not that she was counting), and Jessie still hadn't contacted her. On principle Zoey refused to make the first move, even if that meant she'd never speak to Jessie again. Of course, the thought of not speaking to Jessie, not seeing her or touching her, made Zoey's chest constrict and turned her vision blurry. Jessie would call, she told herself. She had to.

The ringing of her phone startled her, and for a second she believed that she had willed Jessie to call her. But it was only the library letting her know the books she'd ordered had arrived. Fast, she thought. She'd just put the order in on Monday, when she had felt on top of the world and wanted to tackle another research project. Now the thought of a big project just made her weary. She rested her head on her desk, too depleted to cry and too tired to put up a fight with her emotions. Her weariness consumed her. She'd had several cups of coffee—the only thing she'd ingested since the fight—but exhaustion pervaded her entire being.

Sluggishly, she conferred with three students in panics over their final essays, noting in spite of her disassociation that it was never the students who should panic that ended up doing so. She also just made it through a brief but important conversation with her department chair before she closed her office door and succumbed to the tears that had threatened for hours. Finally realizing that she was useless in her current state, she abandoned her office and the school and made her slow way toward the L, hoping there would be a call from Jessie before the long night ended.

CHAPTER TWENTY-ONE

Jessie slogged through her days, working and practicing hard, trying to keep her mind off Zoey. For two and a half days she dwelled in this fog of rigorous labor. Rising each morning still exhausted, she approached her work with a dogged resolve. When she returned to work at the garage on Saturday, her productivity increased, but Marco watched as his sister's energy drained from her, and he worried that she would burn herself out. At home she poured herself into her music just as stubbornly as she faced the challenges of her job, pounding away at her drums, striving for precision and absolute flawlessness in every movement, and even driving the guys a little crazy with her insistence on perfection. They affectionately groaned at her demands, and she found some relief in her renewed focus and their playful resistance. As she continued to improve with her homemade click track and began to regain her old confidence as a musician, she felt certain that her next foray into studio recording would be successful, maybe even laudable.

By the end of the long, lonely weekend, though, her rigorous schedule had depleted her, leaving her exposed to an emotional assault that had been building in intensity the more she had distracted herself from it. Monday was unbearable for Jessie and everyone around her. She spent the entire morning brooding about Zoey, her inner turmoil seriously damaging her social skills. When Junior asked if she could hand him the spark plugs that were right next to her, she told him to do his own goddamn work. Eddie, already freaked out by a girl mechanic, cared even less for a girl mechanic with a temper. He steered more clear of Jessie than usual, even waiting an hour to take a break because Jessie's work space stood directly between him and the little refrigerator where he stashed the lunch his wife packed for him. And when Marco stopped her on her way back from the bathroom and asked when he'd get to meet the missus, Jessie even snapped at him.

"Screw you, Marco. I don't need your fucking approval."

Positioning himself directly in front of her and leaning down to put his face perhaps an inch from hers, Marco jabbed his finger into her chest and said with unsuppressed irritation, "Maybe you don't need your fucking job either."

Scared and sullen, Jessie hung her head and clenched her jaw to prevent tears or another unfortunate outburst.

"Now quit being such a bitch and get back to work."

Too cowed to mope, she hastened back to her work station, where she remained for the bulk of the day, silent and pensive. On her way out, she popped her head into Marco's office to apologize.

"Forget it," he said as his eyes raked over her haggard face and defeated posture. Then, his expression softening, he asked, "Is everything okay, *mija*?"

"No. It's really not." She leaned against the grease-smudged doorjamb, sniffling heartily as tears threatened once again.

He moved around to perch on the front of his desk. Always her protector, he asked, "Do you want to talk about it?"

"Yeah, but I don't want to cry anymore. I think I'll just go home."

She turned to leave but heard him call out, "Can I at least beat someone up for you?"

Turning partway back, she laughed halfheartedly. He looked like a thirty-year-old kid ready to take on the school bully at recess. "You'd have to pulverize me, *gordo*. Thanks though." She resumed her listless shuffling away from her brother, leaving a confused and frustrated Marco in her wake.

Leaving work made her feel no better. From her truck to her home, thoughts of Zoey assaulted her at every turn so that, despite her grimly eye-opening encounter with Marco that morning, Jessie's bitter mood easily reasserted itself. In her bedroom Sheila, the most stubborn cat in existence, still sulked over Jessie's recent and frequent absences, so he offered her no comfort, leaving her to wallow in the torture she found in the room where she'd first made love to Zoey. But the rehearsal space, with its other obvious reminders of Zoey, offered no refuge either. In fact, the sight of Neal revived her anger, and she stewed for over an hour in her own irascibility. Though she played well and, out of habit, insisted on perfection, her heart wasn't in it, and try as she might to rein it in, her mind kept drifting back to Zoey, Neal and her own misery. By the time they finished, she'd become so agitated that she lashed out at yet another innocent bystander.

It started simply enough. Paul, amped about the prospects of the next day, double- and triple-checked their studio schedule and asked four times how and when everyone planned to get there. Normally, he was the most laid-back member of the band, just rolling with whatever came, whenever it came. But with this record deal his efficient, managerial side had emerged, and the rest of them found it endearingly irritating. Mocking Paul's latent attention to detail, Sean went around the room and asked everyone what they were going to wear and if they should coordinate their outfits. He followed that up with "Do you know the songs forward and backward? Have you practiced enough?" That was a mistake.

The other guys laughed and played along, but when he asked Jessie, she attacked him. At first a stream of irate Spanish issued forth from her mouth, but when she realized he had no idea what she was saying, she blasted him with a few choice expletives in his native language.

Her words and steely voice cut through the air, and Neal and Paul stared at her in open-mouthed disbelief. Fortunately Sean had consumed enough beer to ignore her harsh words, turning her outburst into a nonevent. But her lack of control scared her, and instead of staying to get in one more night of practice with her click track, she ran upstairs to hide from the world. A brief but disheartening glance at her cell phone told her that Zoey hadn't called, and though she knew Zoey had no reason to call her, she flung herself facedown on her bed in despair.

Overcome with fatigue and misery, Jessie turned out the lights and tried to sleep. However, she couldn't flip the switch on her brain as easily as the one on her wall, and her racing thoughts plagued her for over an hour.

For a long time she considered the fact that this was all her fault. Over and over she saw herself in Zoey's living room, saying these horrible things that seemed to come out of nowhere. Watching her memory of herself, she could almost pinpoint the moment when she'd lost control of the situation, and it was like a football player watching the tape of his worst game ever, each wrong move recorded and blown up for inspection. She'd said some pretty harsh things to Zoey, so she couldn't really get upset at her response. But, she told herself, those words had sprung from her fear that Zoey didn't care for her. She had bared her soul to Zoey. She'd invested all of herself, put all of her emotions on display. She loved Zoey and let her know without hesitation, but Zoey had never once said how she felt for Jessie. A person can't exist for long in that kind of emotional uncertainty without giving in to fear and doubt. So, Jessie reasoned, in a way Zoey was to blame for this whole ugly situation.

"You're an idiot," Jessie berated herself in the black silence of her room. Even though Zoey had never vocalized her feelings for Jessie, she'd shown how she felt in a hundred ways—amongst other obvious signs, she told herself that a person didn't just out herself to a total stranger over meaningless sex. Maybe Zoey just found it harder to express her emotions than Jessie did. Assuming she could convince Zoey to forgive her, Jessie would wait patiently for an acknowledgment of her love.

Jessie tossed and turned for close to another hour, puzzling over the problem she'd created for herself. She'd come up with no solid plan to win Zoey back before emotional and physical exhaustion overcame her, but she knew she had to find an answer soon or lose Zoey forever.

* * *

Finally home from work on Monday, Zoey collapsed on her couch. She had barely made it through another day of classes, and she didn't know how she would handle the next day if she didn't hear from Jessie soon. All weekend, she had been a mess, sulking in her apartment and refusing to leave in case Jessie decided to stop by. Zoey had jumped every time her phone rang but let it go to voice mail when she saw that it wasn't Jessie calling. She didn't want to miss the call from Jessie that she was sure was coming. It had to be.

But by Monday morning, when she had heard nothing from Jessie, the anger that had subsided into depression returned, now with a different focus. She couldn't believe that Jessie was being so stubborn and cruel.

When her apartment buzzer sounded just after dark, Zoey sprang up and ran to the intercom. "Jessie?"

"It's Grace." Zoey's heart sank with disappointment as she buzzed her sister up. Maybe she had been too harsh when she had kicked Jessie out.

"I'm not interrupting date night, am I?" Grace closed the door behind her and headed to the couch where Zoey sat. Grace sounded weirdly gentle, and Zoey wasn't sure she could handle a sympathetic ear right now. She had talked to no one about her fight with Jessie, afraid of making it more real by vocalizing it.

"No." Her voice was small and tight, barely making its way around the hurt and sadness lodged in her throat. "No date tonight."

She felt the heat behind her eyelids moments before Grace's arms were around her. For several minutes she wept into her sister's shoulder as Grace held her tightly, whispering words of gentle encouragement. Eventually, Zoey relayed the disastrous events of Thursday night. As emotion overcame her sister, stopping the flow of words, Grace waited patiently for Zoey to regain the ability to speak, and when Zoey finally finished her story, Grace still sat quietly with her, just holding her and letting her cry. She didn't judge Zoey's actions or chide her for exhibiting the same selfish behavior that she accused Jessie of. She merely asked, softly and kindly, "Would you rather be right or be with Jessie?"

She didn't wait for or expect an answer. Instead, she elicited a promise from Zoey to try to eat something, if not that night then the next day. An hour later, she tucked her big sister into bed, turned out the lights and left her alone.

Zoey turned over in her bed and closed her eyes, but thoughts of Jessie plagued her. Her bed felt vast and empty, and her heart and mind pained her. For a time she tried to will herself to sleep, but the lonely ache within her kept sleep at bay. "Would I rather be right or be with Jessie?" She repeated Grace's question to the darkness. After several minutes of irritated thought, Zoey shuffled tiredly to her closet, pulled out Jessie's coat and, putting it on, shuffled back to bed. Embraced by the familiar scent of Jessie, Zoey sighed and fell into a fitful sleep.

CHAPTER TWENTY-TWO

First thing the next morning, Jessie sought out Sean to apologize for her behavior the night before. It was awkward, and his gloating response didn't help, but once she'd made amends, she felt more like her old self. Thinking of all of the apologies she still had left to make, she began to feel a little like a recovering alcoholic—twelve steps to absolution. Though most of those steps still stretched out before her, her struggle toward cleaning up the mess she'd made, challenging though it might be, would doubtless end triumphantly. Whether she won Zoey back or not, her efforts at honesty and atonement would only make her stronger. But, she reflected, she fully intended to get Zoey back.

Driving to Dino's studio later that morning, Jessie and Neal both remained quiet and sullen for over half the trip. She knew that Neal still brooded about Zoey. In her selfishness, she had avoided talking to him about the breakup, which he didn't even know that she knew about. Jessie realized that Neal still had no idea that she was the reason that he was single, and since that bit of information would only hurt him more, Jessie considered that she would have to find some way to apologize to Neal without letting him know why. It would take a lot more than an "I'm sorry" to make this right. She'd have to find some real way to keep Neal from hating her forever.

A few blocks from the studio as Jessie ransacked her mind for ideas, Neal cleared his throat nervously. "So," he started hesitantly, "I don't want to piss you off, but are you ready for this?"

She emitted a brief, low chuckle that was as much an exhalation as it was laughter. "I am. I don't think I've ever felt more ready in my life." A strained silence filled the truck as they sat at a stoplight. "Hey," as the light changed, Jessie's suddenly loud voice crashed through the quiet. "I'm sorry about last night. I was a real bitch."

"Yeah, you pretty much handed Sean's balls to him on a platter. What set you off?"

"I can't really say," she answered honestly.

"Well, just try to keep your cool in there." Neal hitched his chin at the squat brick building that housed Dino's studio.

"Don't worry," she said as she opened her door. "I'll be good."

Inside the studio Dino greeted Neal with a hearty handshake and a thunderous salutation. Sean and Paul received less boisterous welcomes, but they seemed positively effervescent in comparison to the quick, expressionless nod Dino sent Jessie's way. Peering behind Dino into his office, she saw Billy Stewart leaning back in Dino's chair with his feet on the desk reading the *Sun-Times*. Irritation washed quickly over her, but she shook it off, confident that Dino was wasting his money and Billy's time.

They got right down to business, and as she'd said, Jessie was ready. She played flawlessly, her drumming perfectly in synch with the click track. Glancing at her bandmates she noted with pleasure their pride in her performance. Neal even high-fived her after she nailed their most challenging song on the first take. He seemed eager to rub her improvement in Dino's face, and she was totally content to let him.

But Dino wasn't happy. He made her replay the song several times, and though she played it beautifully each time, he always found some reason to make her do it over. The first two times there were technical difficulties, and the next time, he claimed she'd slowed down. She knew she hadn't, but rather than argue she said, "Let's go again." He seemed to be trying to push her into mistakes so that he could supplant her with Billy, but she had no plans to give up the driver's seat. If Dino felt like wasting his own money, she'd happily let him. She would play the song over and over for the next twenty-four hours if that's what it took to show him his head was up his ass—maybe he could pull it out with his own ponytail.

After another four takes, Dino said with thinly veiled contempt, "That'll do. Why don't we move on to something else?"

Disappointed by Dino's attempted invalidation of her night-and-day improvement, Jessie, certain he lacked the abilities of a big-time record producer, began to grow angry. Nonetheless, she graciously obliged and played the next song just as eagerly and just as well as the last one. Again Neal, Paul and Sean radiated pride at her performance, and again Dino grumbled about minor and nonexistent mistakes. Two more takes—unsuccessful by Dino's standards—followed before Jessie excused herself to use the bathroom. She didn't have to go, but she needed to gain control of her temper before doing something she would regret. To calm herself she quickly braided her hair and splashed water on her face all the while cursing Dino Ryan.

By the time she emerged from the little bathroom just off the studio, all the men, including Billy, had congregated around the sound board and appeared to be having a serious discussion. As she approached she caught snippets of their talk through the open door, and she wasn't pleased by anything she heard. After phrases like "not right," "amateur" and "novelty act" wafted past her ears, she entered the control room ready for a fight.

Oddly calm, she spoke in an innocent voice. "Hey guys. What's going on?"

They all turned sharply at her question. Dino answered easily, "We're just having a private discussion, Jessie. Not your concern." Then he winked at her, the slimy bastard.

Neal, who had been sitting, flew out of his chair in a rage. He towered over an obviously shaken Dino as he shouted, "It's totally her concern! You're trying to get rid of her!"

Jessie's heart stopped, and the air around her grew thick. It pressed her body downward, constricted her chest and squeezed the air from her lungs. As if from a great distance she heard Dino's voice, a deep rumbling portent she could neither heed nor ignore. "I told you before. She doesn't fit the image."

She watched from outside of herself as Neal, Sean and Paul all roared to her defense. Paul bellowed about corporate destruction of rock music while Sean cried out, "We don't have an image, and we don't care about having an image, especially if it means losing Jessie."

And Neal, poor Neal, went on a rampage about loyalty. "Jessie's a part of the band, has been almost since the beginning when we were playing in shitholes to half a dozen people. She never complained, never bailed on us, and I'm not going to turn my back on her now." He kicked his chair for emphasis.

Slicing through all of their arguments was Dino's clear-cut statement, "I have the right to replace her. It's in the contract."

Again her friends rallied to defend her, all of them shouting at the same time so that most of their arguments blended into one steady rumbling. She did discern Paul's accusation of racism and misogyny, but the rest just seemed like noise. Dino barely listened to each of their protests and then refuted them collectively with a simple, "You signed the contract."

Neal exploded. "Fuck the contract!" Sean and Paul both stopped talking. Their heads flew in the direction of Neal, and panic registered on their faces as they listened to him. "I'm not replacing Jessie, so just fuck your goddamn contract!"

"Neal, wait." Jessie grabbed his arm and spun him around to face her. "Don't do this."

"Listen to her, kid," Dino butted in.

"Shut up, Dino," Neal barked at the little man. Then he turned back to his friend. "Jessie, he wants you out of the band."

"I know. It's okay."

"What?" All three of her boys shrieked their surprise in unison.

"I can't let you do this to yourself. Or to them. You guys deserve this."

"And you don't?"

Pursing her lips, she shook her head a little before answering, "Not lately." Neal's face was a picture of confusion, and she struggled with the knowledge of what she had to do. "I'll quit the band. It's fine. You guys keep the contract without me, but—" she looked around the room, taking in Dino's smug expression, Paul and Sean's open-mouthed disbelief and apprehension and Billy Stewart's peripheral disinterest. She couldn't do this with an audience. To Neal she asked, "Can we talk alone for a minute?" His slight nod hardly registered before she dragged him out the door into the adjacent hallway. Closing the door behind them, she saw Paul's and Sean's faces crowding the window and glared at them, but they didn't move.

Taking a deep, shaky breath, Jessie looked Neal directly in the eye. It was impossibly hard, but she had to handle this head-on, no more hiding, no more lies. "I'll quit right now, leave you guys to Billy and Dino, but I need you to forgive me for something."

"Okay." Neal's confusion and hesitation registered in his voice.

"I'm so scared you'll hate me. Please don't hate me, Neal." She grabbed his hands and squeezed them tightly.

"You're freaking me out. What is it?"

"I know that you and Zoey broke up, and I know why."

His eyes narrowed. His brow furrowed, and he said, "What are you talking about?"

Terrified yet needing to come completely clean, she forced the words from her. "I know that Zoey was cheating on you. I've known since it started because I was there." She paused, gathering courage. "She's been with me, Neal. Zoey and I have been sleeping together."

For a moment everything stilled. Time slowed as Jessie watched Neal's face morph from confusion to all-out anguish and then to fury. Suddenly he threw her hands from him, the force of his revulsion propelling her backward. The doorframe cut across her back, and her head ricocheted off the jamb. Stunned and aching, Jessie shook her head but quickly returned her attention to Neal, who, she saw, was actively kicking Dino's furniture and saying either to her or a leather ottoman, "Go fuck yourself." She felt the door behind her begin to open and quickly pulled it shut with a force that surprised her. She looked through the glass at Sean and Paul and seeing their concern, heard them yelling at her to open the door, but she signaled them to stay out of it.

When she turned back Neal was standing in front of her, staring down at her wild in his wrath. "When did it start?"

"Neal, please." She looked up into his eyes and cowered beneath him.

He punched the wall next to her head, his fist cracking but not penetrating the plaster. "When Jessie?"

"About two weeks ago."

Shoving her again, he screamed "Fuck" once more. Before storming from the building, he yelled, "You don't get to quit. I want you out. Out of the band, the house, all of it." Then he kicked everything he encountered on his way out of the building.

Jessie moved to run after him, but the door behind her opened and her remaining bandmates spilled out into the hallway. Sean grabbed her arm, pulling her back. "Are you crazy going out there? Just let him go, Durango."

"I have to talk to him." She shook free from Sean's hold, but as she moved to the door, Paul stepped in her path.

"You're going to get hurt if you go out there, Jessie. Leave him alone."

"You don't understand. I have to talk to him. I have to fix this." She dodged her friends and ran toward the door.

Outside she found Neal around the back of the building punching the brick wall. Slowly, rhythmically, his fist hit the same bloodied spot over and over again, but he made no sound of pain or anger. He seemed almost unaware of what he was doing to himself. Carefully she approached him. She grabbed his hand, which looked in places like raw hamburger meat, and forced it to his side.

"Leave me alone, Durango." He sounded utterly defeated, and though that saddened her, she took it as a good sign. At least he'd moved past his initial, blinding rage.

"No Neal. You have to talk to me."

"Why?"

"I need to explain."

He spun around. "Explain what? Why I shouldn't hate you? If you were a man, I would beat you senseless. You knew what she meant to me, you fucking knew! How could you do this?"

"I love her."

"You hardly know her." He sank down to the ground, leaning against the wall and stretching his long legs in front of him.

"I don't think that really matters. How long did you know her before you knew what you felt for her?" He made no reply, just stared off into the distance. "Almost from the first day I met her she's been in my head. My whole system was filled with her. I couldn't sleep. I got shaky when she was around and sometimes even when she wasn't. Neal, I tried so hard to fight this. I did everything I could think of to get her out of my mind and my heart, but she wouldn't go." Sitting down beside him, she confessed, "She's not even talking to me now, and she still won't leave me alone. Surely you can understand what that's like."

He nodded a terse agreement then looked her in the eye and asked, "Why did you sneak around? Why didn't you tell me?"

"I wanted to tell you, believe me I did. But Zoey thought it should come from her, and I agreed to let her tell you. I even promised I wouldn't talk to you about it before she had a chance to tell you. *Pendeja*," she cursed herself and shook her head. "But neither of us knew it would be so hard to be honest. Then the more involved we got, the harder everything became." She saw him flinch but ignored it. "I was so lost in love with her—I knew it was wrong, but I let myself believe it would all work out somehow. I was stupid and selfish, and I know it doesn't even begin to cover it, but Neal, I'm sorry. I'm so, so sorry."

She stared at his profile for a long time as, eyes closed, he leaned his head against the wall, digesting everything. He breathed deeply several times as she studied his face for a sign of understanding and hoped that somehow he would forgive her.

His voice just above a whisper, he asked, "Do you love her more than the music?"

Her voice just as soft, she answered, "Yeah, I really do."

"So, are you quitting the band for her?"

"And for you. I can't let you walk out on this over me."

"You didn't have to say anything, you know. We could've gotten another contract." The corner of his mouth twitched up, almost the beginning of a smile. "Like Huey Lewis."

Happy that he was coming further out of his anger, she smiled a little herself. "I want to live honestly, and I want to deserve your friendship. Right now I don't."

"No, you don't." His words stung. "But giving up the dream, that's a pretty big sacrifice."

"Well, you're worth it." Tentatively she grabbed his hand, careful not to touch his wounds, and she was pleased that he didn't pull away from her. "You're worth more than that, and I will find some way to regain your trust and your friendship."

For a little while longer they sat, hand in hand, in almost companionable silence, the only sound that of the birds and traffic. She thought for a moment that Neal had dozed off, but he surprised her by saying, "You know, a part of me always knew she was too good to be true." She was about to offer some words of comfort when he added, "But lesbians are totally hot, so maybe it wasn't a complete loss."

"You're such a pig." She hugged him tightly. "I love you."

Standing up they saw Sean and Paul lingering awkwardly at the corner of the building. Apparently satisfied that the confrontation was over, they approached, and Paul asked, "Are you guys coming back inside? We still have to decide what to do about Jessie and the contract."

Neal said, "And I need to kiss Dino's ass a little." He cast a forlorn glance in Jessie's direction and asked, "Are you coming?"

"Just to get my stuff. I have a lot of work to do." She looked to Neal meekly. "Like finding a new place to live."

"You're not moving out," Sean jumped in, surprising Jessie with the force of his interjection. "Neal doesn't make all of the decisions, and I don't want you to leave."

"Me either," Paul offered.

Jessie was touched and a little surprised by their sentiment until Sean continued, "Who'll translate all the billboards in the neighborhood if you go?"

"And that was almost entirely genuine. Thank you," Jessie said and hugged Sean, something she'd never done before. "But it'll be too hard if I stay."

"I guess you're right," he muttered before he turned away and headed back inside with Paul.

Neal paused, allowing Sean and Paul time to get out of earshot. He cleared his throat a couple of times and stammered a bit, obviously preparing to say something difficult. "Hey." He looked at Jessie, his eyes still full of the hurt she had put there. "Make it work with Zoey. Because if you put me through this and then give up, I'll *really* be pissed."

"I will." She hugged him once more, saying in his ear, "Thank you."

Sometimes Zoey hated her baby sister. That damn question that Grace had asked her had plagued Zoey throughout the night and from the moment she got out of bed in the morning. "Would I rather be right or with Jessie?" It was so much easier, so much more satisfying to stew in her anger and sadness than to be reasonable about the situation. Of course, the satisfaction of being right would eventually wear off, and then Zoey would still be brokenhearted and alone. She knew Grace had a point. She just didn't know how willing she was to accept it and what, if anything, she would do about it.

She failed to come to a decision about anything by the time she entered her office, and she managed to make her way through several revised essays (many of far better quality than she had allowed herself to hope for), three student conferences and a fruitless meeting with the dean before she glanced at her watch and allowed herself to remember that the band was probably back in the studio. She wondered if Jessie had worked on the metronome thingy—the click track—and realized with a mix of pride and sadness that she undoubtedly had poured her energy into her music.

Right now Jessie would be happily proving Dino wrong, not even thinking about Zoey and what she was going through—the sleepless nights, the loss of appetite and the bodily sickness she felt. It enraged her afresh that Jessie could just let her wallow in this misery without even a backward glance at the damage she had caused.

But Zoey couldn't help herself. In spite of her anger, the thought of Jessie in the studio sent her mind back to the night they met and watching Jessie play. She could clearly envision the joy in Jessie's eyes as she made music, not unlike the radiant glow Zoey saw in her when they made love. Jessie's passion for music was carnal and addictive, and Zoey wanted to be near it again. "Would I rather be right or be with Jessie?" she asked herself once more, and the answer came so clearly, so forcefully that Zoey couldn't believe it had taken this long for her to make up her mind.

She wanted to call Jessie right then, but the thought of getting Jessie's voice mail or of a student or one of her colleagues overhearing her as she bared her soul gave her pause. Knowing she would have to wait until she was home to make the call, she checked her watch once more and willed the next three hours to pass quickly, at which point the passage of time seemed to halt altogether.

She hadn't expected to find Jessie waiting for her when she finally arrived home, and she certainly hadn't expected the intense revival of her anger to be her initial response to seeing Jessie for the first time since they fought. But there it was, and underneath it, the hope that, somehow, everything would work out between them.

For four hours Jessie sat on the front steps of Zoey's building poring over the classified sections of three different newspapers looking for a place to live. As they passed in and out, Zoey's neighbors threw quizzical glances at Jessie, who merely smiled and said hello before returning to her papers. One older woman asked Jessie if she'd been locked out, signaling that she'd let her inside the building, and though tempted to answer yes—it was figuratively, if not technically, true—Jessie thought better of such an intrusion into Zoey's life and home. She declined the offer and went back to her search, circling a few promising ads for places that seemed like they might take a drummer with a cat. Ultimately, though, her mind remained focused elsewhere.

By the time Zoey finally walked up to her door, Jessie— long done with both her apartment search and the thoroughly mesmerizing activity of watching a shirtless man with an enormous, hairy beer belly mowing the lawn across the street— had rested her head on her knees in despair. In her tenancy of the cold front steps, she'd worked herself into a panic over Zoey, the storm in her brain blocking out the world. She jumped when she heard Zoey's voice, its honeyed tones tinged with hostility, say, "What are you doing here?"

Jessie's head jerked up, and she bolted to her feet. "I need to talk to you."

Zoey stared at her for a full minute, no happy recognition on her face nor any sound issuing from her lips. Jessie searched her face for any sign of hope but saw none. With her red, slightly puffy eyes and wan skin tone, Zoey merely looked tired and depressed. Her expression remaining neutral, she finally offered a dull-voiced "Okay," as she opened the door.

All the way up the stairs, neither woman said a word. Jessie, terrified about what would happen, couldn't formulate small talk. She only guessed and feared what Zoey's excuse for silence might be.

Once inside her apartment Zoey gestured to Jessie to have a seat. Feeling a little like a criminal awaiting conviction, Jessie perched on one end of Zoey's couch while Zoey took the nearby chair. Increasingly conscious of the dull ache in her back, neck and head, Jessie longed for an aspirin, and while she sat there debating with herself about asking Zoey for one, she heard Zoey clear her throat pointedly. Turning to Zoey, Jessie smiled awkwardly at her own helplessness, but Zoey simply asked in a voice like stone, "What did you need?"

Accepting the challenge that lay before her, Jessie made what she hoped was intimate eye contact and answered, "I need to apologize."

"I'll say," Zoey snorted.

"I know that I was a real asshole the other night."

"Agreed." Zoey, it seemed, wasn't going to make this easy on Jessie.

"I said some pretty unforgivable things. I was a real jerk, and I don't blame you for being angry. Maybe you even hate me." She waited for Zoey to contradict her, and when the other woman merely sat there in stone-faced silence, Jessie's heart sank a little. "But I know that none of what I said is true. I knew that when I was saying it."

"Then why say it?"

Jessie sat quietly collecting her thoughts before she answered, "I was scared. You never said how you feel, and it seemed like you were hiding this from everyone. Like you were ashamed." Zoey opened her mouth to reply, but Jessie held up an apologetic hand to silence her and then forged ahead, needing to explain herself fully. "I was so afraid that you didn't care for me and that you'd leave me when you found out that I'm nothing special, that you could do so much better than me." Sudden and forceful emotion welled up in her, and she sniffled deeply, wiping large, hot tears from her cheeks with the back of her hand. "I've had five days to think about what I did, and why I did it. At first, I was making excuses, trying to justify my behavior to myself, to make myself feel better, but none of that worked because the one thought that kept coming back to me is that, for five days, you've been hurting. Because of me. And there is no justification for that." She folded her hands in her lap and looked at them. In spite of Neal's warning, Jessie felt the hopelessness of the situation weighing heavily upon her. She gave herself over a little to despair. "I guess I was an idiot to think I could talk you into giving me a second chance."

"It hasn't been five days." Zoey's voice had gained some warmth. "And you are an idiot."

"What?"

"I said it hasn't been five days since we fought." She glanced at her watch. "It's only been four days, twenty hours and thirty-seven minutes."

"You've been counting the time?"

"Yes," Zoey answered. "And it was the longest four days, twenty hours and thirty-seven minutes of my life."

"Oh," Jessie said, pleased.

"But it gave me time to think too." She bit her lip, scrunched her face and ran her fingers through her hair before she revealed anything further. "You were right about Neal and how I treated him and the truth, but I wasn't ashamed, and I wasn't hiding. I was scared too, Jessie. I've never felt this strongly about anyone before, and I guess I was afraid to open up to anyone, including you, and lose control completely." Absently she twisted a lock of hair around her finger. "I couldn't help it, though. I actually told my mom about us that day."

"Really?" Jessie, feeling horrible for Zoey's pain and for the wedge she'd driven between them, hung her head in shame. "I'm such a jerk. I'm sorry."

"How could you have known?"

Zoey's voice sounded much lighter than when they'd started talking, and Jessie found herself growing hopeful again. Through the fuzzy cloud of her burgeoning optimism, Zoey's earlier statement penetrated Jessie's brain. She asked, "You think I'm an idiot?"

"A little bit." Zoey leaned forward in her chair, resting her arms on her thighs. "We had a fight—a really, really big fight, and if you ever say anything like that about me again, you won't live to apologize."

Jessie made an X across her chest with her finger, swearing her complete loyalty to Zoey. When Jessie dropped her hand back in her lap, Zoey picked it up, and Jessie's body came alive at this, their first physical contact in days.

"That happens in relationships. More often than it should. But even as livid as I was with you, I was more miserable without you. You're right that I wasn't very demonstrative, at least not verbally, and I'm sorry that that frightened you. But you have to have more faith in me, in us, if this is going to work."

"I know. I'm sorry." Jessie nodded, her eyes still locked on her shoes. Her heart fluttered wildly, but she didn't know whether to trust her ears or not.

Cupping Jessie's chin with her hand and lifting her face so that their eyes were level, Zoey added, "I don't know where all this doubt is coming from, but you are something special, and I could never do better than you. I love you, Jessie Durango."

Wiping more tears away from her cheeks, Jessie offered thanks to whatever god granted her this reprieve. Then, seating herself on Zoey's lap and showering her with kisses, she said repeatedly, "I love you. I'm so sorry." Their kisses grew rapidly in intensity, the passion of reconciliation after a too-lengthy separation surging between them.

Their hands roamed freely over one another, seeking reassurance that they were, in fact, together again. Running her fingers over Jessie's breasts, Zoey made a quiet little grunt as Jessie's nipples instantly hardened. "I missed you."

"I'm so sorry, *guera*. I promise to spend the rest of my life making this up to you."

"Can you start now?" Zoey was nibbling at Jessie's earlobe, running her hands all over her body, "or do you have to go practice?"

Instantly remembering that she still had more to reveal, Jessie sighed, "I definitely don't have to practice. I quit the band."

Removing her tongue from the delicate swirls of Jessie's ear, Zoey sat back and said, "I'm sorry. It sounded like you said you quit the band."

"I did."

"What! Are you crazy? Why would you quit?"

Briefly Jessie explained the circumstances surrounding her departure from Nuclear Boots while Zoey listened attentively, growling in anger at Dino's behavior.

"But you were just about to make it. What are you going to do now?"

"There are other bands. And as long as I've got you, I've got all I need." Zoey's face lit up, and she moved in for a kiss.

"Wait. Before you and your lips make me forget again, I told Neal about us. I had to."

Zoey's face registered surprise, but when she answered, "I understand," she sounded sympathetic. "He wouldn't have let you go if you hadn't. How did he take it?"

"Not well. He kicked me out, and there was a lot of yelling and violence directed mostly at furniture. Dino's wall will need a minor repair—not that I care—and I might have some bruises."

"He hit you?" Zoey seemed incredulous. "I haven't beaten anyone up in about fifteen years, but I will turn that scrawny little shit into hamburger."

Jessie smiled involuntarily at Zoey's protective concern. "Really, I'm okay. It was more of a shove than a hit, and it was more incidental than intentional. Besides, he's not so angry now. He calmed down a lot, and we talked. Our friendship's not what it was, but I think I might win him back someday."

"Let me see." Zoey started inspecting Jessie's bare arms, scanning them for signs of injury.

"Zoey, come on. It's not a big deal."

"Show me," she insisted, so Jessie stood and removed her shirt. When she turned her back to her, Zoey clucked her tongue and whispered, "Poor baby," before her tender lips placed gentle kisses in a stripe along Jessie's injuries. She even removed Jessie's bra to access the entire bluish purple bruise. "You promise you're okay?"

"Yes. And if you keep kissing me like that, I'll be more than okay." Bare breasted and obviously aroused, she turned to face Zoey.

"Oh," Zoey gasped and pulled Jessie to her. Their lips met briefly before Zoey bent to kiss Jessie's breasts. Jessie let out a soft moan of pleasure as Zoey's warm, wet mouth left one breast to travel to the other. The muted whimper that escaped her seemed only to incite Zoey's desire as Zoey carefully but forcefully guided Jessie over to the couch. Straddling Jessie she began an urgent, rhythmic grinding against her. Propping herself up with one hand, Zoey moved the other lightly over Jessie's torso as she kissed her. She gently caressed shoulders and arms and breasts and ran her hand across Jessie's taut stomach, making it jump. She opened Jessie's jeans and slid a teasing hand just inside her panties, and Jessie shivered as Zoey's fingers grazed the wetness between her legs.

As Jessie clung to her, murmuring her pleasure, Zoey slowly stroked, her fingers deft and sure, bringing Jessie to the edge of orgasm, but not allowing her to crest just yet. Zoey slipped a finger inside Jessie, who hovered on the edge, whimpering in her need for a deliciously interminable length of time before Zoey's hot breath kissed her ear in a whisper. "I'm not hurting you, am I?"

In a frenzy Jessie exhaled, "God, no. You're perfect. Please." And Zoey increased the pressure of her hand ever so slightly, eliciting gasping paroxysms of exquisite release from Jessie, who cried out and then shuddered against Zoey for some time.

When Jessie's quaking subsided, Zoey said, "I've missed you."

Jessie kissed her fiercely, pushing herself and Zoey up to a seated position as she did. Pulling away slightly she said, "I don't ever want to be apart from you again." Then she began the slow process of removing Zoey's clothes. As she kissed her with the barest contact of her lips on Zoey's skin, she worked each button on Zoey's blouse with excruciating deliberateness and, opening it, spent several slow minutes kissing her chest, tracing the perimeter of Zoey's bra with her tongue and inching the shirt from Zoey's shoulders. Just as lingeringly, she slipped Zoey's bra straps from her shoulders, leaving them loosely dangling as she nuzzled her neck and trailed her hands behind Zoey to release her breasts from their lacy prison. Dropping the bra on the coffee table behind her, Jessie lost herself in Zoey's breasts. She kissed and stroked each one slowly, eventually taking each firm nipple between her teeth.

"Oh," Zoey exhaled raggedly, elevating Jessie's yearning. Without warning she forced Zoey into a prone position and, her patience spent, yanked down Zoey's pants with animal ferocity. Her mouth came to Zoey again, and as she ran her tongue over Zoey's stomach and thighs, she worked her panties over her hips and flung them from her. Her appetite heightened, she focused her mouth on Zoey's aching need. She tasted her desire and, savoring every sound from Zoey's throat, every flutter of her thighs against her face, Jessie teased and tarried, keeping Zoey's orgasm at bay as long as they both could stand it. Eventually, Zoey thrust her hips and called out her satisfaction. Jessie crawled up Zoey's limp body, laying herself on top of the woman she loved. Zoey's arms held her tightly, and she kissed Jessie and murmured, "I love you."

For some time they remained in this position, silently absorbing the substance and satisfaction of one another. The ugliness of the last few days behind them, they focused on their present happiness. Jessie could feel Zoey's heartbeat against her own, and they seemed to be perfectly in synch. She wondered how she ever doubted Zoey's love and felt that she never would again. Then, remembering a comment of Zoey's, she broke their comfortable silence. "You never mentioned how your mother reacted when you told her."

Zoey let out a soft chuckle. "Now who's bringing up mothers inappropriately?"

"I'm sorry, but it's important."

"You're right. She was surprised, I think, and a little disappointed. She wants to meet you."

Jessie lifted her head to look at Zoey. "Uh, I already met your mother. Remember?"

"You met my mother as my friend and her favorite mechanic. You didn't meet her as my lesbian lover."

"And our relationship changes who I am?"

"To Fiona Carmichael it does."

Jessie shook her head good-naturedly. "Is there any chance she'll forget you mentioned it?"

"None whatsoever."

"Then," sighed Jessie, snuggling her head back into the crook of Zoey's neck "I guess I'm headed back to Rogers Park. Any advice on winning her over?"

"Avoid having your way with me at the dinner table, and you should be fine."

"No sex at dinner. Got it."

Abruptly Zoey sat up, taking Jessie with her. "Are you hungry?" She kissed Jessie, preventing an answer, then rambled on as she extricated herself from the tangle of limbs on the couch. "I'm starving. I don't know about you, but I haven't eaten very much the last few days. I was so nervous and depressed and angry. I just couldn't think about food." Her voice trailed off as she headed into the kitchen. A moment later she returned with the phone and a take-out menu. She was still talking a mile a minute about her hunger and their time apart, taking a break from her verbal onslaught only to place her order. Hanging up she said, "We have an hour before the pizza gets here. What do you want to do?"

"I can think of a few things to pass the time." Jessie ran her eyes over Zoey's body. "But you will have to put some clothes on to answer the door."

"Or we could answer it together and avoid tipping."

Jessie laughed, a delightful sound that echoed her sentiments trilling from her. "You're crazy. I love you."

"Just keep it that way, okay?"

Jessie met Zoey's vulnerable eyes with her own then placed her hand upon her heart in a pledge. "Nothing could ever stop me."

EPILOGUE

"I can't believe they're playing Metro," Jessie exclaimed as, pushed by the crowd, she pressed herself into Zoey. "It's sold out too. This is huge!"

"It was awfully nice of Neal to give us these tickets." Zoey stood behind Jessie, wrapping her in her arms to protect her from the jostling mass of people who chose the brief span of time between the opening act and the headliners to shove their way toward the bar or the bathroom. "Maybe he's coming around."

"I hope so. Sean told me he went a little catatonic when we moved in together, so this is a good sign. Of course, it probably doesn't hurt that you introduced him to his next great love, which is just so weird."

"Tell me about it. As if my mother wasn't already freaked out by our relationship, Grace had to go and fall for my ex-boyfriend."

"It will make your sister's wedding very interesting."

Zoey laughed heartily. "Let's hope Mom doesn't have a meltdown first. Although she likes Neal a lot more now than she did when he was with me. And she loves you. I don't know how you did it."

"Well, I didn't have to resort to obvious brown-nosing, like some people I could mention." Jessie threw a haughty glance at Zoey, whose expression was one of pure innocence.

"Are you suggesting that my Spanish studies are nothing more than an attempt to win your mother's favor?"

"Aren't they?"

"No."

"No?" Jessie seemed incredulous.

"No!" Zoey huffed indignantly. "I might remind you that your mother liked me from the beginning, and since she thinks I'm the reason you started working on your degree, she adores me. It's your dad I'm trying to impress."

"He loves you too, *guera*."

"He has excellent taste," Zoey said, bending her head so Jessie could hear over the crowd that was filling in again. Turning serious, she asked, "Does it bother you that you could have been up there with them instead of down here with me?"

"I'd be lying if I said no, but I think I got the better end of the deal." She kissed Zoey, not caring that those around them stared openly. "Besides, the new band is starting to come together. We'll get here some day. If we ever agree on what to call ourselves."

Just then the lights went down, and as Neal, Sean, Paul and the new guy took the stage, Zoey squeezed Jessie tighter in pride and affection. "I love you," she whispered in Jessie's ear, the endearment momentarily overpowering the cheering of the crowd around them. Jessie kissed her once more then shifted her focus to the band.

They opened with a new song before moving right into the single she'd heard on the radio once or twice since their album came out. She was proud of her friends and their accomplishment, but a part of her hated that they sounded good without her. She lost herself in examining the new guy, watching his technique, looking for flaws and comparing him to herself, so she was only half-listening when Neal introduced their fourth song.

"If you've been following us for a while, you might have noticed a change in the line-up." Jessie smiled a little when a small section of the crowd made its displeasure known. She saw that Neal smiled a little too, and she felt Zoey's arms tighten around her again. "We lost our drummer a while back, but she's here tonight supporting us." Again the crowd interrupted with cheers, raising Jessie's spirits. "Now, we don't usually do covers, but we just couldn't help ourselves. This one's for Jessie and Zoey."

Jessie recognized The Cars song in the first few seconds, and she threw her head back in laughter that subsided into a teary-eyed joyfulness. It took until the chorus for the song, and Jessie's reaction, to register with Zoey. But she understood when she heard Neal sing: "She's my best friend's girl. She's my best friend's girl, but she used to be mine."

They were forgiven.

Bella Books, Inc.

Women. Books. Even Better Together.

P.O. Box 10543
Tallahassee, FL 32302

Phone: 800-729-4992
www.bellabooks.com